Myra

A Twisted Tale of Karma

Myra

A Twisted Tale of Karma

by

Amaleka G. McCall

This is a work of fiction. All of the characters, organizations, and events portrayed in this novel are either products of the author's imagination or are used fictitiously.

 For information, address Melodrama Publishing, P.O. Box 522, Bellport, NY 11713.

www.melodramapublishing.com

Library of Congress Control Number: 2008940450
ISBN-13: 978-1-934157-20-6
ISBN-10: 1-934157-20-1
First Edition: March 2009
10 9 8 7 6 5 4 3 2 1

Previously published as: *A Twisted Tale of Karma*

In Memory

David McCall—Gran'pa—There is not a day that goes by that I don't think about you. My love for you will always remain unconditional. There is no love like it. Your light will always shine constant in my heart. I'll always be Meeka . . . your sweetheart. I love you. Rest in Peace.

Donna Jean McCall—Mommy—When I think of the good times I smile. God had other plans for you, so I won't question it. Your heart was golden and no one could ever say anything different. Thanks for teaching me to always say what I'm thinking, which has proven to be one of the best lessons I've ever learned. Thanks for making mistakes so I wouldn't have to. I miss you, I love you. Rest in Peace.

Acknowledgments

Before any is God . . . Lord, I thank you for bringing me this far; without you I am nothing.

To my beautiful babies, Chynna—remember you will always be my first love. You are a God-given gift. Amaya—my baby girl, God touched my womb when he blessed me with you. Mommy loves you. Ed—the love of my life, there are no words to describe the love I feel for you. If I had to put it all down on paper this book wouldn't suffice. Thank you for believing in me when I didn't, thank you for loving me unconditionally, thank you for being a friend first and a partner always. Although I won't share you, I wish every woman in the world could be as lucky as I am. By the way, "Who' da thunk it!" Daddy—we've had our ups and downs, but thwo things remain constant: our love for each other and our stubbornness. I love you even when I tell you that I don't. Remember when you asked me if I had a "plan" for my life? Well, I have the answer—God had a plan. Love you! Aunty—girl, I did it! Without your push this would all still be a dream. I admire you from your head to your toes; your tenacity is unmatched. I love you like cooked food! Quita—thank you for the years of laughter, partying, and six-hour phone calls! True friends are hard to find, but sisters are forever! If you feelin' like a pimp gon' brush ya shoulders off! Tyra—I'm proud of you! Thank you for always being a sister and never turning your back. Luv you! Renee Leggett—your straightforward approach has taught me invaluable lessons. Thanks for the long walks on Beach 23rd. When I was at one of the lowest points in my life you were standing right there. Luv ya, sis! Gran'ma—not many people can say that they have a grandmother as strong as mine. I love you for teaching me to always stand up for myself. Yvette—you never let me give up. You are probably the first person that really believed in A Twisted Tale of Karma. I know our family doesn't show affection, but, girl, I love you! Joseph—my little brother, although our paths have been separated, we are bonded for life. I pray every day to see you soon. I love you! Mrs. B—my gratitude is running over. I love you. Thank you for treating me and Chynna like we belonged to you from the beginning. Jamol and Mylon—my brothers from another mother . . . you guys make me smile. If you work hard, your dreams will come true. Katie—What can I say? We go back and forth, but you know I got love for you, honey (smile). Grandma and Granddaddy—thank you both for fostering such a wonderful family and making me part of it. Yolanda—thanks for keeping my father at bay. *smile* I love you. Good luck in all your endeavors. You can do it! Mrs. Elamora and Billy—you have enhanced my life over the years. Thanks for always being there when I needed you. LaIvy—someone once told me, "when you love something let it go, if it comes back it is meant to be, if it doesn't it never was"—well, you came back so I guess our friendship was meant to be. Thanks for being you. Kiss Tee for me.

Now for the SHOUT OUTS! Porsche, Lexis, and Mercedes—you girls are my lil' sisters so that means you have to go a little further than I did, I have faith in all of you. PM Family—Pete, Ray, Ralph, Gid—You guys are the truth! Thanks for holding me down when Ed was in FLETC. I will never forget it. I love ya'll man. Nay—girl you've shown me that you don't have to know someone for a lifetime to consider them a friend. PJ—boyfriend, Aunty Leek loves you! My Godchildren—Taquan, Taniah, Tanasia, Jalen—I love you all! My added Godchildren—Darius, Aaron, Jaden, and Janelle—kisses, sweet babies! Cindi—I've walked through doors so you wouldn't have to; learn from my experiences and remember I'm always here if you need me. Evan and Erik—keep up the good work. Luv you guys. Kawana—you have been there for me when times were good and bad, and that says a lot. Don't ever let anyone tell you that you are not genuinely the sweetest person I know. ReRe—girl your babysitting skills are up there (smile). Thanks for your constant encouragement, luv you! Donn aka Dee-Bo—What up! Thanks for never turning your back. The Bell Family—Thanks for making me feel right at home. Ty, Nicki and Maia—my Aeneas Designs Family—you guys inspire me. Keep up the good work. Mima—the craziest Puerto Rican I know—and, yes, I put a Boriqua in the book! Thanks for telling me the story was hot! All of my test readers (you know who you are)—thank you for taking the time to read A Twisted Tale of Karma, and for all of the constructive criticism—I needed it!

Dive—Thanks for being the best graphic artist around. Fatima—thanks for the bomb editing job! All of my aunts, uncles, and cousins (on all sides)—there are too many to name. Although I don't get to see ya'll that often, no matter what, I love all of you. Lacey—Thanks for giving me a chance when you were not accepting any more manuscripts! To all of the writers who have paved the way—thank you! Finally, to the readers—thank you for purchasing Myra: A Twisted Tale of Karma, my first novel. I hope you enjoy reading it as much as I enjoyed writing it. If I've forgotten anyone, please blame my head and not my heart.

Amaleka

Foreword by

Kiki Swinson

"I need a ride or die bitch! *Wifey* that will hold me down by any means necessary."

Those were the words my ex-man said to me a long time ago. He told me to promise that I would do anything for him, and in return he would o anything for me—a big house; shopping sprees; and a hot whip. I was sold. I bet if you're a female from any hood in America reading this, you've heard these same words whispered in your ear before. I don't know about you, but I kept my promise. I rode and rode for my man, until the wheels fell off of my life. I dealt with his lies and cheating and put myself at risk while he hustled my life away. See, I was a ride or die bitch and it got me five years in federal prison.

Fortunately, that five-year prison bid gave birth to a new me. When I walked out of those prison walls, I was broke with nothing but lint in my pockets. But I had a story to tell, and I was ready for anything the hood had in store for me. I took the lemons that nigga left me with and made lemonade. I used my experience to pen my first novel, the #1 *Essence* bestseller, *Wifey.* See, what my ex-man didn't know was, when I rode for his ass and I got fucked over, that experience gave me what I needed to write from the heart. I turned my tragedy into a success story. I've gone on to write six novels, all *Essence* best-sellers. Bet that nigga didn't think I'd be shining like this! Where is he now? Hmm, let's just say, what goes around comes around . . . it's called Karma, baby.

In every hood across America there is a young, impressionable girl who just wants to be loved. She may come from a broken home or a good family; she may have been raised in the streets or raised in the church; she may have been a straight-A student or cut school every day. When it comes down to it, it doesn't matter what her circumstances are, if the girl has low self-esteem and a fine-ass street dude walks into her life with the gift of gab and a shiny dime or two, she will probably give up everything. I've seen chicks throw away their entire college careers to ride for a dude. I've seen chicks stab their own families in the back to be with a dude. I've seen chicks let their kids go hungry for a dude. It is not a game what we will do for these niggas. There are chicks serving life sentences behind "riding" for their man. There are thousands of babies born in prison every day because their mothers were ride or die chicks.

My happy ending is rare. Most females who do prison bids wind up back in the hood on welfare and fucked out of the game. Let me be an example to all my sistas out there. Ride for yourself. If a dude loves you, he ain't even gonna put you at risk. I'm here to tell you: Fuckin' with these dudes ain't gonna get you shit but stiff dick and bubble gum!

Karma

"Whatever we do, with our body, speech, or mind will have a corresponding result. Each action, even the smallest is pregnant with its consequences."

-Sogyal Rinpoche, author of The Tibetan Book of Living and Dying

Prologue

"POLICE! WARRANT FOR MYRA DANFORD AND MILTON ROBERTS!"

Myra heard the words echoing loudly through her apartment door, followed quickly by the brutal force of the battering ram as the door gave away at the hinges. The sound of hard black combat boots thundered unrepentantly down the hallway, reminding her of the rhythmic pounding of a fraternity step show . . . STOMP, STOMP, STOMP. As the hammering of footsteps grew louder and louder, Myra closed her eyes and whispered in prayer, "Please God, take me now I've had enough of this life, I surrender to you."

The warm water enveloped her body, easing her like the comfort only a baby in its mother's womb could feel. Pink tinged water cascaded over the sides of the porcelain tub, forming a waterfall onto the linoleum floor, which ran into a stream under the door. Myra had orchestrated her own watery grave.

"I THINK SOMEONE'S IN HERE!" an officer yelled as he sloshed through the flooded hallway, motioning rapidly for the other officers to bring the battering ram for the door. Voices faded in and out. Myra's heart beat loudly and rhythmically in her ear, like the sweetest African drum music.

Slowly, Myra succumbed to the hypnotic beats, setting her soul free from the confines of her body. Her spirit emerged, hovering over the pitiful sight. "You did it now . . . you fucked yourself outta the game," it taunted. As the door to her self-made sanctuary came crashing down, the reality of her situation became alarmingly clear.

"HEY IT'S THE GIRL AND SHE'S IN A TUB FULL OF BLOOD . . . GET A BUS UP HERE RIGHT NOW!" the sergeant barked orders to the other officers. Navy blue uniforms began to pillage the apartment for evidence of the crime.

"EMERGENCY SERVICE UNIT TO CENTRAL K . . . WE NEED A BUS AT THE LOCATION . . . ONE FEMALE PERP WITH APPARENT SELF-INFLICTED INJURIES, LENGTH OF TIME IN CONDITION UNKNOWN, APPEARS TO BE SEMI-CONCIOUS, STILL HAS A PULSE," the officer shouted into his two-way radio.

The ambulance arrived in less than three minutes. Paramedics rushed Myra out of the building, navigating their way through the gathering crowd of onlookers. A murmur of hushed whispers and speculation passed between the wealthy residents of Dara Gardens as they took in the nightmarish scene. ESU and WARRANT SQUAD were just a few of the titles that the neighbors read out loud as blue and white NYPD vehicles swarmed the area.

The EMTs carefully loaded the stretcher carrying Myra's body onto the back of the vehicle. Doors closed, and the ambulance squealed to life as it pulled away from the curb, leaving behind the wide-eyed and open-mouthed residents of the Jamaica Estates neighborhood.

"She's lost a lot of blood . . . I don't know if she is going to make it. Her blood pressure is steadily plummeting," one of the EMTs reported to the accompanying officer.

"She is important to us right now, so you better find a way to save her," the officer responded coldly.

Chapter 1

THE MORNING AFTER

"Mmmm," Myra moaned as she came into a state of half consciousness. She felt as if someone had a vise around her head, with a piece of metal adorning each of her temples, twisting and squeezing. The pain was unbearable. She tried to open her eyes but they were glued shut—a crusted combination of eye drop medication and dried up tears. As she struggled to pry them open, sharp pains shot through her eye sockets.

Myra had no idea where she was. Panic struck her like a one thousand pound boulder. Frantically, she began trying to move her body. As she tried to sit up, an unknown resistance forced her back down. Dazed and confused, she could barely move her head from side to side and as she tried the throbbing in her head intensified in her right frontal lobe. Myra attempted once again to lift her shoulders and back, but that too proved futile.

"Mmmm," she moaned louder this time. Fear and panic continued to strangle her. After several unsuccessful attempts, Myra finally managed to open her eyes.

Flat on her back, her gaze came to rest on the white ceiling. Myra cringed as the rectangular fluorescent bulbs dangling above blazed unmercifully into her hyposensitized eyes, temporarily blinding her to her new surroundings. Her first instinct was to lift her forearm to shield her eyes, but she didn't seem to have control over her body.

"Shit!" she said to herself as she closed her eyes back. *Why the hell are the lights so damn bright? Where the hell am I? What the fuck?!!"*

Myra began to sweat profusely as she continued struggling to move her limbs. Frustrated, she re-opened her eyes, this time to assess her situation. As she moved her eyes slowly to the left, silver metal railings glared back. *A hospital bed again?*

Peering beyond the railings, Myra saw quilted white padding on the walls and floor. Enduring the pain that racked her skull, she finally managed to lift her head slightly off the bed toward her chest. Forcing air into her lungs with shallow breaths, Myra looked down at herself. A wide, tan leather strap lay across her chest, held firmly in place by silver padlocks attached to each side of the bed.

"Aghhh!!" Myra screamed, and suddenly her body seemed to come alive. She thrashed about fiercely trying to free herself, fighting with all of her might to overcome the restraints. Every inch of her flesh ached. Grunting and gasping, Myra felt like she had been in a twelve round boxing match with Roy Jones, Jr. She tried in vain to move her arms, which were neatly folded across her chest, but they too were impervious to change. Myra's breath got caught in her throat as she realized the problem. *A strait jacket?!* She could no longer control her emotions. Warm tears flowed silently from the corner of her eyes, pooling in her ears as she put her head back down on the bed.

Myra shook uncontrollably, like a wild animal just coming into captivity. She had no idea why she was there. She struggled to recall what had happened to her, but her memory escaped her over and over again.

Myra felt lifetimes pass through periods of drug-induced sleep and wakefulness. During a period of consciousness, Myra heard a noise. Groggily, she turned her head to investigate. The huge door, previously camouflaged by the white padding on the wall, slowly opened.

Her heart beat rapidly, chocking off her circulation. *This is it.*

They're coming to kill me! Wet, hot piss trickled down her legs but Myra refused to take her eyes off of the door even as her vision began to fail her. Exasperated, she rolled her eyes up into her head to try and get her retinas to focus. A voice, low and soft, spoke to her.

"Hello . . . Hello?"

Myra heard what sounded like a chain hitting up against a clipboard.

"How are you feeling today?" the mysterious voice gently inquired.

The voice was definitely feminine. Unclenching her jaw, Myra relaxed a bit, but refused to acknowledge her visitor.

"I'm your nurse I'm here to take your vital signs and help you. Are you ready to talk, Ms. Danford?" asked the nurse.

Myra did not respond. She tried to speak, but the muscles in her face did not want to cooperate. Her lips were dry and badly cracked, and her tongue felt like it was glued to the roof of her mouth. She felt buried alive in her own skin.

"Ok, have it your way," the nurse sighed with exhaustion. "I'm going to come back to take your vitals. I'll bring you something to eat and administer your medication. By the way, my name is Mrs. Tribble, and I will be your nurse as long as you are here on the locked ward. If you need anything, just let me know," the nurse stated and with that she disappeared behind the white padded wall.

Once the door clicked shut, Myra began to sob uncontrollably. She had so many questions. *What the hell did she mean locked ward? What the hell did she mean nurse? Shit, that must mean I'm in a hospital? What the hell did I do to get myself in here?* She scanned her memory but came up empty. Whatever medication they were giving her was interfering with her brain waves. She remembered pissing on herself earlier, but she didn't feel wet anymore. *Maybe I am crazy.*

Mrs. Tribble returned and she came in the same way as before, but this time two men dressed in white uniforms accompanied her. The first one was a short, chubby white guy with red cheeks and a Charlie Chaplin mustache. His counterpart was a tall, skinny white boy with a pimply face, whose elbows seemed to protrude unnaturally through his skin. Both men carried large rings of keys on their belts which jangled loudly as they moved.

"Ok, Ms. Danford. We are going to take you out of this restraint," Mrs. Tribble's soothing voice informed her. "I don't want you to fight or fuss, ok? I'm just trying to get you cleaned up," Mrs. Tribble explained.

Myra stared perplexedly at the trio. She noticed that the skinny boy had moved a noticeable distance away from her bed where he was gawking rudely at her. The fat man was bending over her bed, breathing heavily as he worked to unlock the padlocks which held the leather straps across Myra's chest in place. As he worked on the locks, he cast uneasy glances in her direction.

Huffing and puffing as if he were running a marathon, the portly attendant slowly unzipped the bottom half of the strait jacket to free Myra's lower body. A look of pure disgust contorted his face.

Mrs. Tribble abruptly approached the bed. "Sit up," she ordered, grabbing Myra under her arms and helping her into a sitting position causing the strait jacket to fall from her shoulders. Myra ignored the pain pulsating throughout her body.

The attendants seemed to recoil at the rank smell emanating from her body. Myra herself gagged as the scent of urine mixed with old blood reached her nostrils.

As the attendants quickly backed away from the bed, the sound of jangling keys jarred Myra's ears. The medication may have dulled her mind, but it painfully intensified her senses. She felt like she had acquired animal instincts—dog hearing.

Myra's mouth involuntarily hung open. Drool escaped her lips, running down her chin and onto her chest, mixing with the tears that flowed freely from her eyes.

"Don't waste your time crying. Just get up and fix the problem," the pimply-faced boy chided. Myra's skin grew hot with embarrassment.

"Can you stand up?" asked Mrs. Tribble.

Myra couldn't muster up the words to answer Mrs. Tribble. Twisting her body until her bare feet touched the floor, Myra managed to extend her arms to Mrs. Tribble's shoulders. Just then the skinny boy bent down at her feet with a set of keys in hand. She had no idea what he was doing down there and she did not care. She thought she was getting the hell out of there.

As Myra pushed off from the edge of the hospital bed, she felt like the scarecrow in the *Wizard of Oz.* Her legs shook violently, quaking like a leaf in a wild storm. Mrs. Tribble grabbed her just before her knees buckled, forcing her back up onto the bed. Myra felt like a baby, learning to walk all over again.

Catching her breath, Myra was finally able to take a good look at Mrs. Tribble. A petite black woman with a small frame, the nurse's scrubs were so baggy they seemed to swallow her body. She had a caramel complexion with dusty red hair pulled back in a tight ponytail. Her full lips, tinted bright orange, made her look like a cartoon character.

Mrs. Tribble had very little hair around the sides of her head and she must have used a damn near whole jar of gel to keep those little bird hairs in the back from falling down. Myra, of course, was currently in no position to pass judgment on Mrs. Tribble's looks, or lack thereof.

"Start walking one foot in front of the other . . . I got you honey. I'm sure not gonna let you fall," Mrs. Tribble reassured Myra, as she held firmly onto her arms.

Myra moved around the room as if she were floating on air. As she moved, she noticed the metal shackles cold and hard around her ankles. They served as a reminder that she had to find out why she was there to begin with. *Damn, do I really need to be treated like a mass murderer?*

"I'm going to take you for a shower before you eat," Mrs. Tribble spoke to Myra as if she were a toddler. With Myra in tow, Mrs. Tribble slowly opened the door concealed in the wall. As they stepped out into the sterile white hallways, two NYPD officers jumped to attention. Both officers seemed to scrutinize Myra's every move as she slowly made her way down the seemingly never-ending corridor.

Myra dragged her feet across the floor with short baby steps, one foot at a time. The chains between the shackles dragged with each beleaguered step, making a song against the hard tiles on the floor. The pungent smell of disinfectant invaded her nostrils as Mrs. Tribble steered her toward a bathroom on the opposite end of the hall, located just before the elevators. The female police officer followed closely behind.

A scream of sheer terror erupted down the hall before Mrs. Tribble could fish her keys from her uniform pocket. Wide-eyed, Myra looked to Mrs. Tribble for answers.

"Listen honey, that's just one of the patients acting up. Don't be scared . . . you'll be hearing a lot more of that while you're here," Mrs. Tribble explained as orderlies and nurses rushed to the scene of the commotion.

As the door to the bathroom swung open, Myra was led inside like a helpless child. The bathroom reminded Myra of something she had seen on the HBO show *Oz*. It had white sinks with old fashioned faucets, the kind that had separate spouts for hot and cold water. The tiles on the walls and the floor were all white. The bathroom had no windows or mirrors and the toilets had no partitions. The hard institution paper sat on the floor, instead of on toilet paper rolls. A large expanse of wall served as a community shower, with four shower heads in a row, each with its own soap dish, built directly into the wall. Myra was not going to have any privacy.

Mrs. Tribble removed Myra's foam slippers from her feet and pulled her hospital-issued gown, which was covered in dried blood, over her head.

Myra stood naked, too confused to feel self-conscious. Once flawless, her skin was now bruised with imperfect black, blue, and purple circles.

Mrs. Tribble extended Myra's wrists to the female officer who stepped forward to unlock the handcuffs. It was then that Myra noticed the bulky blood soaked gauze that covered both of her wrists.

"We will change these when you get out of the shower, OK?" And with that, Mrs. Tribble turned on the shower, full blast and forced Myra beneath the cold stream of water.

Myra's skin stung like she was being stabbed with a million tiny needles and she recoiled from the water. Mrs. Tribble caught her just before she hit the floor and quickly set her back on her feet, shoving a soapy disposable washcloth into her hand.

"If your skin feels sensitive to the water, don't worry about it. That's the side effects of some of the medication you've been given," Mrs. Tribble explained. Myra wondered what medication that could be, her mind raced with questions.

Immediately after her shower, Mrs. Tribble escorted Myra back to her padded room. She felt like a normal human being again. She was even beginning to feel hungry.

Myra opened the food tray that had been placed on the end of her bed earlier. *What the fuck is this?* The strained peas—cold, green, mashed—were in a small plastic bowl and looked like vomit. The mystery meat—brown, hard and gravy-less—was chopped into about a hundred tiny pieces, like it was prepared for a two year old child. She wasn't eating that shit.

Myra covered the tray and put her head in her hands. Before she could get a minute of peace to collect her muddled thoughts, the female cop entered the room along with Mrs. Tribble.

The short, dark-skinned female cop approached slowly. That was the first time Myra had taken a good look at the officer. She had a flat chest and a huge butt and hips, with cellulite dimples clearly visible through the fabric of her overly snug uniform pants. Her coffee-stained teeth protruded unattractively over her lower lip and the half-inch of hair that she had looked as if she had left her perm in way too long; it was ruffled and unkempt, sticking up and out. She had two dark circles under her eyes and looked as if she hadn't had a good night of sleep in a long time.

"Are you left handed or right handed?" the cop asked Myra, with an attitude.

Myra didn't answer. The officer sucked her teeth and cuffed Myra's right hand to the bed.

Mrs. Tribble came back one more time to check on Myra before she ended her shift. "You have to eat, if you don't you will never get out of here," Mrs. Tribble scolded, after surveying Myra's untouched food tray.

"Ahem . . . Out of where?" Myra asked, clearing her throat and forcing the words out of her mouth. Her brain had finally sent the message to her tongue.

Mrs. Tribble had a surprised look on her face when she heard Myra speak, but she answered her question as if she answered this type of question regularly.

"You are in Elmhurst Hospital on the psychiatric ward where they bring all female prisoners who have mental issues," Mrs. Tribble said matter-of-factly. When she saw the vacant expression on Myra's face, she continued with the explanation.

"Ms. Danford, this is what I refer to as "the morning after" with all of my patients. You were brought in last night by ambulance, but in police custody. They signed you in involuntarily according to your chart." Pointing to Myra's wrists, Mrs. Tribble continued, "As you can see, you tried to commit suicide. You are also under arrest right now . . . don't you remember anything?" Mrs. Tribble asked.

Myra crinkled her forehead and bit into her bottom lip. *She had tried to kill herself?!? Under arrest*?!? Her mind screamed . . . *WHAT*?!? ...but she remained silent.

"You will be arraigned as soon as they can get a judge to come and do it," Mrs. Tribble explained.

Myra nodded robotically, like she fully understood what Mrs. Tribble was telling her. In reality, she had no clue what Mrs. Tribble was talking about.

As soon as Mrs. Tribble left her room, Myra buried her face in her thin hospital pillow and sobbed through the night. *What the hell is going on?*

Chapter 2

MYRA

I believe I can fly . . ..I believe I can touch the sky . . . I think about it every night and day . . . Spread my wings and fly away . . . Oh I believe I can fly . . .

"I Believe I Can Fly"—that would be their mantra for life. Myra sat with her graduating class singing along with R. Kelley. Sweat dripped from underneath her arms, dampening the inner lining of her graduation gown and staining her thin cotton shirt. The golden tassel that hung from her graduation cap hit her on the side of her face and sometimes in the eye as she shook her legs back and forth anxiously awaiting her name to be called.

Myra's eyes eagerly scanned the latecomers who tiptoed their way inside, searching for empty seats. Over five hundred people filled the huge auditorium and, as of yet, there was no sign of her mother.

Myra's lip quivered as her eyes began to fill with tears. How could her mother not come to her high school graduation? After she had worked so hard. After all she had done for her mother during those crucial years of her life.

Myra painfully remembered all of the times that she had come home from school to find her small, one-bedroom apartment filled with crack heads, dope fiends and any other helter-skelter you could think of. She remembered seeing people shooting up, sniffing lines of cocaine and heroin, and sucking on crack pipes all day long. She remembered having to clear away burned spoons, used needles, and empty crack vials just to have space to do her homework. Myra remembered studying hard with hunger pains practically tearing her insides out, while her mother chased crack or heroin—whichever she could get her hands on.

The thunderous applause brought Myra back to reality. The song had finally come to an end and the principal of Thomas Jefferson High School was speaking at the podium, "And now, I am very proud to introduce to you a young lady who has excelled in every aspect of student life, including academics and extracurricular activities. She is a fine example of what we want our future generation to be. So, without further ado, I present to you the class of 2003's valedictorian, Ms. Myra Danford!" said the principal enthusiastically. The crowd roared with applause.

Before she stood from her seat, Myra carefully scanned the audience once more. There was no sign of Vidal Danford anywhere. Not one person in the audience had come to see Myra. No mother, no father, no grandparents, uncles, aunts . . . no one was there to share in her once in a lifetime moment.

Myra's heart pounded with a dizzying combination of excitement, fear, pride, and sorrow. Wiping her cheeks, she reached under her seat and picked up the five sheets of loose leaf paper that contained her speech. She had spent two weeks preparing it, since she was unable to attend the prom and her senior class trip, due to lack of funds.

As the crowd continued to clap, Myra's ears began to ring. She stood up and moved slowly across the stage to the wooden podium buying time, hoping against hope that her mother would miraculously appear, but no Vidal.

"Good morning, fellow graduates, Principal Bailey, faculty, family and friends," Myra began, with her voice quivering.

Somehow she managed to deliver her speech flawlessly. At the conclusion she started to cry, but most people assumed that it was because she was sad to leave her friends and classmates.

After the ceremony, Myra walked slowly out of the building onto the crowded sidewalk. The graduation had ended and all of the graduates in their red caps and gowns milled about outside with their families. There were proud mothers and fathers, grandmothers and grandfathers, aunts and uncles, snapping picture after picture, singing "that's my baby." Celebration plans were underway.

"Myra . . . Myra!" a female voice yelled above the boisterous crowd. Myra turned toward the sound of the familiar voice and saw that it her best friend, Quanda. Myra and Quanda had been best friends since they were five years old. They met in kindergarten, as finger paint partners, and since then they've been inseparable.

"Was sup girl? Where you going?" Quanda asked

"No where. You know my mother didn't even show up," Myra reported sadly.

"Girl, you know she is sick. Don't sweat that bullshit, you can hang with me and my family, we going to Red Lobster . . . mmmm girrrrrl, I'ma get me some skrimps!" Quanda said playfully, trying to cheer her friend up. Quanda was clearly excited to be the first one of her mother's six children to make it through high school without getting pregnant or going to juvenile hall.

"Girl, I don't have any money, and I can't ask your mother for any more help," Myra said contritely.

"I'ma ask her then . . ." Quanda began, but Myra cut her off.

"No . . . no that's alright, it's all good. I'll just go home and get some sleep because girl I was too nervous about my speech to sleep last night," Myra lied.

Myra didn't sleep well at all because her mother moaned and groaned all night in pain with withdrawal. Myra refused to perform her usual to get Vidal high the day before her big day. So, feeling guilty, she stayed up watching her mother scream and writhe in pain, coupled with cold sweats and vomiting. Myra tried to make her mother as comfortable as she could, just as she had done so many nights of her young life. But at 5:00 a.m., she finally relented and gave Vidal enough money to get a small bundle of smack to get her over the sickness. Myra had done this in the hopes that her mother would show up to her graduation the next day.

"I'll be there . . . uh uh you said 9:30 right?" Vidal asked, snatching the money from Myra's hand and rushing toward the door. She knew that the dope man would be waiting for her. "Yeah 9:30 and you can wear my old blue dress; it should be small enough to fit you," Myra instructed, as the apartment door slammed.

That was the last Myra had seen of her mother that day.

"Girl, you sure? I mean . . . my mother just got her check yesterday so she got a lil paper," Quanda reassured her.

"No girl, I'm sure. I'll come over later so I can change my clothes and stuff. We'll kick it then," Myra said putting Quanda at ease.

"Aiight then girl, later," Quanda said with a smile.

Myra walked to the A train station on the corner of Liberty and Pennsylvania Avenues. Her school Metrocard allowed her through the metal turnstile for the last time.

When the train, resembling a silver bullet, made its ear-piercing stop, Myra stood at the edge of the platform waiting for the doors to open.

"Congratulations," a lady said to her, gesturing at her cap and gown.

"Thank you," Myra replied, as she maneuvered her way into the crowded train.

She rode one stop to Broadway-East New York. She walked up the stairs in the bustling junction stop, rode the escalator up to the elevated platform, and transferred to the J train, which would take her home.

"BLACK SOAP! OILS! INCENSE! ALL ONE DOLLAR!" Myra

waved to the friendly Muslim salesman, with his small folding table of Muslim-made products. Myra had been one of the petitioners who had fought to save his small business after Mayor Giuliani's so-called 'quality of life' laws tried to run him out of the subway. In fact, Myra thought sadly, this would probably be her last time seeing him. She was out of school and about to embark on a whole new life. At least, that was her plan.

As Myra sat on the nearly empty J train her eyes welled up with tears. She couldn't hold it in any longer . . . she couldn't believe that her mother couldn't just show up. After all Myra had done for her, Vidal couldn't do one damn thing for her daughter.

Myra glowered at the thought of her mother's betrayal. Myra decided to ride the train to the last stop and back, as she always did when she wanted to clear her mind. She stared up at the rectangular advertisements posted across the train, just above the doors. GOT ACNE? SEE DOCTOR ZIZMOR . . . PREGNANT? . . . NEED HELP? PLANNED PARENTHOOD . . . IN DEBT? . . . FILE BANKRUPTCY FOR ONE LOW PRICE OF $450.

She read every one of the posters, wondering if they put these kinds of ads in trains that went through white neighborhoods. Myra let herself daydream . . . back to a time when things were good...

The Christmas tree stood six feet tall, illuminated brightly with glowing white lights and adorned with white and gold glass ornaments. Vidal and Myra had spent two whole days decorating it. There were piles of gifts wrapped in beautiful gold and silver shiny wrapping paper spilling from under the tree, most of which were for Myra, who was an only child and extremely pampered.

"Wake up Myra . . . it's Christmas. Look what Santa Claus brought you," Vidal chimed, shaking her daughter gently, waiting to see the look on her daughter's face when she saw her gifts. Myra jumped out of bed and ran straight for the Christmas tree.

"Ooooh mommy, I got the Barbie Dream Bus . . . Oooohh look and

the Etcha-Sketch Animator . . . and the . . . " Myra rattled on and on.

"See. Didn't Mommy tell you if you were good Santa would come?" Vidal said, proud of what she had accomplished.

"You did," Myra said.

"Gimme a hug. Who is the best daughter ever?" Vidal sang, as she gave Myra a big squeeze.

"Meeeeeee!" Myra sang back

"Daddy is coming home soon, so let's go make him some cookies," Vidal suggested. "Yeaaaah! Let's go," Myra cheered, grabbing her mother's hand as they both ran toward the kitchen.

"PLEASE STAND CLEAR OF THE CLOSING DOORS!" the conductor's voice boomed, snapping Myra out of her trance. She was still on the J train. Peering over the scratch graffiti that riddled the windows, Myra could see tinges of pink and purple in the dusky sky as the sun began to set. But she needed more time to think . . . to try to remember how and when it all went wrong. *One more ride to the last stop and back should do it,* Myra rationalized, closing her eyes.

"Mommy can we eat the cookies now? Daddy is taking too long," Myra asked impatiently.

"Look, let's just give him a few more minutes. Ok?" Vidal said slightly annoyed. It had been twelve hours since they'd baked the cookies.

"Ok," Myra answered disappointedly.

Three more hours passed. "Myra, you go to bed now. Mommy has to make some phone calls," Vidal said with a hint of urgency in her voice.

"Ok, Mommy. Why are you crying Mommy?" Myra asked, looking at the tears streaming down her mother's beautiful face.

"I'm not sad, honey. I just have something in my eyes," Vidal lied, as she puffed on her twenty-fifth Kool cigarette.

"Goodnight," Myra said, satisfied with the answer.

"Goodnight baby girl," Vidal replied, kissing her daughter's forehead.

There had been no sign of Myra's father and no phone calls explaining his absence. At first Vidal worried that something bad had hap-

pened to him. But after three days passed with no sign of Travis, Vidal finally realized he wasn't coming back.

Myra looked down at the small rectangular leather case that held her diploma. She wiped the tears from her eyes, making excuses for her mother's absence—rationalizing her behavior. *It wasn't her fault. He left because of me and she couldn't take it.*

Vidal Avis was a strikingly beautiful fifteen year old girl when she met Travis Danford. She had a slightly sun-kissed complexion, with freckles perfectly aligned on both of her cheeks. Her skin was smooth and delicate with no acne or scars—flawless.

Her eyes were almond-shaped and many people often mistook her for Asian. Her hair was jet black and hung all the way to the back of her knees. She had a perfect hourglass shape, 36/24/36, with breasts that most women envied and most men admired. A plastic surgeon could not have duplicated such perfection.

They met at a basketball game. He was a six foot three inch tall high school basketball phenomenon with skin the color of black velvet, straight pearly white teeth, and muscles on every inch of his frame. He was a star and he knew it. Whenever Travis played, screaming girls would fill the bleachers and even the guys would come out to admire his game. Travis was the most sought-after player, and Vidal the most sought-after girl. Their paths were bound to cross.

When Travis first spotted Vidal at one of his games, he thought he was hallucinating. The girl with the long ponytails, wearing a soft V-neck sweater that revealed just the right amount of cleavage, had piqued his interest. This beautiful Nubian queen would be his.

It was love at first sight. They both knew it. Theirs was a whirlwind love affair which resulted in Vidal getting pregnant. Travis had to grow up fast, but he willingly accepted his responsibility. When

Vidal's mother, Fran, found out about her daughter's condition, she had only one word to say, "OUT!"

And out Vidal went . . . straight into the arms of Travis. He moved her out of the Fort Greene projects, where they had both grown up, and into an apartment in Flatbush Brooklyn—a relatively uppity neighborhood at the time. Travis graduated from high school with a basketball scholarship to Fordham University. Vidal put off her schooling and dreams of being an artist and settled for being a wife and a mother instead. Travis told her that she didn't need a high school diploma because they would be rich and she would never have to work outside the home; and she believed him. Travis Danford had promised her the world.

Myra Tranece Danford came into the world on March 10, 1985, a healthy 7 lbs. even. She was gorgeous, with a beautiful pecan complexion, a cross between Vidal's light skin and Travis' ebony skin. Her hair was wavy and jet-black. Her eyes were like half moons, and when she smiled they would close completely.

Travis and Vidal both adored their beautiful daughter. Sometimes they would put her in the middle of their king-sized bed and just stare at her.

Time went by and Travis graduated from college. He was picked up by several NBA teams. He'd receive a signing bonus, get cut, receive another offer, and then get cut again. It was a vicious cycle and Travis secretly blamed his marriage and the stress of fatherhood for his unstable and unsuccessful career.

On December 20, 1988, Travis left home, giving his wife and child their customary kiss on the forehead. He was going to try out for the Detroit Pistons as a walk on—that was his story anyway.

He promised that he would be home for Christmas, just in time for Myra to open her gifts. He never came home. He never called. Vidal was devastated by his desertion. She never recovered. She couldn't afford the expensive apartment in Flatbush, and her mother had disowned her years ago when she ran off pregnant with Travis' child.

Vidal lived out the security deposit that Travis had put down when they first moved in. Once that ran out, she took her daughter to the Department of Homeless Services Emergency Assistance Unit, located in the Bronx, where they slept on the floor for three days before they were assigned to Latham Hotel, the worst welfare hotel in New York City's history.

Vidal tried to survive without mingling with the likes of the people in the hotel. It was hard. She had to get used to living off of the one hundred and nine dollars in cash and the ninety five dollars in food stamps that she received from welfare. It was a far cry from the money she was accustomed to receiving from Travis.

Before she knew it, she started seeking comfort in hanging out with some of the other females at the hotel, all mothers or crackheads or dope fiends. Crack was plaguing the city, but heroin was also still around from the seventies. Before long, Vidal had slowly been lured into the drug world. Heroin was her drug of choice, mostly because the high lasted much longer. The first time she used, she overdosed and had to be brought back with a whole lot of slapping and cold water. But that didn't dissuade her. Vidal was hooked. She turned to drugs for comfort, but mostly to forget the past. But it was hard to forget the past when her daughter's face was the spitting image of Travis,' a constant reminder of his abandonment, sometimes making her blood boil over with anger.

Vidal took her daughter and her drug habit along with her to the projects. After her name came up on the Housing Authority waiting list, she moved into the Tompkins Projects in the Bedford-Stuyvesant section of Brooklyn. Drugs had taken over her mind, body and soul. They robbed her of her motherhood, her ability to nurture, her ability to love, and most importantly, her morals.

Myra, come on! You gotta go with me somewhere," Vidal urged Myra, pacing back and forth. "But I'm sleepy," Myra whined. "Look gotdamitt! I gotta go somewhere and you gotta come. So wake the fuck up!" Vidal yelled.

Myra had been noticing a drastic change in her mother over the years since her father had left. It started with her waking up late to take Myra to school. Eventually, Vidal stopped cooking, cleaning, and taking care of Myra's needs. Myra watched as huge sores began popping up on her mother's inner forearm, thighs, and on her shins right above her ankles. Vidal, who was once worshipped for her beauty, was now losing her hair; had dangerously dropped weight, in what seemed like increments of 10 pounds a day; her teeth were rotting; her skin appeared dry and wrinkled, adding several years to her actual age; the bones in her face seemed skeletal, without an ounce of fat on her cheeks; and her eyes had begun to sink into her face and underneath were dark circles, which prominently outlined the wretchedness of her soul.

Like a good daughter, Myra followed her mother's instructions. They walked at a feverishly fast pace. Myra had to run alongside Vidal just to keep up. Her heart pounded and her mouth was dry . . . she couldn't seem to keep up with her mother's pace. The cold early morning air stung the inside of her nose, causing tears to involuntarily run down her eyes.

They finally arrived at the building. It was an old-fashioned brownstone that needed major repairs. The front gate hung off its hinges and had to be lifted slightly in order to open. The large steps had been re- painted with bright red paint, but the paint was chipping off which made them look rundown. The front doors weren't the usual glass doors that you would see on a brownstone; instead a plank of wood replaced what should have been doors. The windows had no curtains and were extremely dirty. Myra looked around confused. Where was her mother taking her?

Bang! Bang! Bang! Vidal knocked hard on the makeshift front door . . . no answer. She looked around suspiciously, pacing back and forth. Bang! Bang! Bang! she knocked again, harder this time. "Who is it?" a man's voice yelled back in response. "Quincy, it's me . . . Vidal. I came back for what we talked about," Vidal replied anxiously.

Myra watched as the door cracked open. The man behind the door peered out to investigate his visitors, exposing only the top half of his face. "Damn, girl, you is a real fiend," he said with a sly grin on his face, as he let Myra and Vidal inside.

"So Quincy, is you gonna do that or what?" Vidal asked as if she were in a great deal of pain, rubbing her arms like they itched really badly. Myra stood there, quietly.

"Let me see what you got here first. Don't be jumping no gun," the man named Quincy warned her mother.

"Aiight. Look at her . . . she ten," Vidal began, but before she could finish he cut her off. "Ten . . . bitch is you crazy?!? I ain't fucking with that . . . nah," said Quincy shaking his head. Myra was really confused now. Why was her mother telling this man her age?

"Pleaaaaaaseee," Vidal begged shamelessly.

"Bitch, I might be a pervert but I ain't that fucking low," Quincy declared.

"So take me . . . pleasssseeeee" Vidal begged, now on her knees.

"I told you I don't fuck no dope fiends . . . so getcha ass outta here," Quincy spat. Vidal had used up her chances at selling herself for drugs. She looked so bad now that she could barely make five dollars anymore. Myra watched in anguish. She wanted to help her mother . . . she loved Vidal so much. She began to cry. She was afraid and she didn't know what was going on.

As usual, Vidal refused to take no for an answer. Myra could not see the man's face—the hallway was very dark—but she could see his wide frame. Mr. Quincy, as he became known to Myra, started to wear down. He couldn't take this dope fiend grabbing at his legs. "Aiight already. Come on, bring her upstairs," he said giving in to Vidal's pleas.

"Ok, you gonna see. Come on, Myra, go upstairs," Vidal said pushing her daughter forward.

Myra obeyed. She had no reason to believe her mother would do anything to harm her. She climbed the weak wooden stairs, one at a time, terrified that the staircase would collapse from all their weight. As she neared the top, the smell was unbearable—a mixture of dog odor, cigar smoke, body odor, and rotting garbage. Myra covered her nose with the sleeve of her sweater.

When Quincy opened the door to the second floor apartment, Myra stood at the threshold, eyes wide with disbelief. There was nothing in the living room except for a 19-inch television with a hanger as its antenna and a reclining chair that looked like it had been to war—foam hung out of both arms and the seat cushion was worn in the middle. Flies stuck to a long brown strip of fly paper hanging from the ceiling. Myra had never seen so many flies in her life—dead or alive. The floor was filthy. Myra heard the sound of dogs barking and scratching behind a door to her right. She was terrified.

As Mr. Quincy moved toward the TV, Myra finally got to see what he looked like. He reminded her of a gorilla. His face was large and round and he had huge jowls instead of normal cheeks. His nose seemed obsolete, except for the two holes in his face that served as nostrils, which were larger than any she had ever seen on a human face. His face was so black that the whites of his eyes seemed to glow from the light of the TV. He had no teeth on the top, but little jagged rotten ones on the bottom. He was short and fat, resembling a woman pregnant with triplets, and his legs were so bowed that when he walked they looked like they would break at the knees. His clothes were filthy. He had food stains all over his shirt and pants, especially around his belly and crotch area. As he walked past Myra, his stench made her gag.

"Take her to the back room and make her take her clothes off," Quincy instructed Vidal. Myra couldn't believe what she was hearing—he couldn't be talking about her.

"Gimme the shit first Quincy," Vidal insisted. "Bitch I'ma give it to you. Just hold the fuck on!" he said irritably.

"As a matter of fact . . . here . . . take dis shit and git da fuck outta my house," he shouted at Vidal as he handed her a small foil package. Examining the package, Vidal acquiesced. "Aiight...here," she said, pushing Myra toward him before she turned on her heels and scurried out the door.

Myra was all alone with the beast as she watched her mother rush out of the door. "Come here, brat!" Quincy ordered as he approached. Horrified, Myra turned to run, "MOMMY!" she howled as his hands closed tightly around her throat.

"NEXT STOP MYRTLE AVENUE!" the conductor belted out. Myra had relived her nightmares enough. She decided that this time she would get off the train and see if Quanda was home yet so she could change out of her graduation dress. All of her clothes were at Quanda's house because if she left them at home, Vidal would find a way to sell them.

Myra had to work for everything she had because her mother had stopped buying her things a long time ago. She worked Summer Youth Employment every summer since she was fourteen, and during the school year she helped out at Dominican Salon, the Dominican hair salon on Liberty Avenue, in exchange for a little cash and free doobey's. Myra had become a pro at saving up her money to buy outfits and sneakers so no one would tease her about her clothes.

Quanda had always been there for her—always loyal. Quanda's mother, Ms. Brenda, had helped Myra on numerous occasions. She would let Myra hide in her house whenever somebody in the neighborhood got tired of Vidal's shit and decided to call Child Protective Services on her. Ms. Brenda even kicked Vidal's ass a few times over the way she treated Myra. She also provided Myra with hand-me-down clothes from her children, and fed her from the time she was six years old until Myra was able to take care of herself. Ms. Brenda did that so that the school wouldn't figure out what was going on in Myra's home.

Ms. Brenda had six children and she was ghetto-fabulous. Who else would have six children whose names all started with the same letter? Quesha, Quanda, Quadir, Quame, Quilleta, and Quashan. She was a single mother by circumstance and on welfare, but with the way she took Myra in under her wing, it was really like she had seven children. Besides, Ms. Brenda had always wished that her dumb ass kids would excel in school like Myra did.

"Girl, where the hell you been all this time?" Quanda asked as she opened the door for Myra.

"Oh, you know my usual, riding the iron horse," Myra answered quietly.

"You better stop that shit before somebody rob your ass one a' these days," Quanda scolded.

"How was Red Lobster?" Myra asked, changing the subject as she stepped inside.

"Girl, it was good until Quil decided she gonna curse out the waiter for taking too long to bring some a those cheesy garlic biscuits. Girl, we almost got throwed out," Quanda laughed.

"Thrown out you mean," Myra said, correcting Quanda's grammar. She hated to hear her friend say stuff like throwed . . . likeded . . . loveded . . . etc.

"Whatever. What we gonna do now that we outta school?" Quanda asked.

"I'm waiting on my acceptance letters. I'm going to college. I have to get the hell up out of here," Myra explained.

"Well girl, my SAT scores wasn't high enough so I'ma have to go to community college and then to a regular college," Quanda complained.

"That'll work . . . at least you'll be doing something besides staying around Tompkins," Myra replied.

"Girl, shit . . . I'm thinking 'bout finding me a rich man, one that's on a serious paper chase, letting him wife me out and just livin' like that cause school really ain't for me," Quanda said giggling.

Quanda had a secret but she knew that Myra would not approve. She never told Myra about her affair with a hustler named Rell from around the way.

Myra didn't respond to Quanda's comment. She didn't find it funny. She knew what waiting on a man could get you. Look at her mother.

"Girl, let me change my clothes and then we can go watch the basketball games in the back. Tompkins is playing Marcy tonight. You know they leave the good games for night time", Myra said.

"Yeah girl, that's wassup but let's go early before . . . *gunshots, gunshots,*" Quanda sang, with a fake Jamaican accent, trying to sound like a reggae singer.

"I know that's right," Myra said, laughing as she headed for Quanda's room.

Myra opened the plastic Rubbermaid tub that contained her clothes. She took out her red velour Lady Enyce sweat suit and a white baby tee. She sat on the bottom bunk bed, Quanda's part of the room, as she got dressed.

"Damn girl, since you wearing your sweat suit I'ma wear mine 'cause it did get a lil chilly out," Quanda said as she walked to the small closet in the left corner of her room and took out her baby blue Rocawear velour suit.

Myra and Quanda were so close they often did that . . . wore the same type of clothes—just not the same color. Myra topped her outfit off with red Diesel sneakers and Quanda with her all-white Nike Air Force One's. Both girls stayed current with the latest brand names; although they saw girls in their projects wearing Gucci, Prada, Fendi, Chanel, Dior, and other high-priced designer labels, they knew that most of them put up with a lot of bullshit to get it. The two of them were happy staying modestly fashionable with clothes from DKNY, Guess, Rocawear, Enyce, Baby Phat, and Diesel; sneakers by Nike; shoes by Steve Madden, and Nine West; and bags from Coach. They both worked real hard to get the things that they liked. Neither of them had anyone giving them shit on a silver platter.

Myra and Quanda joked and laughed, having a good time. Leaving Quanda's house, they cut through the path between their buildings—since they were right next to each other. The only thing separating the two buildings were small patches of grass, adorned with chain link barriers that made small C shapes as they looped from one small silver pole to another.

As the girls walked, they received many cat calls from the hustling guys loitering outside—profiling—leaning up against their Cadillac Escalades, BMW 745's (quarter to eights as they were referred to in the hood), and a number of other high-priced luxury vehicles that lined the side of the street. This activity was known as the "floss show," and during the summer time basketball games, the highlight of the event were the cars and guys outside, more people watched the cars and the occupants than they did the basketball games.

Myra and Quanda had already decided that they were not dating or messing around with any drug dealers. Myra because she hated what drugs had done to her mother and Quanda because Ms. Brenda had threatened her life if she ever caught her with one of them again. Quanda had tried it once before and her mother had beat her within an inch of her life when she found out. Needless to say, Quanda immediately ended her relationship.

The guys were beguiled by Myra and Quanda's looks. Myra had a pecan complexion, with the most beautiful half moon shaped eyes that were adorned with long, dark eyelashes. Her skin was flawless and she had perfectly straight, white teeth. They were so perfect, that it looked as if she had Da Vinci veneers placed on them. Her hair was shoulder length and curly, but whenever she got a doobey, it would fall perfectly straight. Unlike other girls, she never needed a perm. Myra had grown to be very voluptuous. Everyone who knew Myra said that it was because of what Vidal had made her do at a young age. In the projects, the older gossipy women always said, "fucking makes ya blow up." Myra's breasts were a 36 D cup and they sat up perfectly on her chest. Her stomach was flat and her hips rounded 40 inches, with an apple bottom to match.

Quanda had a dark chocolate complexion. She was also striking in her own way. She had a short hair cut which her mother kept done in small stiff curls. She was skinny, with small breasts but she had sexy Tina Turner legs which made her appealing. With those legs, she could wear almost anything and look sexy.

They were the most coveted prizes in the projects, but only because they ignored the guys, which gave them an alluring and mysterious aura. Most of the other girls around the way who were the same ages had drug dealer boyfriends . . . or baby daddies by now. The fast money, fast cars, and name brand clothes appealed to the other girls but not to Myra. She thought it was ludicrous to live in the projects carrying an $850 pocketbook. Unlike most of her peers, Myra dreamt of earning her degree so that she could make a career for herself and buy a beautiful house with a big back yard, a nice car, and go on vacations to places with white sandy beaches. She wanted the "American Dream."

"Yo graduates!" Knowledge yelled when he saw Myra and Quanda approaching. Knowledge was one of the bigger hustlers in their projects. He was only three years older than them and had moved up from street peddling to boss. Most of the guys on the Avenue worked for him. He was the most notorious nigga in Bed-Stuy. People said he would kill his own mother if she shorted him fifty cents. He came around the way to collect his money, and to scope out the chicks. He had three baby mothers and counting . . . and he was definitely fly, wearing nothing but Prada, Gucci, Louis Vuitton, Rocawear, and Sean Jean . . . to name a few, and donning only platinum and diamond jewelry. He drove more than one luxury car, but today he had his black BMW 760, top of the line joint, fully loaded with 20 inch

Lexani rims, which he kept so shiny they looked like mirrors. He had definitely bought into everything rappers rapped about these days. Myra and Quanda looked at him and rolled their eyes. They remembered when he was just a dirty little snotty nosed nuisance trying to play feel-the-butts with them.

"Oooooooh they plaaaaayed you son!" his friends sang out in unison, teasingly.

"Fuck those stuck-up bum bitches . . . especially that bitch Myra. She ain't shit anyway. Plus, if I really wanted her I could have her ass anytime. You know her dope fiend ass mother be selling that pussy for a 20," Knowledge announced loudly, hoping to mask his embarrassment.

"Fuck you, Knowledge!" Quanda yelled back, defending Myra. Myra put up her middle finger. She knew how many times Knowledge had tried to get with her and that he was just bitter from the rejection. She didn't care about his money or his gear. Both girls began to speed walk to get away from him and his cohorts.

Myra and Quanda finally made it to the concrete path that separated their buildings, noticing for the first time the ambulances and several NYPD cars parked in front of Myra's building.

"Damn what happened now?" Quanda asked. Neither of them had heard any gunshots while they were in Quanda's house. Myra stayed quiet. Whenever she saw police cars or ambulances at her building she always worried about Vidal.

They rushed toward the building but stopped when they saw Myra's neighbor, Ms. Taylor, whom everybody called Bambi, flailing her arms wildly and screaming "NO! NO! Oh God, NO!!!"

Myra slowed down her pace and her heart raced. Bambi had lived across the hall from Myra since she and Vidal had moved in. She was a short woman with midget-like features. She was nicknamed Bambi because of her beautiful, big round eyes with long eyelashes. Bambi had raised her three sons in Tompkins and, one by one, she'd lost them to the streets. At one time, she lived the highlife profiting greatly from son's hustling. She had furs, Italian furniture, and trips to Atlantic City almost every week. People in the projects nicknamed her and her sons "three thugs and a little lady." But that life was short-lived. She had now resigned herself to staying in the house—this after two of her three sons were gunned down a year apart, in Tompkins—one on the path leading to her building and one directly across the street, in the order they were born. Bambi had become a notorious recluse, only leaving her apartment to cash her SSI check once a month. Her baby boy, Farel, was all she had left. She begged him to leave the game and he promised that he would, but like all hustlers his promises proved empty.

Myra and Quanda looked at each other and instinctively they knew what had happened. Bambi's last son, Farel, who they attended elementary school with, lay dead in front of the building. His mother watching helplessly as she waited for the morgue truck to pick up his body, because EMT's are not allowed to remove a body after a person is already dead. The scene was gruesome and bloody. Farel had been shot over a dozen times in his chest, head, face, and legs . . . only about twenty feet from where his last brother had met a similar fate. His teeth lay scattered on the hard pavement and his face was almost nonexistent.

Bambi had no one. Her children were casualties of the street war that raged in their neighborhood. Myra cried for Bambi's loss as Quanda put her arms around her shoulders for support. "Yo, put a fucking sheet over him!" someone in the crowd yelled at the homicide detective standing over the body. Bambi fainted.

Myra, Quanda, and damn near everyone from the block sat on the benches in front of Myra's building talking about what had happened until the sun came up. They all had plastic cups filled with Hennessy mixed with Hpnotiq, what they called the "Incredible Hulk" in the hood. One of Farel's boys had gone to the liquor store in tribute to his fallen comrade. Everyone poured a small amount of their drinks onto the ground in remembrance of their friend. The group sat next to the yellow police tape, as if it were a regular part of the scenery. The homicide detectives had come and gone; unwilling to devote time to investigating the murder of a well-known drug dealer.

Farel's death only served as a reminder to Myra. She had to get the hell out of Tompkins. But where would she go? She hadn't figured that out just yet, but at this point in her life, anywhere would do.

"Yo Myra, I'm mad tired. I'm goin' upstairs," Quanda said yawning and stretching. Myra remained silent. She knew her options—go cram in at Quanda's house or go upstairs to her apartment, which on any given day could be completely empty or filled with addicts. She decided to take a chance and hope that no one was in her house. She wanted to be alone tonight.

"I'm goin' upstairs to my house," Myra told Quanda. The girls hugged each other as they parted, saying good night and good morning to all the mourners who remained outside on the benches watching the sun rise.

Myra entered her building and decided to check the mailbox before she caught the elevator. She used her key to retrieve three letters from the small, silver box. Bill collector . . . Bill collector . . . St. John's University! Myra's heart skipped a beat with excitement. With shaking hands, she tore at the envelope making sure not to tear the letter inside. Myra hoped it was what she had been praying for.

Dear Ms. Danford,

It is my pleasure to inform you that you have been accepted to St. John's University for the Fall of 2003. I am further elated to inform you that based on your superior academic achievements, we would like to present you with the St. Vincent's Academic Scholarship.

This is by far one of our most distinguished scholar-

ships. The scholarship covers the cost of tuition and books your entire undergraduate career. You will not be required to fill out a FAFSA this fall. This scholarship will remain in effect as long as you maintain a 3.5 overall GPA.

If you are going to accept this offer, please fill out the enclosed application, have your parent(s) sign and date it, and return it using the enclosed envelope by July 10, 2003 .

Thank you and congratulations again. We look forward to hearing from you soon.

Sincerely,
Robert Harriman, President

Myra could barely contain her joy as she stepped onto the urine-ridden elevator. She placed one of the bill collector envelopes over the spit-covered elevator buttons and pressed 5. She knew she had no one to share her news with at that moment, but she also knew that this was her ticket out of there! Myra had a plan—she was going to get her education and get out of this hell hole . . . the right way.

Chapter 3

MILTON

"Aaaaaaaaaaaah!" Milton released a blood curdling scream. Pain shot through his entire body. He felt like someone was tearing him apart from inside out. The burning was unbearable. "Aaaaaaaaaaaah!" he screamed again, high-pitched this time, like a little girl being beaten.

"Shut the fuck up!!!" his older cousin whispered in his ear, panting as he spoke. He reached over with his large hand and violently covered Milton's nose and mouth. "Mmmmfffff!" Milton moaned into his cousin's hand as he tried to break free. He was sobbing now and his heart was racing. His cousin began pumping faster and faster, shredding away more and more of his flesh. Milton passed out from the pain.

"HUH, HUH, HUH," Milton panted as he jumped out of his sleep. His chest heaved in and out and sweat soaked his wife-beater undershirt causing it to stick to his muscular chest and stomach. His boxers and sheets were also drenched. He swallowed hard, looking around to make sure he was still in his apartment. Milton touched himself to confirm that he was a man, and not a twelve year old boy. It was just another nightmare, he reassured himself. Milton had been plagued with nightmares since his childhood. Sometimes they would subside for a month or two, but for the most part they were a constant in his life.

"Damn!" he said angrily. He hated the fact that he let his dreams get the best of him. He sat up and looked around his bedroom, picking up the football that he kept on the pillow next to him. He clutched it tightly to his chest, "Nobody can take this shit from me," he consoled himself.

Milton was surrounded by colorful framed posters of his favorite NFL players: Jerry Rice, Walter Payton, Lawrence Taylor, Barry Sanders and Emmitt Smith. Just looking at their pictures motivated him and instantly made him feel better. In his mind, he'd already made it. He had a full scholarship to play football at St. John's University, which included a monthly stipend, free books, and a fully-furnished luxury apartment. The cable box that sat atop his 36" flat screen Sony Wega TV read 4:25 . . . it was morning. He had practice in an hour and he had to pull himself together. He had to be focused.

Milton got up and went into the bathroom to wash his face. He flicked on the light switch and examined himself in the large vanity mirror that hung over the sink. Wiping the sweat from his smooth mocha colored skin; Milton opened his round hazel eyes and moved closer to the mirror to examine the large bags that were developing under them. He looked like shit. Just as he moved over the toilet to relieve himself, the telephone began to ring.

"Bliiiinnnnggg . . . bliiiinnnnggg . . ." Milton jumped, accidentally missing the toilet. "Who the fuck is calling me at this fucking time?" he complained as he sucked his teeth and ran out of the bathroom. He leaped stomach first onto the bed reaching for the phone, but just before he could pick up the receiver, the phone stopped ringing. "Fuck!" he shouted angrily.

He turned over onto his back and stared up at the ceiling. He often thought about going to therapy to work out his issues, mostly so he could stop having the nightmares, but when he considered his promising NFL career, he always decided against it. That's all he would need to end his career . . . some paparazzi taking a picture of him coming out of a shrink's office. He could see the headlines now,

"MILTON ROBERTS IS MENTAL" or "STAR QUARTERBACK IS ONE TOUCHDOWN FROM NORMAL." Right now the most important thing to Milton was his career and he would do anything in his power to protect it. He wasn't going to let anyone or anything stand between him and it.

Milton was in his senior year at St. John's University and the star of the football team. He was slated to enter the upcoming NFL draft, and assured that he would be the number one pick, or at least be drafted in the first round. Never before did a Division II school have NFL scouts knocking down its doors for a player. The scouts usually stuck to schools like Oklahoma State University, University of Miami and Tennessee State University for football players, but Milton had made St. John's the exception.

Milton Roberts grew up in the Red Hook projects in Brooklyn. His mother gave birth to him when she was 12 ½ years old and rumor had it that she had gotten pregnant by her stepfather. Milton was raised for the most part by his grandmother, Bertha, and led to believe that his mother was his sister, so he called her by her first name, Dorothia.

Dorothia ran the streets; she had no time for her baby boy. Bertha resented Milton's presence in her home; she had believed all the rumors about her husband and her daughter, and his presence reminded her of them every day. Bertha beat Milton's ass for everything and anything. She hardly ever bought him any clothes, so he was always the "bum" kid in the projects. His sneakers were always so run down they would flap open, or "talk" as the kids used to tease.

There was no hope for Milton—or that's what he'd always been led to believe. His grandmother constantly reminded him that he was a worthless piece of shit; and at one point, he came very close to fulfilling that prophecy. Milton often sat and thought about that one fateful night that changed is life forever.

"Gahead man, hurry up! Take it out," Milton's best friend, Brownie, urgently instructed. Milton nervously fumbled with the bee bee gun. "Gimme ya money bitch," he said with a cracking voice, as he continued to fumble with the toy gun. "HELLLLP!" the lady screamed. "Shut the fuck up," Brownie barked, punching the lady in her chest as he snatched the gun from Milton. He'd scare her himself. "What a punk-ass," he thought to himself about Milton. Thud. The woman crumpled to the ground under Brownie's punch. She didn't move.

"Yo grab her bag man!" Brownie demanded of Milton. Milton was frozen with fear; the lady was still not moving. "Yo, I think you killed her Brownie," Milton said nervously, shifting his weight from one foot to another. "Yo, fuck that come on," Brownie yelled as he snatched the lady's bag off of her limp body and began to run.

Milton stood motionless as he stared at the lady's fallen form. He could tell that she was dead. Maybe she had a heart attack, he thought to himself. The police sirens soon interrupted his train of thought, which finally spurred him into action. Someone had called the cops . . . Shit!

Brownie was a block ahead of him. BAM! BAM! BAM! Milton heard shots ring out, nearby. He saw Brownie's body lurch forward and then fall face forward to the ground. Milton cut across the grassy patches in the projects. He ran non-stop up twelve flights of stairs to the roof of the building next to his. He crossed the roof onto his building and went into his apartment unnoticed.

Brownie, his best friend since birth, was dead. Shot dead by the police at fifteen years old. Milton cried for days over his loss. "Shut da fuck up wit dat cryin' boy. Actin' like some puredee fuckin' faggot. I done tole you, ain't no faggots bein' raised 'rown here. Muthafucka, I said shut up!" Bertha yelled spewing with anger as she cracked her hard leather cowhide belt over Milton's grieving body, letting it land where it pleased.

After Brownie's death, Milton decided that a life of crime was not for him. He learned to channel all of his pent-up energy into sports, namely football. He joined the football team at George Westinghouse High School and dedicated all of his time to playing football. Most of his friends had picked up on the hustling trade. In the projects, there were basically three ways a guy could make money: become a hustler, a rapper, or pro athlete, mostly basketball or football. A select few went to school, got degrees, and obtained profitable, legitimate jobs. Most chose hustling or rapping as their career choice because the money came much faster.

Early on Milton had made up his mind that he was going to the NFL. After all of the years of abuse he had endured at home, he'd become angry, sometimes borderline evil . . . but he made sure that he put all of his energy into his sport. Milton hated his grandmother and hated his mother even more. He hated all women. Milton always vowed that when he got older he would make all women's lives a living hell. His grandmother's beatings actually didn't really even bother him all that much . . . he was a man after all, and could take it. But Milton never forgave her for what she let happen to him when he was twelve years old. He often contemplated killing her in her sleep after it.

"Come on here, boy . . . Scriggy on his way upstairs. We bout to say surprise," Bertha said, ushering Milton to the apartment door. He didn't know his cousin Scriggy who everyone was so excited to see. Apparently, he'd been in jail long before Milton was even born. Scriggy had done 16 years in Elmira Prison in upstate New York, but he was released on parole. The family was throwing a party to celebrate his release.

KNOCK, KNOCK, KNOCK! The door to apartment 9G rattled. Everyone inside scrambled to get in their positions. "SURPRISE!!!" they all shouted in unison as Bertha pulled opened the door. Scriggy jumped on cue, but he knew what was going on. Cousin Scriggy stood six feet tall and was two hundred and fifty pounds of solid muscle. Scriggy had the blackest skin that Milton had ever seen in his life; and his face was riddled with several raised scars. His biceps bulged with his every move, and seemed to beg for mercy under the tight sleeves of his shirt. The crowd of expectant aunts, uncles, cousins, and friends surged forward with hugs, tears, and handshakes. Scriggy blended right on in.

"Come on now, let him get settled down and get soma this down home cookin' now . . . he ain't goin' nowhere no more. Ya'll can do all that later," Bertha commanded, shooing away the crowd that had gathered around Scriggy. Bertha's favorite nephew would get the royal treatment today.

Scranton Philip Roberts was Bertha's baby sister Joannie's—only child. Bertha had been taking care of Scriggy since his mother died while giving birth to him at home. Bertha always had a special place in her heart for him, and was devastated when he went to prison. She visited him religiously, whenever he wasn't in the hole for committing infractions.

Milton sat by taking in the scene in silence, afraid that if he opened his mouth Bertha would beat his ass. He watched as Scriggy shoveled the food into his mouth, chucking it up with the family. He watched as his aunts and other relatives, who always complained about not having any money, handed Scriggy several twenty dollar bills and a few ten's on the sly. Milton wished that they loved him the way they did Scriggy.

Milton realized that Scriggy would be living with them in their two bedroom apartment, which meant that he would have to share his room. At first he liked having Scriggy around because with Bertha preoccupied, she didn't have time to beat on him. But his feelings toward Scriggy would soon change.

One day, about two months after Scriggy's arrival, Scriggy and Milton were alone in the apartment together. Bertha had run out to take care of business. As soon as the door closed behind Bertha, Scriggy turned to Milton.

"So whatchu like to do, lil cuz?" Scriggy asked.

"Play football," Milton replied.

"Oh yeah? Ya any good?" Scriggy asked, seeming genuinely interested.

"Yeah and I'm goin' to Little League Panthers this year," Milton boasted proudly.

"Well I'ma show you a new game to play, Ok?" Scriggy said, slyly.

"What . . . how it go?" Milton asked eagerly.

"It's called 'Booties Up,'" Scriggy said.

"Oh I know that game. You stand facing the wall and see who can punch in the butt the hardest," Milton explained.

"Nah cuz, this one is different. Lemme show you," Scriggy said, motioning for Milton to come closer. Milton went to him.

"You gotta take off ya pants and ya drawers," Scriggy instructed.

"WHAT?" Milton said, alarmed by his cousin's request.

"You wanna learn or not, shithead!" Scriggy yelled.

"Ok," Milton said reluctantly as he took off his stuff.

"Turn around," Scriggy instructed. Milton obeyed.

"Bend over," Scriggy commanded. Milton obeyed, thinking that the worst his cousin would do was punch the shit out of his naked ass.

Milton got more than he had bargained for. That day and all the days to follow would change the rest of his life.

"Bliiiinnnnggg . . . bliiiinnnnggg . . ." the phone rang just as Milton was headed out the door. He ran back in to answer it; he never knew when an agent trying to get him to sign would call. They sometimes offered nice gifts as signing incentives and he didn't want to miss out on anything.

"Hello," he answered.

"What the fuck is up, bitch ass nigga?!?" the man's voice at the other end asked, dripping with venom.

"Yo nigga I told you I got you," Milton answered, obviously well-aware of who was calling.

"Look, I been waiting two weeks now for my payment. I know you don't want that fucking draft press conference to get what I got on you nigga—it would be a wrap fa ya ass," the man on the phone threatened.

"Yo, Damien, son, why you doing this shit? When I get drafted, as soon as I sign my contract I told you, I was gonna hit you off lovely," Milton whined.

"Look nigga, I invested mad time and money in you. When you decided that you wasn't using my manz as ya agent, that shit cut my pockets. So now I got some shit on ya ass nigga . . . and you won't play ball nowhere til you pay up," Damien stated flatly.

Milton was silent. He bit into his bottom lip until he tasted blood, and sweat drenched his brow. He wasn't even sure what Damien had on him but he knew he couldn't chance it. Milton had big time skeletons in his closet, and he'd pay any amount to keep them there.

"Oh yeah, nigga, and ya payment just went up to $1,500 a week," Damien shouted into the phone before he hung up.

Damien Fuller was a hustler, but not the kind who sold drugs. He was a professional predator who hung around the top high schools in all five boroughs of New York, seeking out the top athletes before they went to college. Damien worked for a sports management agent on the low, and his job was to shower the talented kids with expensive gifts—cars, furs, women, jewelry, name brand clothes—things these poor kids from the projects had never seen or experienced. And the recipients of these extravagant gifts paid the price— when they made it big, they were obligated to sign with Damien's boss. And if they didn't sign? Damien found ways to make them pay.

Milton had accepted numerous gifts from Damien throughout his high school years. Milton was slow to realize that Damien wasn't really a generous man, but a man with ulterior motives, who took just as quickly as he gave.

When Milton found out what Damien had in mind for him, he rejected the idea. Besides, he had researched the Stringer Danford Management Firm that Damien worked for and wasn't very impressed. They took a five percent cut, when all other agents took only one to three percent, and they had a dismal record when it came to endorsement contracts. Milton wasn't going to risk his career by signing with them.

When Milton informed Damien of his plans, everything went sour. Damien began his reign of terror, extorting Milton for large sums of money. Milton couldn't let it go down like that—he knew what he had to do. Just thinking about it made Milton's stomach churn. Before he could make it to the door, he ran into the bathroom and threw up.

Where the fuck I'ma get $1,500? Milton thought to himself. The monthly stipend he received from the school was $1,300, which he could double if he hosted a gambling party at his house, but even that wasn't a sure bet. The other alternative was that he could contact some of his boys back home and get a package to hustle, but that would mean admitting that he wasn't the big star that he portrayed himself to be. Milton picked up his cell phone and dialed, feeling desperate, but playing it cool.

"Yo," he said into the phone.

"Wassup, why you be calling me talking like that?" the woman at the other end replied.

"Yo . . . wassup? You messing with me ta night?" Milton asked smoothly.

"Oh you decide to call me now afta you pulled one of ya disappearing acts the otha night," she spat angrily.

"Yo save dat shit for the next man. Ya ass always talkin' breezy . . . you fucking wit me or not?" Milton asked irritably.

"Only if it's gonna be me and you, Milton . . . I ain't doin' no gambling party . . . this shit has gone too far now," the woman scolded.

"Whatchu mean? You be complaining, but don't ya ass be spending that fuckin' money?" he yelled into the receiver. This is why he hated women; they were all a bunch of ungrateful bitches, stupid too. They'd rather fuck a nigga for free in the name of love instead of getting paid to do it.

"Yeah, I be spendin' it alright muthafucka but I be makin' it," she shouted back.

"As a matter of fact, Milton . . . fuck you and the money. I ain't doin' that shit for you no more. Fuck a draft . . . fuck a big house . . . fuck a marriage . . . all that shit you be promising. You ain't no star player. You a fuckin' pimp. Anyway, I got money. Remember, my family ain't fuckin' poor! And I ain't no thirsty ass bum bitch! I did all this shit outta love for ya ass and you dissing me . . . FUCK YOU, MILTON ROBERTS!" she yelled right before she hung up on him.

Milton was furious. His nerves were standing on edge. The hairs on his skin stood up. *Wait til I see that bitch . . . I can easily find a new vic . . . bitches love me. Fuck her,* he thought to himself.

The new school year was about to begin in a week and Milton knew that meant star-struck freshmen girls would be arriving on campus in droves. He made up his mind that this time he would find one who would be loyal, one who would bend to his will, one he would mold to his liking, or one who had no choice.

Chapter 4

THE ARRAIGNMENT

Myra had no idea what time or day it was. When Mrs. Tribble entered her room wearing a different pair of scrubs, Myra assumed that a day had passed. Her mouth was pasty with white curds of dried saliva balled up in each corner. It was still hard for her to remember the particulars of her current predicament and the last time she tried to force herself to recall, she ended up with a massive headache. Today, Myra actually felt a lot better.

"Good morning, Ms. Danford. How ya feeling?" Mrs. Tribble asked amiably, as she wrapped the blood pressure cuff around Myra's arm.

"I'm ok . . . I guess," Myra mumbled in response. Her tongue felt heavy, like she had just eaten a whole jar of Elmer's kindergarten paste. "Do you think I can take a shower by myself today?" Myra inquired.

"No honey, on the locked ward all activity is supervised. This is jail. But you will see a judge and a doctor today and it's up to them to decide whether you stay here or go to Rikers Island," Mrs. Tribble explained. Myra wasn't sure what to make of what Mrs. Tribble had just told her.

Today, Myra had breakfast with the other patients/inmates in the cafeteria of the locked ward. Two correction officers stood guard at the entrance. The trays—orange, blue, and yellow—were all glued to the tables. Myra figured that was to keep the nuts from throwing them at each other. The utensils were plastic—go figure with the tough-ass food they served. Even the chairs were chained to the floor. As always, the food was lukewarm—probably to prevent any of the staff from being badly burned in the event that one of the inmates decided to throw her food at them.

Myra didn't have an appetite, especially after looking at her peers—if that's what they were now—drooling and nodding over their plates, too medicated to give a damn. *Damn what the hell are they giving them up in here?* she wondered.

"Can I leave now?" Myra asked one of the correction officers standing at the door. She wasn't eating in there.

"No, you have to wait until breakfast is over. Everyone leaves together," he said, flatly dismissing her request.

Oh, hell no! What fucking part of the game is that?

"I ain't crazy and I shouldn't even be in here," Myra mumbled under her breath as she headed back to her table.

Once breakfast was over, everyone was allowed to make their phone calls. Myra had fifteen minutes to use the phone. She didn't really know who to call. The one thing Myra did remember was her beautiful baby boy...Kyle. Tears came to her eyes as she tried to picture his face and remember the last time she'd seen him. Myra thought long and hard, trying to remember phone numbers to call. Her brain was still not functioning properly.

After staring at the keypad on the phone for a while, a phone number popped into her head and she dialed it. It was the number to the apartment where she and her boyfriend, Milton, currently lived. "Yo, I ain't here, do ya thing at the beep," the familiar voice on the answering machine instructed. Myra didn't leave a message. *Where the hell is he?* She couldn't really remember the last time she had seen him either. *Shit! Who else, who else?* Myra didn't have much time. She had to track down Milton. As her fingers starting dialing numbers that they instinctively knew, things slowly started to come back to her in flashes and she zoned out.

POP! POP! POP! Six rounds from the nickel plated 45mm Heckler and Koch handgun sounded off into the still morning air. Myra watched as bright blood gushed out of the hole in the recipient's neck. With pure terror etched on every line of the man's face, his body folded like an accordion to the ground. Milton jumped into the passenger seat and she floored the accelerator.

"Hello!" the deep voice on the other end of the receiver barked, snapping Myra back to the present.

"Uhhh, Hi. Um . . . who is this"? Myra stammered, forgetting who she had called.

"Who you called?!" the voice responded angrily. It wasn't Milton, that was for sure.

"Oh, hey Craig. This is Myra . . . is Milton there?" she asked, finally associating the voice with a name. Craig was one of Milton's teammates—one she had spoken to on the many occasions when Milton decided he wouldn't be coming home for the night.

"Nah, that nigga ain't been here," Craig replied, saying it like Myra should have known that.

"Oh, ok. Well, I'm in the hospital and—" Myra started, but before she could finish he cut her off.

"Yo, I know some of the story and that shit is fucked up! If I see that nigga, I tell him you called. Aiight?" and with that, the line went dead. He had hung up on her!

Craig seemed nervous on the phone, like Myra was the last person he wanted to speak to. *What was up with that?*

Myra remembered her baby boy again and started to cry. Her fifteen minutes was almost up and she would have to wait until tomorrow to use the phone again. She stood at the console, contemplating who to call next, when a tall, skinny Spanish chick with wild hair and razor scars all over her face came running head-on at Myra screaming.

"BITCH! GET DA FUCK OFF DA PHONE! YOU DON'T KNOW

THE RULES UP IN DA FUCKING PENTHOUSE. I RUN THIS SHIT. YOU BETTER FALL BACK AND ACT LIKE YOU KNOW!" the crazy female inmate yelled at Myra as her deep-set evil eyes hooded over with ill-intent. *The penthouse . . . what is she talking about?* Myra wondered as she watched in horror as the girl ran straight at her. Before Myra knew it, she was sprawled on the floor and the crazy Spanish girl was straddling her. It took the correction officer—a huge Suge Knight looking black guy—a minute or two to pull her off of Myra.

"Don't fuck around, Jenny, unless you wanna get locked down for the night!" the Suge Knight look-a-like shouted. With a blink of an eye, the big, bad bitch's mood went from pure rage to complete calm. The other inmates/patients knew exactly what the girl meant by 'the penthouse'—the mentally ill female inmates called the Elmhurst Hospital prison ward the "penthouse", because the food was better there than in was in any of the other city jails. They got snacks for free and way more privileges than they would if they were on Rikers Island or in any of the borough detention centers.

After the incident, Myra was visibly frayed and her hands shook uncontrollably. By now her telephone time was up. She still had no information about her baby boy or about the whereabouts of Milton. She left the phone area crying hysterically.

Mrs. Tribble was helping another patient/inmate. Myra felt alone and desperate for answers. She dropped to her knees and started to scream, acting like a real crazy person. The Suge Knight look-alike and fat ass Charlie Chaplin came bursting out of two side doors. In one scoop, Suge Knight swept Myra up off of her feet like a rag doll. Myra flailed and kicked and attempted to bite him a few times. But he wouldn't loosen his grip on her. In fact, his hold remained steady, reminding her of a move she had seen in an episode of *WWE* wrestling. As Suge held her stationary, Charlie Chaplin stuck her leg with a needle. Her body instantly went limp, making her damn-near catatonic. Unable to move or speak, they carried her into the locked padded room. Her free time was over.

TAP! TAP! TAP!

Myra was startled out of her sleep. Someone was hitting the railing of her bed. She opened her eyes wide, trying to get them to focus. Two men stood on either side of her bed looking down at her. They were dressed in trench coats and suits. Myra was starting to put the pieces together. She immediately knew who they were—detectives. The detectives had raced to the hospital, hoping to arrive before Myra was arraigned and assigned a lawyer. They knew that if she obtained a lawyer, their chances of receiving any information from her were slim to none.

Myra's heart raced, but she decided to play it cool. She'd heard enough hood tales about people getting arrested, talking to detectives without a lawyer, and living to regret it. The results were often the same—the poor young guy or girl would "confess" to the crime before they were assigned a lawyer, and then they'd be fucked for life. *What the fuck do they want?* she thought as she rubbed the sleep from her eyes. She didn't trust anybody.

"Hello, Ms. Danford. I'm Detective Wheeler," said the bald, black guy.

"And I'm Detective Paskins," the fat, white one followed. He reminded Myra of Tony Soprano from the HBO show, *The Sopranos.*

"We are from the major case squad in Brooklyn North Task Force," they said, almost in unison.

"We need to ask you a few questions about what happened," Detective Wheeler started. Myra just stared at them.

"You understand?" Detective Paskins asked. Myra didn't respond.

"How this works is we ask the questions and you answer them. Do you understand?" Paskins asked again. Myra still did not respond.

"Ms. Danford you are facing serious charges here, so you better start talking . . . and fast," Detective Wheeler castigated, getting up-close and in her face, trying to intimidate her. His behavior reminded Myra of a bad cop scene from a movie.

"You recognize this . . . huh? You fucking waste," Detective Paskins interjected angrily, showing Myra a picture of a gun. There would be no good cop/bad cop routine today, they were both seething over the crime and wanted a piece of her.

Myra finally grew tired of their so-called interrogation, which bordered on abuse.

"I don't remember shit . . . so I can't help ya'll," she said coldly dismissing them.

"Listen here girl . . . you need to try 'cause your life is on the line here. All of the evidence right now points to you," Detective Wheeler stated with conviction in his voice.

"I told you I don't remember shit," Myra reiterated.

"You remember who this is, don't you?" Detective Paskins asked mockingly, placing a picture of Myra's infant son on her lap. "If you don't start talking now, you will never see your baby boy again. He'll become another foster care statistic. You better start talking. Judges and juries don't look too kindly on mothers who abandon their children at birth," Detective Paskins threatened, chuckling evilly.

Myra began to cry. *How did they get that picture of Kyle?* She knew that there had to be a better way. The picture of her son seemed to jolt her back to reality. *I must be in deep shit,* she reasoned.

"Where is Milton Roberts? He left your dumb ass holding the bag, huh?" Detective Wheeler interjected, refusing to give up.

"I don't know, gotdammit!" Myra yelled at them both. "I can't remember shit! This medication got me all messed up; and even if I did know, I wouldn't tell ya'll asses anyway!" she assured them. *Where the fuck is Milton?*

"Looks like you done made shit worse for yourself," Detective Paskins retorted, finally giving up as he turned on his heels and stomped out of the room.

Myra cried herself back to sleep. That was all she could do lately . . . cry and sleep.

"Good afternoon. Uhhh . . . Ms. Danford is it?" a man's voice roared in Myra's ear, jolting her out of sleep once again. *Damn, what time is it? Not again!* Myra groaned inwardly. The detectives had just left.

Myra looked up at the short, balding, middle-aged man standing at her bedside, flanked by two court officers.

"My name is Judge Weitz. I'm here to conduct your bedside arraignment," he explained as he clicked on a small tape recorder. "We are on the record now, ok?" Myra nodded like she understood. "Normally, this is done in a courtroom, but since you're hospitalized, we'll have to do it here. Do you understand what I am saying to you?" he continued.

"Arraignment?" Myra asked, puzzled.

"Yes, Ms. Danford, that's the formal reading of your charges. I will let you know what you are charged with; ask you how you plead; offer you the services of an attorney; and set a date for you to come back to court. Shall we begin?" he asked.

"Ok," Myra answered, still confused.

"Ms. Danford, you are being charged with first degree murder, conspiracy to commit murder, grand larceny, robbery, and possession of a weapon for an unlawful purpose, as outlined in the New York State Penal code, for the crime that took place. How do you plead Ms. Danford?" the Judge finally asked.

"I can't remember a crime taking place," Myra insisted, sitting up in her bed.

"Ok Ms. Danford, I will enter a "not guilty" plea on your behalf," the judge replied as if he were in a rush to go somewhere else.

"Ms. Danford, do you have an attorney?" he asked perfunctorily.

"No," Myra answered.

"Ok. Do you work or have any significant income?" he inquired.

"No," Myra replied flatly.

"Then the court can appoint an attorney to represent you in regard to these charges. Do you wish to have an attorney appointed to you at this time?" he asked.

"I guess so . . . if I'm being charged with all of that," Myra responded uncertainly.

"Here is the card of an eighteen B attorney. His name is Mr. Shepoweitz and he's a public defender," the judge informed Myra as he placed the card on her lap. "I am refusing to set your bail at this time. Your court date is set for thirty days from today. Your attorney should instruct you on everything else," the judge said. And with that, he was gone.

Myra had now been formally charged and turned over to the Department of Corrections. She was facing serious jail time and she couldn't remember a thing. They were going to have to lower her medication in order for her to think properly. They had her on 500mg of Prozac (twice a day) for her "manic" symptoms, 10mg of Depakote (twice a day) for anxiety, and 20mg of Seroquil (at night) to knock her out.

After Myra's morning ritual of a supervised shower followed by breakfast, Dr. Shapiro came into her room for their scheduled one-on-one. She had met the psychiatrist the week before, right after the detectives and the judge left. She hadn't spoken to him either. Paranoia had gotten the best of her.

Myra could tell by his body language that he didn't have very high hopes for this particular meeting. He probably expected her to act like an asshole like last time, when she ignored him during the entire session.

"Hello, Ms. Danford. How are ..." he began his spiel, but Myra cut him off before he could continue.

"Hello, Doctor," Myra replied.

Dr. Shapiro looked up from his notepad, taken aback. Myra had finally realized that if she didn't cooperate, she would never figure out what really happened, and never figure out how to get herself out of there.

"Glad you found your voice," Dr. Shapiro said with a smile. "How's the medication working for you?" he continued.

"I don't really like the way it makes me feel. It messes with my head. I can't remember anything," Myra complained.

"Well that may not necessarily be a direct result of the medication. You may be suffering from post-traumatic stress disorder, which sometimes suppresses the memory, as a coping mechanism, if you will. That's what the medication is intended for—it helps give your mind time to relax," he explained, rubbing his chin.

"I'm ready to find out why I'm here. I want to remember," Myra pleaded with the doctor.

"Ok, maybe we can arrange to have your meds gradually lowered. But that all depends on your behavior, Ms. Danford," Dr. Shapiro explained.

"I want to get off all of it," Myra insisted.

"Are you still feeling like you want to hurt yourself?" he asked, ignoring her request without even looking up from his notepad.

"I don't remember ever feeling that way, so I guess not," Myra said with an attitude.

"Ok, that's good. Do you feel like hurting anyone else?" he asked.

"No!" she responded, frustrated by his line of questioning.

"Do you know what depression is?" he asked.

"I know that people say they're depressed when they feel sad. Why?" Myra asked suspiciously.

"Well Ms. Danford, right now that's your diagnosis...major depression with manic symptoms and suicidal and homicidal ideations," Dr. Shapiro continued in his doctor lingo.

"How did you come to that conclusion?" Myra asked, questioning his diagnosis.

"You were brought in after attempting to commit suicide. You cried for an entire week straight. You've experienced several mood swings while you've been here, which are indicative of manic depression, and in the beginning you refused to eat or bathe. These are all signs of major depression with suicidal ideations," he explained blandly.

"I heard that the police brought me in," Myra started, but the doctor abruptly cut her off.

"Yes, you are still under arrest, but it is mandatory that all prisoners with mental illnesses be treated, diagnosed, and evaluated to determine if they can stand trial and so forth," he expounded.

"Do you know why I'm under arrest?" Myra asked candidly.

"You mean you can't remember that either?" Dr. Shapiro asked disbelievingly, scribbling wildly in his notepad.

"Didn't I just say this medication is making me lose my damn memory?!" Myra barked angrily. An uneasy feeling invaded her psyche as she read the doctor's face. *Shit . . . did I kill somebody?*

"Like I said, post-traumatic stress often makes people forget things. In our next few sessions we'll go over those traumatic events, and deal with them one at a time. Right now, given all the medication you are on, I don't feel comfortable having you recount any events that might cause a major set back," Dr. Shapiro explained rationally.

Myra sighed loudly and rolled her eyes. *Who the hell do they think wants to be locked up with a bunch of nuts and not know why!?!*

"Ten, eleven, twelve, thirteen . . ." the burly Puerto Rican correction officer mumbled as he went up and down the aisle of the caged bus counting heads. Myra stared out of the gated windows. She could not believe that she was there, handcuffed like a true criminal.

She had remained on the locked unit for two weeks, but with good behavior and great group therapy participation, the psychiatrist had finally deemed her sane enough to be released from the hospital. They were transferring her to the Rose M. Singer jail, where they housed female prisoners on Riker's Island.

Myra was scared stiff as she sat among the most masculine women she had ever seen in her life, some of whom you wouldn't be able to decipher their gender if they weren't on a bus strictly for females. Myra decided as soon as she stepped onto the orange and blue Department of Correction bus that she would keep to herself and not associate with any of the criminals staring back at her.

As of late, Myra had been experiencing irrepressible flashbacks of the events that had led up to her arrest. Myra knew that she would have to tell her story eventually, if not to save herself, then to save her soul.

She couldn't believe that Milton would leave her for dead like this. He had promised her so much, and she had believed him. The mere thought of his deception made her both angry and sad. Myra had never contemplated vengeance until now. She would pay Milton back. She wasn't going to let him get away with this.

Myra was processed through the Rikers Island receiving section. She was assigned to live in Dorm 9 at the Rose M. Singer jail. It was up to her to get in contact with the attorney she'd been assigned.

After about twenty unanswered calls and numerous phone messages from Myra, her attorney finally came to see her. Myra approached the council visit area apprehensively. The stranger had pulled up two colorful rubber-seated chairs, one for himself and one for her. When she finally arrived, she stepped into the small cubicle biting her nails. He wasn't exactly what she had expected.

"Hello, Ms. Danford. I'm Mr. Shepoweitz," said the skinny Jewish boy, dressed in a cheap blue pin-striped suit, with a black yarmulke on his head. He had a long nose that hooked at the end. His face had so many pimples that he appeared to have no clear areas on it.

"You look too young to be a lawyer," Myra said unimpressed and truly concerned about her case.

"I might look young, but I'm good at what I do," he assured Myra.

"Why are you here? It can't be for the money, because I don't have any," she said.

"I can assure you it's not for the money . . . public defenders don't get paid a lot of money anyway. In fact, looking at the severity of your case, I might as well be doing this pro bono," he said gravely.

"Oh," Myra said, somewhat satisfied with his answer.

"Ok, Ms. Danford let's start," he said as he opened her voluminous file.

"Ok," Myra complied.

"From the looks of it, you are in big trouble here. Why don't you start by telling me your version of what happened" Mr. Shepowitz began.

"Everything from the beginning?" she asked.

"I think that would be best," he replied.

Myra thought for a minute about the events that had led to her predicament. Myra realized that her life had taken a drastic turn. As she pondered her lawyer's request and prepared to tell it all, she asked herself, *How did things get so twisted, so complicated?*

Chapter 5

HOW IT ALL GOT STARTED

"Myra! How you gonna leave me like this today?" Vidal whimpered, sick with withdrawal, laying her usual guilt trip on Myra.

"Look, I gotta go. It's my first day of school . . . do you even care?" Myra replied angrily. She still hadn't told Vidal the news about her scholarship.

"Ughh! I'm sick, MyMy. I'ma be dead by da time you get back," Vidal griped. She only used Myra's nickname when she really wanted something. Vidal knew that scaring Myra with her impending death had worked in the past, but Myra was grown up now. She knew that Vidal's death was inevitable, and she still prepared herself every day for the moment.

"I can't help you! Don't you ever think about me when you sell your food stamps for less than half of what they are worth, or when you get your check on the first and the fifteenth and use that money to get high!? Look around here, there's no food, no soap, no nothing!" Myra yelled, angry at her mother's nerve.

"Look I gotta go . . . I'm not being late for anybody," Myra slammed the door and left. She still had to make her way to Quanda's house to shower and get dressed.

The train ride from Brooklyn to St. John's was long, but Myra was determined to be on time. She arrived at the campus with about ten minutes to spare. As she stepped off of the Q23 bus, Myra took in her surroundings. The campus was enormous. Myra whirled around, taking in every bit of the environment. "Damn, this is a far cry from the hood," Myra murmured to herself, as she gawked at the beautiful houses with freshly manicured lawns, gardens, garages, and some with little bird houses in front.

Myra strolled through the gates of the campus, taking in as much scenery as she could. She walked until she reached the front of a glass-paneled building, with a sign that read "ALUMNI HALL." She had read about this place in her new student bulletin; it was the gym where all of the school's sporting events took place. Myra knew that great athletes like *Chris Mullin* and *Mark Jackson* had played right in that very building.

She smiled to herself. She, too, would be famous one day. After all, she was destined for greatness. She planned to be a world-renowned lawyer, just like *Johnny Cochran*, except she would defend kids like herself—kids who had nothing going for them; kids who got caught up in the criminal justice system because they had to steal to eat, or kill to survive.

Myra had to report to the financial aid office to pick up her full scholarship package and book vouchers. She sat through freshman orientation daydreaming about her future. She had so many opportunities . . . the possibilities were endless now that she had her foot in the door. She would get her degree, have a fabulous career, buy a car and a house. Yes, she was on her way. The thoughts excited her.

Myra attended her classes diligently. She wouldn't have missed them for the world. After her Friday afternoon Trigonometry class; she went to find something to eat. She had a long break and needed to kill time. Myra had worked at the Dominican hair salon for a whole week and saved up enough money for carfare and lunch money.

Marillac Hall was where all of the cool people hung out, or so she had heard. Yeah, that's where she'd go.

Myra walked into the huge cafeteria and looked around. *Damn, so many people up in here,* Myra thought to herself. Feeling slightly intimidated, she found an empty seat in the corner. She couldn't eat in Marillac . . . not with all of those guys around.

Myra sat in her corner and observed others—eating, laughing, and talking—enjoying themselves. Feeling a little isolated and lonesome, Myra wished for companionship. Just then, the doors to the cafeteria opened wide and a solitary figure entered. Myra's heart skipped a beat; she recognized him immediately. *Oh shit is it really him? Wait til' I tell Quanda this shit,* Myra thought to herself. Her palms became sweaty. Milton Roberts, star quarterback for the St. John's Red Storm, was staring directly at her.

Myra examined Milton's majestic form from head to toe. He wore an orange and blue Houston Astros fitted cap, a fresh white tee, Rocawear jeans, and a pair of Timberland construction boots. His eyes were beautiful, hazel, and round. His skin seemed to glisten. He had the most beautiful gapped-tooth smile, complete with straight white teeth. *The girls must be throwing themselves at him left and right.*

Myra couldn't image Milton ever being interested in her. She quickly diverted her eyes away from him, but she couldn't help but notice he was returning her gaze. It became increasingly difficult for Myra to pretend that she wanted to look elsewhere, so she decided to take a chance and test whether Milton was still watching her. Myra turned her head slowly, pretending to look at the wall on the opposite side of the room. Yup! Milton was still eye-balling her. She started to feel a little squeamish. *Why is he looking at me? She* pondered. *What would Quanda do?*

Confidently, Myra stood up, letting him see the entire package.

Even though it was the first of September, the weather had been reminiscent of a hot day in July. Myra donned a fuchsia wife-beater with no bra underneath. As she stood, she pretended to remove her jean jacket, tantalizing Milton with just an eyeful of her perky nipples. She wore the tightest *Guess* jeans she owned, which emphasized the curves of her rotund hips and ass. Just yesterday, Nidia from the Dominican salon had hooked Myra's hair up; it was wrapped and hanging long and smooth. Myra wasn't into makeup really, she always wore the bare minimum—just enough mascara to lengthen her dark eyelashes and just a touch of light pink M·A·C lip gloss to give her mouth that soft, slightly seductive look. Yes, Myra had come through dipped.

Myra decided to further test out her theory. She moved from the table slowly and seductively, and walked past Milton, smiling at him as she exited the doors of the cafeteria. Myra had learned at the tender age of ten years old to manipulate situations to her advantage using what God had given her—her beautiful face and, as she got older, her well-developed body.

When Myra entered into the hallway, she felt foolish. *Damn, you're acting like a groupie. You ain't here for that. And anyway, you know how men are,* she berated herself. Myra was no nun, but she had promised herself that she wouldn't get involved with any men until she finished school. Myra had suffered enough at the hands of men. She had been used and abused by men all her life. But there was definitely something different about this one, something that separated him from all of the other men that she had encountered during her brief life. It was odd how Milton had affected her so. Nevertheless, she decided right then that if she saw him again she would totally ignore him.

Damn she is fine, Milton thought to himself as he stared at Myra's gorgeous profile, knowing that she was doing the same in her peripheral vision. She was someone he could get to know better. Being from the projects, Milton knew an around the way girl when he saw one. She looked young, probably a freshman. He couldn't remember seeing her on campus before anyway. *Yeah she wants it. I got this one,* he said to himself confidently. She'd be the perfect addition to his collection of women.

Myra didn't have anywhere to go after her little stunt, so she went upstairs to the second floor and took a shortcut through the building to the other side of the campus, in the direction of the library.

Along the way, Myra ran into Angie. Angie had gone to the same high school as Myra and Quanda, but they hadn't been really close in high school. But in a sea of unknown people, Angie was a welcome sight.

"Hey Myra," Angie greeted. Myra had spotted her first, but she felt that she was definitely the cooler of the two, so she waited for Angie to speak first.

"Wassup Angie, you just get here?" Myra asked.

"Nah, I been here since eight, what about you?" Angie answered and asked simultaneously.

"I had an 8 a.m. class but I got up here early," Myra said.

"I'm about to be out . . . my classes are done," Angie replied.

"Not me. I got a long-ass break. I just left the cafeteria in Marillac. It seems to be the jump off," Myra reported.

"So why you left?" Angie inquired. Myra chose not to tell her about her little coquettish flirting scene with Milton.

"I just decided to cruise the campus and take in the sights," Myra lied.

"Oh I hear that . . . alright. Well, I'm going down there now, so see ya lata," Angie said as she waved goodbye.

"Aiight," Myra said, as she did the same.

Myra went to the library but couldn't seem to concentrate on her work. She kept daydreaming about her encounter with Milton. *Snap out of it dummy! You know where dreaming of a man can get you,* she scolded herself. She hadn't come this far to blow it all on a guy. She filed the episode away in her memory and considered the matter dead and over with.

Myra was proud of herself. She was excelling in school and enjoying her daily escape from the projects. Myra secretly hoped that one day Milton would notice her again. But as hard as she tried not to think about him, he kept popping up in her thoughts. Her hormones were on overload. She'd even gone out and purchased an entire new wardrobe of sexy clothing.

During the gaps in her class schedule, Myra hung out with Angie. Angie had become a Marillac regular, and Myra used her mostly for information about Milton. She was always subtle about her inquiries, never giving away her true feelings.

Angie was a good source of information. Myra knew that Milton had a girlfriend, but for some reason that didn't change her feelings toward him. Secretly, she hoped that he had noticed her sexy, new clothes. The day came sooner than Myra had anticipated.

"Yo Myra!" Angie called to Myra from the other side of cafeteria, waving excitedly at her. Myra walked over to Angie's table and sat down.

"Girrrrl . . . guess who asked about you today?" Angie asked mysteriously. Myra already knew the answer, but she played stupid.

"Who?" Myra asked innocently.

"Bitch, don't act like you don't know! Your ass only been flirting like a muthafucka with him since day one," Angie said laughing. Myra began to blush, embarrassed that it had been so obvious.

"So what did he say?" Myra quizzed, continuing to play it cool.

"He was like, 'Yo, wassup with your girl...she be lookin right,'" Angie repeated in a man's voice. Myra sat in silence, hanging onto Angie's every word. She tried very hard to hide her excitement.

"And I said to him, 'I don't know. Why? Whatchu saying?'" Angie prattled on, relaying the conversation.

"And he was like 'Yo, hook it up.' So here girl, this is his number," Angie continued, pulling a small piece of ripped off paper bag from her purse. "He said to call him tonight. He gonna be home at seven after practice," Angie said with a grin.

Myra nonchalantly took the piece of paper and put it in her bag. She told Angie that she had class and quickly excused herself. She was lying through her teeth. Myra's mind whizzed. She thought about the possibility of having a man. She thought about having a normal sexual experience with a man, the kind she heard other girls bragging about. Up until now, Myra had only had sex for one reason—to get money or drugs for her mother. Myra let her imagination run wild . . . *Mrs. Milton Roberts had a nice ring to it.*

"I can't believe ya ass hid this from me for so long," Quanda scolded Myra after she finally confessed her feelings for Milton.

"Well girl, you know me . . . I'm not with getting with a man. They are nothing but trouble, but girl I'm telling you there is something different about him," Myra beamed.

"Hell yeah girl . . . it's called 'ching! ching!'" Quanda said, making the sound of a cash register.

"No Quan, I'm telling you it's more than that," Myra explained on cloud nine.

"Look, girl, he is going to be number one in the next NFL draft. You better do ya thang with that. If you don't, shit, I will," Quanda said, teasing her.

"But you know my problems with men," Myra whined, sadness creeping into her voice.

"Myra, you gotta get over that shit one day. All men ain't like that and you gonna hafta have sex for pleasure one day. I know it's hard, but forget all of that shit that happened in ya past. You older now, ya body belongs to you now, not ya mother," Quanda stated convincingly.

"Look," Myra said, pulling the number out of her bag.

"Girrrl, you ain't tell me you had the digits!" Quanda squealed. "Here you go, call him right this minute," Quanda instructed, handing Myra the phone.

"I want to wait a while. I don't want him to think I'm on it like that," Myra said.

"Get to dialing! You ain't letting this pass you by, not while I'm alive anyway," Quanda said, snatching the paper from Myra's hand and dialing the number.

Myra listened as the phone rang through the receiver.

"Damn," she complained. No one was picking up.

"What...he ain't home now right?" Quanda asked, pressing her head up against the receiver.

Just as she was about to hang up, a voice came on the line.

"Whatup?" Milton said into the phone. Myra's heart skipped a beat.

"You tell me," she said in the sexiest voice she could muster. Something had come over Myra. She had never acted this way; she never flirted or tried to be sexy for any guy.

"Who this?" Milton questioned, annoyed.

"Oh you give your number out to that many people?" Myra asked playfully.

"Yo, say who this is or I'm hanging up," he barked.

Damn calm down, she thought to herself. "This is Myra. You gave my friend Angie your number to give me," she explained nervously with the words tumbling out of her mouth.

"Oh shit. Shorty with the fat ass...wassup?" he said.

"Nothing you tell me," Myra replied, excited that he wanted to talk.

"Nah shorty, I just like your style, you know. You don't be hawking and shit...you ain't no groupie and you fly as hell," Milton said, thinking he was paying Myra a compliment.

"Well, thank you," she said, smiling from ear to ear.

"So what's the verdict? I'm not really the phone type. I'm more about action, not much of the talking type," Milton crooned.

"Oh I like that... a man who knows how to take charge," Myra said without thinking, covering her face in embarrassment when she realized what she said. She'd learned all of these lines from listening to Quanda talk to men on the phone.

"I wanna get to know you, ma. You seem to have that glow," Milton said, getting his game on. He knew he could have her hook, line, and sinker.

Although Milton said he wasn't a phone person, they talked for three hours that night. Myra spent the night at Quanda's just so she could talk to him. She got cozy on Quanda's bed—the bottom bunk, right up against the wall and carried on the conversation.

Myra and Milton spoke about everything and anything. They were both born in March...his birthday was the fifteenth, hers was the tenth. Both had come from drug-addicted parent homes, his mother had abused drugs too. Milton told Myra how his mother had him when she was twelve and how he had grown up thinking she was his sister. He confessed that he never knew his father, and that his grandmother raised him. He said he was looking to settle down soon . . . maybe even get married before he went to the NFL.

Milton was selling pipe dreams and today he had caught an unsuspecting smoker. Milton wanted Myra to feel sorry for him and it worked. Myra was a little more cautious. She only told him half of her story—about how her father had left, how she and her mother moved to the projects afterward, and how her mother started to abuse drugs. Neither of them went into too much detail about their childhood...mostly because it was too painful, but they exchanged enough information in one night to feel like they had known each other for years.

Milton and Myra talked on the phone whenever they weren't with each other. He invited her to sit in on his practices and she gladly accepted his invitations. Myra began to do something that she had never done before—let her guard down. She began thinking about things she never thought she would think about—love, marriage, children, how Milton could save her from her life . . . about leaving

Vidal behind. Myra wasn't thinking about overcoming her situation through school anymore. She had convinced herself that she would be the wife of Milton Roberts—an NFL wife.

Myra beamed with pride over her relationship with Milton. What she was most proud of, though, was the fact that she had managed to get a man who was not a hustler, a man who was going places the right way.

Milton liked her and he had big plans for her, but he kept his distance emotionally. He would never fall in love, no matter how beautiful the girl. Women were still women, and they were all the same. He didn't rush to spring for the sex because he knew that she was going to give it up eventually. Milton had no intention of having a wife, kids, or anything of the sort. All he needed was a way to keep his pockets laced with cash and a way to pay off his debts.

"You are really good," Myra complimented, as she approached Milton on the football field after practice ended.

"Thanks," he replied, kissing her on the lips.

"So, what's up for today?" Myra asked, wondering if he was going to finally invite her over to his house or do his usual and drive her home.

"Don't know," Milton started as his phone rang and cut him off. "Hello," he said into the small *Samsung* cell phone. "You a dead man!" a man's voice warned on the other end.

Milton clasped the phone shut. He knew who it was. He decided that now was the time to start his pitch to Myra. Myra did not ask any questions about the abrupt phone call; she didn't want him to think she was the kind of girl that would be all up in his business.

"Look baby, I want to take you out tonight," Milton said, lying. He really wanted to say, 'Look bitch, I need you . . . so fuck all the small talk.' But instead he bit the side of his cheek, masking his deceptiveness.

"Ok. Where we going?" Myra asked.

"How bout we take a ride to the city . . . check out *Jimmy's Downtown*," Milton suggested.

"Ok, but I gotta go change," Myra stated, excited. She had never been to a restaurant in the city before, but she had read about *Jimmy's* in all of the hip-hop magazines.

"Aiight, I'll go home to change first and then take you to your crib and we'll leave from there," Milton explained.

Myra didn't think she'd heard him right. *Did he just say we would go to his house first?* She was really excited now. This was the first time he had suggested going to his place. He'd usually drive her straight home after school. She felt like she had moved up in status with him.

They climbed into Milton's *Lincoln Navigator.* He switched his cd disc changer to play *"LOVE"* by *Musiq Soulchild.*

Loooove so many people use your name in vain. Myra threw her head back and closed her eyes to the sweet music. She was quiet and content as they headed toward Milton's house. Myra felt a dizzying mixture of fear and excitement. Never before had she been alone with a man, in his house, at her own will. She wished that she could call Quanda right now for advice. But Myra opted to wing it and let her instincts take her where they may. She let the wind beat on her face, inhaling deeply as she thought about what might happen.

When they arrived at the gates of the apartment complex, Myra was flabbergasted. A gated community complete with security guards, valet parking, manicured lawns, and a huge water fountain with a sign reading *Dara Gardens,* greeted her. She had always dreamt of living in a place like this.

Milton pulled up to the security console. "Hey Musin," he said to the Arab-looking security guard on duty.

"Ah Mr. Roberts, good evening," the swarthy guard responded in his deep Middle Eastern accent.

"Park it in my spot; I'm in for the night," Milton instructed.

"No problem," the guard answered.

In for the night?!? What the hell does he mean 'in for the night'?

I thought we were going out! Myra thought to herself, but chose to remain silent.

They both exited the vehicle and walked in silence down the grassy path to Milton's building; 127-49 was the address on the front. Milton swiped a card to open the front door, holding the door open for Myra to enter inside. Myra stood in the marble vestibule, waiting for Milton to lead the way.

"I walk up. It's good exercise, but you can take the elevator if you wanna," Milton said.

"No, I'll walk up too," Myra said.

"Oh an active woman, I like . . . I like," he said, appreciatively smacking her ass.

Myra felt her body temperature rising and her insides melting. She didn't know if what she was experiencing was embarrassment or sexual tension. They walked up to the third floor and stopped in front of his door. It was adorned with gold plates that read "3S04." Milton pulled out the key card again and swiped it at a pad on the side of the door, punching in several numbers to open the door. *This is some high tech shit,* Myra thought, impressed.

When she stepped inside the apartment, she was shocked by its beauty and style. It reminded her of something out of the *MTV* show, *The Real World*. There were so many colors, but they all seemed to be in harmony with one another. The kitchen was painted yellow, with beautiful flower pots hanging above the window. The marble counter top and cherry wood cabinets were ultra modern; the stove and refrigerator were black and shiny. The appliances all looked new and expensive. The living room walls were painted in a very soothing shade of brown. The sofa was high-backed and red and was adorned with brown and beige throw pillows to offset the walls. It looked like it was purchased from one of those fancy Italian furniture stores. The off-white throw rug that lay atop the parquet floors looked as if no one had ever stepped foot on it. Colorful *Martha Stewart Liv-*

ing candles adorned the coffee table, which had a glass top shaped like an "S." Myra was fascinated with her surroundings, which made Milton even more attractive in her eyes. This was the kind of life she had dreamed of living.

"I'ma go change. You wanna stay in here or you wanna go in my room?" Milton asked suggestively. He wasn't one to beg for sex.

"Oh I'll take the tour," Myra said, not wanting to say the words "wanna" and "bedroom" in the same sentence.

"Aiight, come on then," Milton said, smiling to himself, thinking how easy this was going to be.

Myra followed Milton down the hallway to his bedroom. This place was a world away from 220 Throop Avenue. Milton went about lighting candles, until the entire room was illuminated by candlelight. He had no intentions of changing his clothes.

A light aroma of lavender and chamomile tickled Myra's senses, soothing her jittery nerves. Myra's gaze strayed to the bed, covered with a white duvet trimmed with lace. Ten large fluffy white pillows were stacked high at the headboard, reminding Myra of a sultan's lair. Myra was so nervous that she tripped on the edge of an expensive fur carpet.

"Oops, who put that there?" Milton said playfully as he laughed and grabbed her around the waist.

"Shut up, silly," Myra responded teasingly, holding onto his strong arms. The smell of his cologne was intoxicating.

She could feel her pussy getting wet and her nipples growing hard. Milton put his hand under her chin and slightly lifted her head toward his face. He looked into her eyes and kissed her deeply, sensually probing the inside of her mouth with his tongue. Myra felt her body going limp as she returned the kiss, pulling on his tongue gently with her lips. He continued to kiss her as he pushed her toward the bed.

Once they reached the side of his bed, he gently lifted her onto it, moving his mouth from her lips down to her neck, kissing and sucking. Myra began to breathe heavily. Milton continued on down to her breasts. He slowly opened her bra taking each breast into his hands, massaging the delicate skin. He suckled each one, running his tongue around and around her areola, biting them ever so slightly. Myra panties were wet and hot. She could feel his manhood pressing up against her legs as he lay on top of her administering the most wonderful tongue massage. It was time. Milton stood up on the floor and removed his shirt, exposing his wonderfully muscular chest, complete with a six pack stomach.

Myra didn't know what to do with herself. She watched in amazement as Milton removed his pants, displaying his strong, powerfully built legs. His body reminded her of something she'd seen in an Iron Man competition. Myra wasn't ready to see his penis yet; so she quickly closed her eyes when he removed his boxers. Curiosity got the better of her though and she slowly opened her eyes to check out what he had in store for her. It was the biggest thing she'd ever seen . . . and she'd seen a lot of penises.

Now fully undressed, Milton moved toward her like a lion toward its prey. He began kissing her breasts again, licking down her stomach until he reached the buttons of her pants. Adroitly, he unfastened her jeans exposing her sexy black panties.

Myra's thighs quivered with anticipation. Milton was getting a kick out of watching her expressions.

"Lay down and relax," he whispered in her ear when he felt her tense up. But she couldn't relax. Myra had never really had proper sex. She didn't know what to do.

With her panties and jeans removed, Milton climbed on top of her and prepared to enter her. She could feel his dick hitting up against her inner thighs.

"You need a condom," Myra said, finally getting her brain to work.

"We're exclusive right?" he asked.

"Yeah," she conceded, feeling good about what he had just said.

Myra knew that she knew better than that, but her head was in a different place. She was in complete ecstasy for the first time in her life. Milton grabbed the head of his penis and pushed up against Myra's trembling body until he entered the warmth of her wet vagina. He put his hands on her shoulders for support and made his way in gently.

Myra felt a slight pain shoot through her vagina and buttocks as Milton plunged further into her depths. He began to move in and out of her; slowly at first, but gradually picking up the pace. Milton breathed heavily in her ear, nestling his face in the soft skin of her neck. Myra suddenly froze, as her mind inadvertently took her back to the past.

"Where my mommy went?" Myra asked Quincy, crying hysterically.

"She left you here with me. I'ma show you some stuff," Quincy replied.

"I don't wanna," Myra screamed.

"I got somethin' for ya little ass," Quincy said, as he wobbled toward the door with the dogs scratching behind it.

He opened the door and brought back two huge Rotweilers. They had the biggest heads Myra had ever seen and they were foaming at the mouth, snarling and barking, fighting against their leashes to reach her.

"See these? They gonna eat ya ass if you don't do what I say," Quincy threatened, pushing the dogs toward Myra menacingly. Myra began to cry even harder.

"Get to the back room and take off ya clothes," Quincy instructed. Myra moved further into the dark, dirty house. She had no choice but to obey.

She took off all of her clothes, and stood in the middle of the floor, displaying her underdeveloped ten year old body to the old pervert.

Quincy brought the dogs with him. He tied them to an old fashioned heating pole in the far right corner of the room, making sure Myra knew what would happen if she didn't follow through. He sat down on the bed.

"C'mere," he beckoned. Myra stepped forward. He touched her flat chest with his rough and dirty fingers. Growing bored with her small buds of breasts; he turned her body around and began probing her anus with his fingers.

"Ouch," she screamed in pain.

"Shut up before I put these dogs on your ass . . . they eat kids like you," he warned.

"Get down on ya knees, NOW," he ordered. Myra complied.

She could hear a zipper going down. Next thing she knew, his penis was in her face.

"Touch me," he commanded. Myra reluctantly touched his penis. It felt all wet and mushy to her.

Ewwww, she thought to herself. The smell was making her sick.

"Put it in ya mouth," he demanded.

"NO!" Myra said, crying and pushing his penis away.

Quincy bent over the side of the bed and began reaching for one of the dog leashes. Myra was afraid for her life so she did it.

"Suck it like a lollipop," he said, wheezing and breathing hard with excitement as it grew hard. Myra obeyed. She did this over and over until she received something bitter in her mouth. She gagged and gasped for air, wanting to throw up.

"Swallow it!" he yelled as he watched her eyes go wide, getting turned on by the minute.

Myra wretched all over his floor. He slapped her so hard blood shot out of her nose.

"You aiight ma?" Milton asked, noticing that Myra had stiffened up, making it nearly impossible for him to continue the rhythm he had started.

"Yeah I'm ok, it's just that . . ." Myra started to explain but decided against it. She had never confided in anyone about the horrible things that she had endured, not even Quanda knew the whole story of Myra's life.

Myra didn't want Milton to think she was a dirty freak. She also didn't want to destroy her chances of being with him.

"What is it?" Milton asked, feigning concern.

"It's nothing, baby . . . let's continue," Myra said as she grabbed him and pulled him on top of her. She was afraid to lose him.

Milton picked up right where he had left off. They made love for the first time that night, and several times after that. Myra spent the night at his house, sleeping on his chest. She was in love. She knew this was where she was supposed to be—in the arms of Milton Roberts. That is how it all got started.

Chapter 6

THE DRAMA BEGINS . . .

Myra was ecstatic as she descended from the high step of Milton's SUV. For the first time in her life, she had had sex because she wanted to, not because she had to. It was hard for her to wipe the semi-permanent smile from her face.

She contemplated walking straight to Quanda's building to share the news with her best friend, but instead she went upstairs to her house to check on Vidal.

Myra entered the building, speed walking and avoiding eye contact with the usual hustlers in the front playing dice. She never spoke to them, but their stares always unnerved her. She didn't pay them any mind as she walked by, oblivious to several of the guys giving each other hand signals and motioning to someone sitting in a darkly tinted vehicle.

Myra pressed the button for the elevators and stood waiting. A Puerto-Rican lady named Ms. Madi who lived in the building entered the hallway. Ms. Madi was short and round with a head full of soft, thinning silver hair. She always wore slippers, no matter what the weather. She did so to combat the gout in her legs and ankles that she had acquired with old age. She was like everybody's nana in the building, and she especially loved Myra. Ms. Madi had fed Myra on several occasions when she was younger.

"Aie mami, the elevators is broken since two days," Ms. Madi complained in her thick Puerto Rican accent to Myra.

"Dag, they always broke," Myra groaned, being careful not to curse. Ms. Madi was a devout Catholic, and everybody in Tompkins knew that she would preach an entire church sermon if she heard anyone swear.

"Yes mami, the kids, they so bad 'round here," Ms. Madi said rolling her r's, as she dragged her swollen legs and slippers across the floor and prepared for her painful walk up the stairs to her second floor apartment.

Myra followed Ms. Madi into the stairwell. Myra hated walking up the stairs. So much shit went down in the stairwells in project buildings that there was no telling what she might find. People fucking, smoking crack, shooting up, or buying drugs; you name it, Myra had probably seen it. Not to mention the high smell of piss that burned her nostrils whenever she entered the stairwell.

As they made their slow climb up the stairs, Myra and Ms. Madi prattled on about this and that, with Myra right on Ms. Madi's heels. Ms. Madi finally made it to the second floor. "Alright Ms. Madi, take care," Myra said as she picked up her pace and continued to climb the stairs to her floor.

Myra looked up at the "5" painted in black on the beige cinder block wall, pulling open the graffiti-riddled metal door, stepping onto the fifth floor. As she moved down the hallway, Myra heard the squeak of the exit door opening behind her, and then footsteps. She turned to see who it was, but before she could turn fully around a sharp pain penetrated through her skull. "Aaaahhhhhhh!" her scream was short-lived, and then, utter blackness.

The person who Myra had never gotten a chance to see put what appeared to be a black pillowcase or some kind of bag over her head, and pulled it tightly around her neck and face, as if they were trying to smother her. The bag was pulled so tightly around her face that her profile was imprinted on it. Myra tried to scream again, but the sound wouldn't come out. She began gasping for air, ferociously kicking and clawing at her assailant, trying to break free.

After a few seconds Myra was able to sense that she was in the presence of more than one person, although her vision was obstructed by the bag. She could feel someone behind her and in front of her body. The second person snatched her keys from her hand, as the first continued smothering her with the bag, dragging her along. Myra continued to struggle fiercely, now digging savagely at her neck, trying to get her fingers under the material to relieve some of the pressure around her neck. She felt as if her esophagus would crumble under the pressure of the perpetrator's grip.

Myra finally managed a muffled scream, but it fell on deaf ears. The person holding the makeshift hood of death tightly around her head dragged her, kicking and screaming, into her apartment. She got a few good kicks in at the heavy metal door, causing it to make a loud BANG! as it hit up against the hallway wall. But to Myra's dismay, her assailants managed to drag her inside. She was too afraid to think logically, so she continued to fight for her life. She figured that if they were going to kill her, at least she would go out with a fight. Myra continued to thrash about, still under the tight grasp of one of the attackers, trying to make out the muffled voices of her assailants as they conferred about her fate.

After a few seconds of unnerving silence, Myra heard faint ripping noises, like heavy duct tape coming away from the roll. The next thing she knew the material that covered her head was being tightened—around the top of her head and then around her eyes and neck. The goons had taped the black bag over her face and sealed it by placing the tape around her entire neck. She could barely breathe through the material, and she definitely could not see or speak. She was going to suffocate.

Manhandling her, one of the anonymous attackers grabbed her under her arms and lifted her up, placing her on one of the raggedy wooden kitchen chairs in the apartment. One of the few things that remained after Vidal's numerous "yard sales" of their belongings. They held Myra's arms behind her back, in the arrest position, causing her shoulders to bulge and lock. Her wrists were taped together to hug the back of the chair and each of her ankles were affixed to the front legs of the chair.

Myra made several futile attempts to scream. Suddenly, a sharp pain pervaded the side of her head. *CRUNCH.* Myra felt a fist connect with her right temple. She felt as if a piece of her skull had been knocked loose. Several punches followed the first.

"Where ya mother at bitch?!" one of the deep-voiced assailants boomed, sounding like Lou Rawls. Myra wasn't given an opportunity to respond before the same deep-voiced attacker grabbed her head through the bag and repeatedly punched her on the other side of her face. Her head and face were wet and sticky with blood, which seeped the material that surrounded her head. Tears rolled down her face, further dampening the cloak of death around her head. Myra had no idea why they were assaulting her.

"TALK!" one of them yelled at her.

"I don't know," Myra mumbled through the bag, taking in mouths full of material and blood, making her response entirely inaudible. It was difficult for her to breathe, much less speak. Suddenly, Myra felt as if her chest was going to cave in. The beating had intensified and moved to the center of her body. Myra's ribcage buckled under the potency of the closed fist punches. She'd had the wind knocked out of her. She moved her head wildly in circular motions, trying in vain to get her lungs to fill back up with air.

"I said where ya fuckin' thievin' ass dope fiend mother at?!?" the deep-voiced assailant barked.

Myra was drifting in and out of consciousness. *Crack . . . slap . . . punch.* Myra felt a barrage of punches, kicks, and slaps raining down on her body.

"Look bitch you gon' die for that fucked up mother of yours that be pimping you out?!? Just tell me where she at. That bitch robbed me, and either she gon' die or you gon' die. I'ma let you live today, but if I don't have five thousand dollars by Wednesday next week, to replace my product and my money, I'm coming back to finish this shit!" the deep voice threatened.

They left Myra's unconscious body—still taped to the chair, bleeding from her face, head, and body—for dead.

"What's all that slamming over there?" Bambi asked herself as she looked out of her peephole. She heard several doors slamming, followed by a torrent of thumps, and then some more slamming. The walls in the projects seemed thick, but you could hear everything that went on in your next door neighbor's apartment if you listened carefully. Bambi watched as Knowledge and his worker Rayon left the apartment across the hall in a hurry. She could see that they left the door slightly ajar.

"That damn Vidal is a mess. Wait til I see Myra and tell her about her momma. Now she done added drug dealers to the mess of people she got in and outta there," Bambi said to herself. She went back to her couch, feeling sorry for herself.

"Ma, did Myra call last night while I was out?" Quanda asked Ms. Brenda.

"No," her mother answered.

"Anybody know if Myra called?" Quanda yelled out to her brothers and sisters.

"NO!" a few of them yelled back.

"Damn . . . that's suspect. It's not like her not to hit me for a whole twenty four," Quanda said worriedly to her mother.

"Maybe she studying somewhere," Ms. Brenda replied pointedly.

"Ho boyeee, here we go," Quanda retorted. "I'ma go to 220 and check for her," Quanda continued.

"Alright, let me know," her mother replied.

Quanda sped across the path to Myra's building. None of the hustling guys who held down the front of the building were out there, so she couldn't ask them if they'd seen Myra come in. She hated going to Myra's apartment, because she hated running into Vidal. But Quanda was going to have to do it today because she was really worried about her friend.

Quanda pressed the elevator buttons frantically, getting nervous. "This bitch probably at her new man house laid the fuck up and I'm worrying for shit," Quanda said out loud to herself. The elevator was taking too long. She didn't have time for this shit, she was taking the stairs.

When Quanda arrived on the fifth floor, she noticed that one of Myra's earrings was laid up against the wall just outside the stairwell door. Quanda picked up the mangled piece of gold, and her heart sank into the pit of her stomach. Quanda bolted down the hallway to her friend's apartment door. She could see as she approached that the door was ajar. She broke into a run, pushing it wide open. Quanda's jaws fell open at what she saw. Myra was tapped to the chair that had now fallen over. Blood had completely soaked the black material over Myra's face, staining the floor and the front of Myra's shirt.

"Ahhhhhhhhhhhhhh . . . OH MY GOD, HELP! HELP!" Quanda screamed at an ear-shattering pitch. There was no phone in the apartment. Quanda nervously fumbled with her jacket pockets, trying desperately to locate her cell phone. *Shit! I must've dropped it!* Quanda didn't want to leave Myra in the condition that she was in to go look for her phone. So she continued to scream for help, all the while calling out to Myra. "MyMy . . . come on MyMy. Can you hear me?!" Quanda cried, frantically tearing at the material around Myra's damaged head.

"Please Myra, please. You can't die. . . I need you . . . PLEASE HELLLLLP!" Quanda began screaming again, crying more hysterically. Quanda gently put Myra's head down and ran to the kitchen to get a knife to free her friend from her duct tape captivity.

Finally, Bambi appeared in the doorway. Terrified by what she saw, she quickly turned and ran back into her apartment. "Bambi, wait!" Quanda screamed. But Bambi slammed her door; she couldn't deal with any more pain . . . or death. And she damned sure wasn't telling anybody who she had seen leaving from there. Bambi guiltily realized that she had heard the whole incident going down, but didn't know that Myra was involved. As minutes ticked by, Bambi finally came to her senses though and dialed 911.

Quanda was in hysterics by the time the ambulance arrived, so much so that the EMTs had to give her an oxygen mask to regulate her breathing. The police asked Quanda several questions, none of which she had answers to. She had no idea what had happened to her friend, but she figured Vidal was involved, directly or indirectly. That day, as Quanda watched Myra cling helplessly to life, she vowed that she would find out who did this to her friend—they would have hell to pay.

As Myra lay heavily sedated in the hospital, rumors circulated around Tompkins about what had happened. The final version of the story was that Vidal robbed a dealer's stash of drugs and money from a small opening in the paneling over the elevators on the fifth floor. The story didn't seem too far fetched. It was possible, of course. It wasn't unusual for some of the hustlers to stash their drugs on a different floor every day, just in case a jump out team of narcotics cops ever decided to make a sweep.

According to the story, Vidal had waited until the hallway was empty first. Then, with the expertise of a high-priced jewel thief, she tipped out of her apartment, took the money and the drugs, and casually walked out of the building and disappeared. She never thought for a second about the danger she had put herself or her daughter in, but then again "thinking" was not one of Vidal's strong suits.

Everyone, including Quanda, wondered who had stashed their goods on the fifth floor of 220 Throop Avenue the day that Vidal boosted the stash. Quanda's first instinct told her that it was some of the little flunkies on the come up that worked for Knowledge. Quanda promised herself that as soon as Myra recovered she would find out who was responsible for what had happened to her.

Quanda stayed at Myra's hospital bedside around the clock, leaving only once a day for about an hour to take a shower and change her clothes. Quanda had put herself down as Myra's sister so that the doctors would update her on Myra's progress. The doctors informed her that Myra had suffered a concussion, several subdural hematomas, two fractured ribs, a fractured nose, two broken fingers, and a fractured eye socket. The doctors felt very good about Myra's prognosis—they expected her to recover fully. They said that after a few weeks of healing, Myra would look like her normal self again.

Quanda cried every time that she looked at her friend's swollen, bruised face. She knew that Myra could never return to Tompkins. The next time, Myra might not be so lucky.

Quanda got in touch with Angie, who gladly took Myra's hospital paperwork to the financial aid office at St. John's to ensure that she didn't lose her scholarship. The school sent their well wishes and informed Angie that Myra should take her time to get better and that she could return to school next semester and still be eligible for her full scholarship benefits.

Angie also tracked down Milton to let him know what was going on; and when she found him, he was walking with a girl. Thoroughly disgusted, she figured there was no better time to interrupt his flow.

"Yo Milton can I rap a taste wit you?" Angie asked. Milton looked at her like she was crazy. Didn't she see he was otherwise involved?

"Nah yo . . . I'm busy," he replied. Milton hadn't heard from Myra in a few days and he didn't want to talk to her friend. Even though he knew that Myra's extraordinary beauty increased his potential to make money with her, he had already written her off as a flake.

"Look . . . pull ya'self away from the groupie for a sec, it's about Myra. It's serious," Angie said, boldly pulling Milton's arm away from the girl.

"What the fuck?" he protested, shocked by Angie's bravado.

"Look asshole, Myra was almost killed. She in the hospital. She got a bunch of injuries n' shit . . . she in real bad shape. You might wanna go check on her . . . you know how she feels about you," Angie softened her tone a bit.

Milton's mind raced. *Killed? Hospital? Injuries? What is going on with that?* he thought to himself.

"Uhhh, thanks for the info . . . I'ma go check her on the real . . . damn that shit ain't cool," Milton said sincerely.

"Just go up there. She in Woodhull Hospital—it's on Flushing Avenue, up the block from her crib. She needs everybody right now," Angie said pointedly, and walked away.

Milton had to admit that there was something about Myra that made him tick. He wasn't one to be all over any female, but visiting her in the hospital was the least he could do. Anyway, he never knew what might come of it. He had thought long and hard about making her his next money maker. She was young, naïve, and most of all, needy. Yeah, he was going to make it real good. He would visit her and help her in anyway he could. And to make himself feel good about it, he would just think of it as an investment; in which case he would have to put in a lot of work to reap the benefits.

Knock . . . Knock . . . Milton tapped lightly on the door to room 211.

Quanda jumped up from her makeshift chair/bed to investigate. She was like a guard dog at Myra's side.

"Who you?" Quanda asked, cracking open the door.

"Umm, I'ma friend of Myra's," Milton started, but before he could finish Quanda jumped on the defensive.

"Friend from where?" she asked angrily. She didn't trust a soul when it came to this situation.

"Take it easy, ma. I'm from St. John's. Me and ya friend been keeping company for some time now," he explained.

"Oh, you Milton?" Quanda asked, calming down. *Damn he is fine*, she thought to herself. She scanned him from head to toe. He reminded her of one of the hustling guys on the street—baggy jeans, NBA team jersey over a white tee, and Timberlands—but from what Myra had told her Quanda knew that Milton had his shit together.

"Yeah . . . it's me," he said, a little annoyed.

"Oh sorry bout' that, but you know I gotta protect my girl," Quanda explained apologetically.

"Don't sweat it. I feel you. So what happened . . . who did this shit?" Milton started. He had lots of questions.

"Yo, it's still a mystery, and fuckin' Five-0 ain't got a clue. She ain't deserve this shit . . . not at all. It's all good though, 'cause now the drama begins, that's my word," Quanda said, bursting into tears.

"Nah, she definitely didn't deserve this. She a trooper though. She gon' pull through," Milton reassured her.

He walked over to Myra's bedside. He hung his head and closed his eyes in disbelief at Myra's condition. He could barely see her face through all the bandages. What little he could see was riddled with black and blue. Even though he had conditioned himself to think of women as hateful bitches, he truly felt sorry for Myra. He couldn't believe that someone could do that to such a beautiful face.

Moved by an unknown emotion, Milton grabbed her hand and kissed it. He told himself that it was just a front for Quanda. He whispered words of encouragement in Myra's ear, although he knew she probably couldn't hear him. "Hey baby, it's me. I'ma be here for you, just pull through this shit, I got plans for us," Milton spoke softly. He gently kissed Myra's hand again. She was so heavily sedated; it seemed as if she were in a coma.

When Milton stepped away from Myra, he saw Quanda looking at him sympathetically. He was glad that he had sold Quanda on his concern for Myra; if not, she could be a serious obstacle to his plan.

"You wanna go get some food or somethin'?" Milton asked Quanda.

"Nah, I don't leave my girl alone at all . . . unless one of my brother's or sisters is up here to stand guard," she maintained.

Ok, I understand. Well . . . you need somethin'?" he asked considerately.

"Nah, I'm aiight," Quanda said, surprised by his thoughtfulness.

"Look, I know you don't trust nobody right now . . . but I'm on ya side, ma. I really dig ya friend. I don't know what she told you about me, but it was gettin' serious with us. I just want to know what went down and how I can help," Milton said, telling half truths.

Quanda had to think about it. She didn't trust anyone and she wasn't just going to act in haste and give Milton free reign.

"Look, give me ya number and I'll hit you up and we'll talk later," Quanda said. At this point she just wanted Milton to leave so she could be alone with Myra. And so she could think.

"Aiight . . . here I'll write it down," he said, scribbling his number on the top of the Patient's Rights brochure that sat on the food tray next to Myra's bed.

"Aiight, I'll hit you tomorrow," Quanda said.

To make it look even better, before he left, Milton went over to Myra and kissed her bruised lips.

His mind was heavy; and for the first time since he was twelve years old, his heart was heavy as well.

"HELLLPPP!" Milton sat in his room, listening to the young girl's screams. He could hear the men cheering and laughing in his living room. He found the sounds reassuring. He was making some good money tonight. *Good fa the bitch*, he thought to himself. But he knew he was going to have to stop them before they went too far; he could catch a case if the unknown girl decided to turn on him.

"Yo, party over," Milton yelled over the music and loud voices.

"Hey man, you give the best fucking parties," said a tall white man dressed in a two piece *Brooks Brother's* suit, as he handed Milton his money for the night.

"Yes . . . yes," some of the other well-dressed business men agreed as they handed over their share as well.

As they filed out of his apartment, Milton looked down at the girl on the floor. She was clearly very young. He tried his hardest to remember her name, but after a few minutes he realized that he didn't give a shit enough about her to even remember it. All he knew was that he had made a bundle, enough to pay off his extortion debt to Damien for approximately two weeks. The money he had earned at the young girl's expense made her that much more insignificant in Milton's twisted mind.

His original plan was to have Myra where he wanted her by now, but he got a little sidetracked for obvious reasons. For now, he had to find vulnerable, young girls to fill in. Milton did not consider himself a pimp, nor did he believe what he was doing was criminal in nature. In his mind, it was party promoting, and nothing more.

"You aiight, ma?" he asked as he bent down to check on her. The girl lay balled-up in a fetal position. Milton noticed that her entire latex-like outfit was ripped to shreds, with pieces of it strewn all over his couch, floor, and coffee table.

"Come on sit up. You can wash up in the bathroom," Milton said, grabbing her arms and forcing her upright.

"DON'T TOUCH ME MUTHAFUCKA!" the girl came to life screeching and pushing Milton's hands away. She was clearly in shock from the ordeal. Milton noticed the bruises that were forming on her face. *Yo what the fuck these white boys did to her . . . these niggas are wild fa the night. They are fuckin' freaks,* he thought to himself.

He had booked a gambling party with some high-rolling Wall Street cats that his friend Tom had told him about. Tom was famous for his get-rich-quick schemes and told Milton that these guys liked to "party" with girls. Milton figured that he would get the young girl to strip, maybe fuck a few of them like usual and then he'd get his money. He knew they liked freaky sex, but he never expected them to beat the girl, sodomize her with beer bottles, hangers, and a broom stick, and then fuck her brains out.

Damn what I'ma do if she decides to go to the police? he thought worriedly. He felt kind of sorry for her too. He was going to have to make it right.

"Look, ma . . . I didn't know they got down like this n' shit or else I would a came out here. I thought they just wanted a stripper," Milton assured the girl, who continued to lie in a putrid heap of strange-smelling body fluids.

"Let me help you up. You can stay here a few days. I got ya paper too. I'ma take you back ta Red Hook in a few days, when you feeling better," he promised her.

"Mmmm," the girl just moaned and cried, still not moving. He seriously contemplated dumping the young girl off on a corner somewhere in Brooklyn. He didn't have time for this shit.

Milton punched at the air, and chastised himself. He vowed that next time he would get somebody that he personally knew to perform his infamous gambling parties, just like he had in the past. He would do it like a real pimp, have the unsuspecting female live with him and be his one and only hoe. That way he could provide her with protection, in case anything like this ever happened again. Whoever he chose would be loyal to him and only him.

Myra was laid up for six weeks. Milton and Quanda had been at her bedside constantly during that time. Just as they predicted, she had made a full recovery.

The doctors stopped sedating her when the swelling in her head went down. All that remained of her ordeal were a few remnants of nicks and scratches on her face, a splint on her two broken fingers, and a wrap around her torso to help her ribs heal properly.

"So my nigga how does it feel to finally be going home?" Quanda asked, smiling from ear to ear, happy to see her friend leaving the hospital.

"Girl, I think I got bed sores. I can't wait," Myra answered enthusiastically.

"Well, ya boo will be up here in a few, so let's get you dolled up," Quanda chimed, pulling out a comb and brush to repair Myra's wild, untouched hair.

"Girl, I can't believe he has been here like this for me," Myra beamed, feeling good about her relationship with Milton.

"Yeah girl, he is the truth. And you know I don't say that 'bout no nigga," Quanda agreed. "He taking you in cause you can't go back home. That's some stand-up shit for real, Myra . . . you betta hold on to a nigga," Quanda said bluntly.

"I know, girl, but I will miss your ass," Myra confessed.

"Please believe I will be having my skinny ass parked right up in ya new crib," Quanda assured as she parted Myra's hair into four sections so that it would be easier to comb out.

"So, has anybody heard from my mother?" Myra asked. She had been concerned about Vidal. Although she realized that her mother was the cause of all her pain, deep down she still loved Vidal and worried about her.

"Hellll no! Her ass did a fuckin' Hoffa n' shit," Quanda responded angrily.

Myra fell silent . . . the news didn't surprise her.

IS THIS LOVE?

"Girl this shit is tiiiiiight," Quanda whispered to Myra, referring to Milton's apartment.

"I know girl, right" Myra responded, smiling proudly.

"Ok ladies, can I get ya'll anything? Soda, food, anything?" Milton asked, as he came down the hallway after putting away the last box of Myra's belongings.

"Ummm, hell yeah. I'll have whatever alcoholic stuff you got," Quanda requested with a smile.

"Aiight, I got Henny, Remy Red, some P to the B (Parrot Bay) and some Heinekens," Milton said over his shoulder as he peered into the refrigerator.

"Gimme some Remy straight on the rocks," Quanda replied like a pro, excited about her selection.

"I don't want anything," Myra chimed in.

Myra couldn't wait to be alone with her new man in her new home. Myra was going to be the best thing that ever happened to Milton . . . and hopefully, one day, the best wife.

The three of them laughed and talked for hours before Quanda decided she had freeloaded on enough of Milton's liquor stash to get a good night's sleep. She hadn't slept too well since the incident with Myra occurred.

"I love you girl. You my sista—my life. I'd kill fa you, you know,"

Quanda said emotionally, slurring her speech as she held tightly onto Myra. The Remy had taken its toll on her.

"Ok girl. I'll call you tomorrow," Myra said barely getting the words out. Quanda had her in a death grip, like she was afraid to let go.

"You gon' be aiight? You gon' be aiight, sis? You trust this nigga? Cause' I could kick his ass. . . word, MyMy. I will kill a nigga for you," Quanda declared with her speech sounding like a drunken sailor during Fleet Week.

"I'm ok for real. I promise to call you tomorrow," Myra reassured her friend.

Milton watched, waiting patiently for his drunken guest to leave his home so he could go to bed.

Quanda finally made it to the door after a bunch of stopping, stumbling and hugging. Milton called her a car from the exclusive Jewel car service that the football team used. He gave the driver Quanda's destination, and as usual payment was never discussed. Quanda was gone.

Milton was glad. "Well it's just me and you against the world now, baby girl," Milton said turning to Myra.

"Yup," she answered, blissfully throwing her arms around his neck.

"We gonna have it all baby. NFL . . . here I come," Milton announced with his game plan in mind.

"Let me ask you a question. Why me? Why did you pick me?" Myra quizzed, moving her head so that she could look up into his eyes.

Milton was initially thrown by her probing questions, but he recovered quickly.

"I told you, ma . . . you got that glow," Milton said after a moment's pause, avoiding eye contact.

Myra smiled at him, kissing him on the lips. She laid her head on Milton's shoulder. She had never remembered feeling this kind of comfort from another human being in her life.

Milton had taken a chance by moving Myra into his home. All of the other women would have to take a back seat now. He also knew that he would have to be extra careful with all of his "extracurricular" activities. Milton was banking on the fact that Myra had no one else to turn to, and fearing for her life would provide him the assurance he needed that she would stay. He felt a sense of satisfaction knowing that Myra had no place else to go. He held her life in his hands, and he planned to manipulate that fact to his advantage.

"Last one to the bed is a rotten egg," Milton said playfully, running toward his bedroom.

"I can't run . . . you know that you a cheater," Myra griped, giggling as she limped to the bedroom.

"You see this gun, this is for you if you ever tell," Scriggy threatened. Milton sat on the bed frozen with fear. He felt his feces moving down to his sphincter muscle. Clenching the muscles in his butt, he fought hard to hold it in. "Now c'mere, lemme show you somethin' new," Scriggy said, holding the gun close to Milton's face. Milton obeyed, afraid for his thirteen year old life. "You gonna do somethin' to me dis time," Scriggy affirmed. Milton remained silent. He wanted to grab the gun and kill his perverted, deviant sexual predator of a cousin. "Get down on ya knees and open ya mouth," Scriggy instructed with a sinister grin on his face. Milton obeyed, feeling the cold steel against the side of his face the entire time.

"Uhhhhh!" Milton squealed, jumping out of the bed and whirling on his heels like a deranged lunatic.

"What happened?!" Myra yelled as she sat up, scared half to death by Milton's outburst and his sudden jolt out of the bed.

"Nothing," he said calmly, realizing that he was just having one of his nightmares.

"You ok?" Myra asked, both concerned and terrified by what just transpired.

"Yeah, I'm aiight . . . go back to sleep," Milton said jadedly, climbing back into the bed.

Milton lay with his back toward Myra and she did the same. He was angry and embarrassed that Myra had witnessed one of his nightmares. Myra couldn't immediately fall back to sleep, for several reasons: her new surroundings, concern for Vidal, and confusion about what had just happened with Milton.

As soon as Myra began to doze off, she heard Milton's voice say, "I'm leaving for practice, be back later." He didn't wait for a response from Myra, nor did he make any eye contact with her or kiss her goodbye. All of a sudden, Milton seemed different—distant.

He was probably just stressed out with the football season coming into full swing and with the draft looming, Myra reasoned. After convincing herself that she was not the problem, Myra decided she would do something special for Milton. *I'll make dinner, set the table really nice, and light some candles*, she thought romantically.

Myra got up that morning, excited about her plans for the night. She flitted around the apartment making preparations, being careful not to over exert her still-healing wounds. She opted to prepare a couple of steaks that she found in the freezer, complete with sides of mashed potatoes, and vegetables. *He'll appreciate a good home cooked meal for a change*, she reasoned.

Myra watched just about everything there was to watch on cable. Milton told her that he would be back early today. His practice ended at three-thirty. "He should have been home by now," Myra said to herself, getting concerned. It was six o'clock already.

Myra tried calling his cellular phone numerous times to no avail. He hadn't responded to any of her messages. *Where the hell could he be?*

The remainder of the evening seemed to drag. It was now eleven o'clock and still no sign of Milton. Myra contemplated calling the police, but instead she called the only other person that she could depend on for comfort and advice.

"Hello. Who this? Oh hi Quil. Is Quanda there?" Myra asked Quanda's younger sibling.

"Nah, she went out . . . call her cell," Quanda's sister instructed.

Just as Myra pressed the TALK button on the cordless handset to disconnect the line, the phone began to ring. Her heart skipped a beat; she wondered if she should answer it. *Damn, I do live here now . . . but he didn't tell me to answer his phone. But what if it's him*? Myra argued with herself. She decided not to answer it. She set the phone back in the charger cradle and let the answering machine pick up. The person did not even bother to leave a message. Myra gave up on calling Quanda. She didn't need to get Quanda all caught up in her problems.

Myra finally fell into a fitful sleep at two o'clock in the morning. She had long since eaten the dinner that she had prepared, putting his share into a Tupperware container in the refrigerator. So much for a nice, quiet dinner for two.

Myra opened her eyes when she heard the apartment door creak open. The cable box read 5:00 a.m. She could hear Milton moving down the hallway toward the bedroom. Myra closed her eyes and pretended to be asleep. She didn't want to deal with him right now. She was really hurt by his no-show. Milton took off his clothes, trying to be as quiet as possible. He knew that Myra would probably have lots of questions for him. He put his game face on and prepared himself for some Academy Award caliber acting.

"Hey, you sleep?" Milton whispered, climbing into the bed, moving his chiseled body close to Myra.

"Hmmm," she moaned, still pretending to be asleep.

"I'm sorry baby. I got caught up in a important meeting with a agent," Milton said in the lowest baby voice he could muster, lying through his teeth.

"It's ok, but next time call," Myra grumbled turning toward him, wincing in pain from her bruised ribs.

"I gotchu for next time," he said charmingly, kissing her on the lips to seal the deal. Myra immediately felt better. *See, he had something important going on.* She scolded herself for ever thinking something negative about her knight in shining armor.

"C'mere," Milton requested, tugging her gently toward him, hugging her body close. He moved his body under the comforter, nestling his face comfortably between Myra's legs. He began nibbling gently on her clitoris, as she melted into a gentle rhythm pushing her body and love juices toward his tongue. Milton skillfully darted his tongue in and out her pussy and nibbled on her clit for over thirty minutes. Oh! Oh! Myra screamed over and over again as she experienced her first orgasm. Myra was instantly in love. *Yeah I got her ass now. She will take my word for anything,* Milton thought to himself, grinning as he watched her tremble with the after shocks of the explosive experience.

Milton promised Myra the world. He told her that when he was drafted they would get married the following week. He said that they would move to whichever team's state drafted him and offered him the most lucrative contract. Milton assured Myra that she could have any car she wanted, any house she liked, and a fat diamond ring. He told her that the world was hers, and all she had to do was stick by him—to love him no matter what.

Loving Milton was easy. Myra was very tempted on several occasions to say to hell with her scholarship and school. Just being Mrs. Milton Roberts was enough for her. But when she thought about her mother and father and what had happened to them, she reasoned that getting her degree was still the smartest thing to do. Myra was ready to juggle school and being an NFL wife. Milton was her savior, her life, her sole source of happiness.

Milton continued to suffer with nightmares. When Myra grew concerned enough to inquire about them, he refused to talk about them. She decided not to push the issue. He continued his daily routine of practice and school. Some nights he came home and some nights he didn't. Myra, filled with promises and blinded by love, remained silent about his iniquities, just as she did about a lot of other things that were going down.

"Yo ma, I'm out," Milton yelled as he grabbed his bag and started toward the door.

"Ok . . . are you coming home?" Myra asked with a hint of attitude in her voice. She was getting tired of his disappearing acts.

"Look, you here, right?" he asked rhetorically, annoyed by her question.

"But I'm—" Myra started, but Milton cut her off.

"You here, you got all of this, and you gonna have more when I get drafted so fall back and play ya position," he said flatly, turning on his heels and continuing toward the door. Myra remained silent, not wanting to piss him off before he left, for fear that he would not return.

Bliiinnnnng . . . Bliiinnnnng . . . the phone rang. Milton ran back into the apartment like a bat out of hell.

"You want me to get it?" Myra asked, as he came barreling toward her in a hurry.

"NO!" Milton screamed as he ran toward the phone like it was a matter of life or death that he answered it.

"Hello," he panted breathlessly into the receiver. Milton had made such a mad dash for the phone his chest heaved in and out fiercely. The person had already hung up.

"Don't ever answer this phone . . . you understand? Ain't nobody calling here for you!" he barked, leaving Myra behind with a forlorn look on her face. She felt rejected and dejected—lost.

Myra realized that Milton had some issues. *Is this love?* she wondered to herself, unaware of how long she was going to be able to stay quiet about his behavior. She missed Quanda and the projects already.

Chapter 8

ON A MISSION

Dressed in all black like the omen . . . have ya friend's singin' this is for my homey . . .

Quanda sang Lil' Kim's lyrics as she slid into an all-black leather cat suit. Adjusting the halter top around her neck to ensure that the deep cut in the front was positioned appropriately—enough to expose the sides of ech of her breasts. Quanda primped and prodded until she got it just right. "Aiight, aiight . . . smoking," Quanda said to herself as she looked into the full length mirror hanging on the back of her bedroom door. Turning her back, she looked over her shoulder into the mirror to check out her ass—she had to look just right for her mission tonight.

Quanda was moving alone tonight. She had the Notorious B.I.G.'s theory on the brain. *"real niggas move in silence and violence."* She knew she had to go at this alone in order for it to go down just as she planned. Quanda checked her cell phone to make sure that Myra hadn't called. No calls. "She must be honeymooning n' shit," Quanda said out loud to herself.

Quanda arrived at the 40/40 Club, Jay-Z's new spot on West 25th Street in the city. Stepping out of the yellow cab, she complained, "Damn thirty dollars for a damn ride . . . a bitch need a car."

The cold November air stung her exposed back, sending a chill through her entire body, pushing her nipples hard against the leather of her cat suit. She had a jacket with her, but putting it on ruin the effect of her outfit.

The line was off the hook, but Quanda knew she didn't have to wait. All she had to do was get to the front and tell them her name. One of her home girls, Chantel from Marcy, was down with Roca-Fella, Jay-Z's record company. Well she wasn't exactly down with Roca-Fella but she had dealt with Memphis Bleek for a minute. She apparently grew up with him in Marcy, one thing led to another . . . and yada yada yada. To make a long story short, it had all worked out for Quanda.

Quanda had prearranged for this night after finding out that Bleek was celebrating his birthday and a big fight was coming on. That combination alone guaranteed that some of the major players from around the way were going to be up in the spot. Even though legend had it that guys from Marcy and guys from Tompkins didn't get along, Quanda knew that the person she was looking for had people up in Marcy and he was always keeping up with the rappers. She knew for sure he would be there.

"Yo sweetheart, there is a line. Don't you see it?" the three hundred fifty pound bouncer barked at Quanda.

"I'm on the guest list," Quanda replied ostentatiously.

"Hold up a sec. Yo, Bee! Bring me the guest list. This little hottie says she's on it!" the bouncer said, yelling to his partner as he undressed Quanda with his eyes. Quanda impatiently shifted her weight from one foot to the other. Her ass was freezing. "I'm right here," Quanda said pointing her name out on the sheet.

"Aiight," the bouncer conceded, unhooking the clasp of the velvet rope.

"I don't know whatchu heard about me . . . but bitch can't get a dollar outta me . . . 'cause I'm a P-I-M-P . . . the 50 Cent lyrics resounded loudly off the walls as Quanda slid into the club; she could feel the bass vibrating through her body. The place was packed, just as she

expected. She felt like all eyes were on her—probably because they were. There were several other scantily clad women inside, but none of them resembled cat woman. All of the men were scoping Quanda out thinking *all she needs is a whip*.

"Lemme get a Mojito," Quanda told the bartender. As her drink was being prepared, she turned from the bar so she could check out the scene.

The club was hot. It was decked out with suspended eggcup swinging lounge chairs, Italian marble floors, and huge Plasma screen televisions. The dim lights gave the place a classy, yet seductive aura.

"Here you go . . . that'll be ten dollars," the bartender said as he placed Quanda's drink on the bar. Quanda paid for her drink and left a generous tip. She had prepared well for this night. She wasn't half-stepping. It was important that she be able to hang with the best of them tonight. Like a sophisticated woman would, she nursed her drink for another half-hour.

Finally, it was time. Roy Jones Jr. tussled it out with Antonio Tarver on the big screen and the crowd in the club was going crazy. Quanda looked around and decided that even if she didn't see Chantel, she was still going to make her way up to the VIP lounge.

Just as Quanda got up from her seat to move, she spotted Rayon, Knowledge's right-hand man, coming down the stairs. She suddenly became hot with anxiety. *Bitch this ain't no time to get shook . . . you got this . . . you got this . . . be easy*, she comforted herself. Rayon walked toward her and stood between her and the stool next to hers. "Yo, give me another bottle of Courvoisier V.S.O.P.," he demanded of the bartender.

Quanda stared at the side of his face hoping that he would notice her. She watched as he pulled out a stack of bills—about the width of a big block of welfare cheese—and peeled off several bills to pay for drink. When he turned to leave the bar, he finally noticed her. *What this hood rat doing up in here*? Rayon thought to himself. Instead of confronting her, he decided to be nice, thinking he might get some ass from Quanda tonight. The guys back on the block would never believe it if he did. What he didn't know was that Quanda wasn't after him. He had just become a pawn in her game.

"Yo what up? Whatchu' doing up in this spot? You a sports fan?" Rayon asked, talking to Quanda like she had been his friend forever.

"Yup, and I came out for my manz Bleek," she replied.

"Oh word? So, why you ain't up in there wit us chillin?" he inquired.

"I just got here," Quanda lied.

"Oh aiight, come on then," Rayon said, gesturing for her to follow.

Perfect! Just what I needed . . . an invitation! Quanda thought to herself, hiding her excitement. "Aiight, but who up in there?" she asked cautiously, sliding off her stool.

When she stood up Rayon almost dropped his $200 bottle of cognac. His eyes bulged out of his head. He had never seen her look so damn right.

"The whole crew up in the spot," he reported, unable to take his eyes off her curvaceous body. He had an instant hard on.

"Oh, that's what's up," Quanda said pointedly, the hairs on her neck stood up, she was so excited.

Quanda and Rayon walked together, both of them preoccupied. When they approached the VIP door the bouncer in front stopped them. The bouncer recognized Rayon, but he didn't know Quanda. So many groupie chicks tried to get in that room it was unbelievable.

"Yo, who this?" the bouncer asked, pointing to Quanda.

"She wit me man," Rayon said, hoping that would impress Quanda enough for her to go home with him.

Quanda just kept quiet and slid right on in. Everybody was up in the VIP room—rappers, hustlers, and groupies—all having a hood rich good time.

Quanda looked around at the tables adorned with bottles of Cristal, Belvedere, Remy Red, Hennessy, and Moet. She was almost blinded by all of the bling; diamonds sparkled from necks, wrists, fingers, ears, and teeth. Quanda took it all in like she was like a special agent on a covert operation. Her eyes scanned the crowd . . . she spotted her mark.

Knowledge was sitting comfortably on one of the white leather wrap around sofas. On the table in front of him lay a stack of cash, a bottle of Cristal, and a plate of jumbo cocktail shrimp. His crew surrounded him like he was the damn president. Quanda knew that his table was invite only, so she had to get herself invited. Rayon was Knowledge's best friend and business partner. Quanda knew that Rayon was feeling her, so she played on it.

"Yo, so I'm sayin, can I have a drink wit ya'll?" Quanda asked surreptitiously.

"Come on over," Rayon said with his own ulterior motives in mind.

As they approached the table together, she noticed all of the guys staring at her, especially Rell. That was the effect Quanda was going for, but a sudden wave of discomfort invaded her stomach. She felt like the acids in her stomach were sitting right at the back of her throat. She walked behind Rayon to hide the fact that her legs were feeling unsteady. Before her legs gave way, Quanda quickly found a chair close to the table. She took a long, deep breath and sat down on the soft, cushioned chair.

Quanda knew she was treading very dangerous ground when it came to Knowledge. He was good at what he did, and he planned on keeping it that way. It was not going to be easy to infiltrate his operation, but she knew that was exactly what she had to do. She'd never felt such an overwhelming need for revenge in her life.

Knowledge whispered something to Rayon and then they both looked over at her. Quanda quickly turned her head away, pretending not to notice. Out of her peripheral vision she could see Rayon moving toward her.

"Yo Quanda, Knowledge said wassup. He wants to holla at ya," Rayon said, leaning in close so that she could hear him over the noise of the club.

"Me?" she asked, playing dumb. *Damn, how easy was that*? Quanda thought, smiling to herself.

"Yeah, man. He said for you to join him at the table," Rayon replied.

"Word? Aiight, that's wassup," Quanda beamed, acting excited. She was trying hard to hide the fact that she was so nervous she was about to piss on herself.

Quanda got up and walked over to Knowledge's table. Knowledge was talking and laughing with his crew as she approached. He looked up at her, clearly intoxicated. His eyes were low and he had a lazy grin on his face. It was the first time, since they were young kids, that Quanda had really taken a good look at him. She stood there, not knowing what to say.

Knowledge had the smoothest mahogany brown skin, a square chin, and a noticeably chipped front tooth which he was forced to display after gold fronts played out. His hair was cut low and perfectly lined-up, which seemed to emphasize his rather large head. Knowledge had broad shoulders and a barrel chest, and was beginning to get a small bulge in his stomach area, probably from all the good eating and alcohol he consumed. His clothes were pristine. He wore a black linen *Sean Jean* dress shirt, a black *Gucci* monogram belt, a pair of neatly creased *Armani* slacks, complete with black *Gucci* loafers. Money could make the ugliest person look good.

"What the deal is ma?" Knowledge asked Quanda.

"You tell me playboy," Quanda responded teasingly.

"I'm sayin' you up in here looking like . . . whoa. You rollin' by ya self?" he asked

"Yeah," Quanda responded, batting her lashes.

"So where ya girl Myra at?" he asked.

Quanda eyes suddenly hooded over. *The fucking nerve of this bastard!* she screamed inside of her head, but continued to play it cool.

She had a mission to carry out.

"She around . . . I guess," Quanda replied vaguely.

"Around?" Knowledge asked, trying not to reveal his real intentions for inviting Quanda to the table.

"Yeah . . . around. You wanna talk about her or us?" Quanda asked, trying hard to hold onto her composure. She really wanted to jump on him and gouge his eyes out. But she realized that if she did just that, she would receive a good old fashioned Brooklyn beat down. Quanda decided that Knowledge's punishment would be long and painful. He thought he was so untouchable—that he would always be on top.

Quanda was on a quest tonight. She was convinced that Knowledge was the person responsible for what had happened to Myra. And since no one seemed to find time to right all of the wrongs that had been done to her friend, Quanda decided that she would do it herself. Besides that, Quanda had another old score to settle with Knowledge.

When Lamont Trady a.k.a. Knowledge was just a little bum scrounging for food in the projects, a big-time heroin dealer named Akbar gave him his first job—delivering packages. Akbar was Quanda's father. He was a 5 percenta Muslim and he had all of Bed-Stuy on lock down. He even had the Muslims that occupied Bushwick Avenue on his team. Drugs weren't his only hustle; he sold Muslim oils, incense, bean pies, Black soap—you name it, he had people selling it. His operation ran like a well-oiled machine, sort of like the Carter in the movie New Jack City. Akbar was a no-holds barred type of guy. He believed in an eye for an eye; everyone who had crossed his path feared him. He provided everything for his wives, one of whom was Brenda. When Brenda was with Akbar she used her "Queen" name, Naimah. Akbar provided generously for his six children with Naimah. Quanda's life was complete when her father was alive and around.

Years of hustling had proved fruitful for Akbar; he had a strong, loyal crew. Or so he thought. Rumor had it that Knowledge was the one who played both sides of the fence and did away with a great deal of money from some weight that Akbar had been moving for a Cuban cat name Rohelio from Harlem.

Rohelio thought he was Tony Mantana from Scarface; he prided himself on murder and mayhem. Akbar had no idea that Rohelio was short on his payment; he had given the full payment to his little runner, Knowledge. The Cubans didn't play. One day, Akbar sat in his champagne colored Cadillac El Dorado with its white wall tires waiting for Naimah to come out of the building. Just as she emerged from the front exit, heading toward the car where her king awaited her, she heard the loud buzzing sound of a motorcycle. Before Naimah could react, she heard shots ring out. Akbar had been shot over thirty times by two unknown assailants on a green Ninja motorcycles. Naimah fell to her knees as she watched in horror as all of her dreams washed away with Akbar's blood.

Naimah was devastated from losing Akbar. She changed her name back to Brenda and became extremely overprotective of her children. She forbid her girls from dating drug dealers. She did not want them to suffer the pain of having everything one minute and losing it all in the next. Brenda was never able to recover Akbar's assets because the police seized everything as evidence during the murder investigation. She and her children had been left to depend on the system.

As far as Quanda was concerned, Knowledge had set her father up by not delivering the money and by dropping dime to the Cubans that Akbar was skimming off the top. Growing up without a father was painful; but seeing her mother cry at night because she missed Akbar just added fuel to Quanda's fire.

"Calm down . . . I'm just asking," Knowledge said laughing, snapping Quanda back into the present.

"So anyway, wassup? Where you going when you leave here?" Quanda asked.

"Breakfast somewhere probably . . . and then to a telly if you coming with me," Knowledge replied, flashing a crooked smile.

"I don't know about all of that but I will come to breakfast with you . . . but only if it's me and you," she said softly, gauging his reaction.

"We'll discuss that. For now, why don't you sit here and keep me company?" Knowledge said, patting the empty space on the couch next to him.

"Aiight," Quanda complied, sitting down as he poured her a glass of Cristal. She tried very hard not to look over at Rell who was sitting directly across the table from her. Quanda knew that Rell was the jealous type, but right now she didn't have time to deal with his hurt feelings. She sipped the expensive champagne, bidding her time.

Over the next two hours, as Quanda sat at the table, she figured a few things out. First, Rayon was next in line after Knowledge; he was the "lieutenant." Second, she learned that Budda, Robbo, and Rell were all referred to as "soldiers." But while their small "army" of men seemed to be doing well, none of them seemed to be doing as well as Knowledge.

Quanda and Knowledge talked off and on for the remainder of the night. Even though Knowledge was a well-known hustler and product of the streets, Quanda was actually impressed by his leadership skills and shrewd business sense. He told her that he had changed his name while doing a bid upstate and that he was down with the Gods. He also said that he had learned many self-improvement and empowerment principles from reading books when he was locked up. She thought that was a real contradiction, considering the type of lifestyle he led.

Knowledge told her that he never tells anyone where he lives, and that he takes care of all of his children, even though he is not with any of his babies' mothers because they were all "birds." He told Quanda that he was looking for a shorty to ride with him, but so far he hasn't found anyone strong-minded enough. Quanda took mental notes.

Maybe he doesn't know about what me and Rell had? She kept reminding herself to stay focused on her goal, and not be distracted by her surroundings or the temptations of finer things. Quanda learned a lot that night. She was pretty confident that she could quickly gain his trust. Yes, things were moving along just fine.

Milton grumbled and cursed under his breath as he left the house. "I took this bitch from the gutter and she got the nerve to be questioning me? I'll stay out ten fuckin' days if I want to," he mumbled about Myra. He needed to clear his mind and relieve some of his stress.

Milton pulled up in front of Webster Hall, his favorite club. The line was almost going around the block. He scanned the line, observing all of the so-called thugs with their hats turned backwards, jeans hanging low, crisp team jersey's over white tees, wearing Timbs or Air Force Ones. A few had that metrosexual look going on, dressed in tight-fitting striped dress shirts and slacks. But for the most part, the thug look was the trend for tonight. He would fit right in.

Milton drove around on several side streets before he found parking. He hit his alarm, locking the doors and headed toward the club. The line was moving slowly, but he wasn't waiting on it. He maneuvered through the guys standing on the sidewalk in front of the blue police barriers that separated the line, and made his way to the front door.

"Yo, wassup Dauid," Milton asked the tall, slender host at the door.

"Hey you," the guy answered, with a very feminine overtone in his voice.

"Anything good tonight?" Milton asked.

"Yeah your type up in there . . . you know the ones that don't believe yet," Dauid said with a smirk.

Milton got a little pissed at his sarcasm, or maybe it was the truth behind his words that pissed him off. The lanky host rolled his eyes and stepped aside. Milton entered the black door. His lungs quickly filled with marijuana smoke.

Beautiful . . . I just want you to know . . . you're my favorite girl. Snoop Dog featuring Pharell was blaring from the speakers surrounding the club. Milton put his hands in his pockets and found a spot in a darkened corner. That was his usual routine. He didn't want to get noticed by anyone he didn't want noticing him.

Milton watched as all of the "thugs" got their groove on, some with doo rags, some with fitted caps and some with 360 waves. Some of them danced alone and some with each other. Milton wasn't with that. He wasn't gay; therefore there would be no dancing with other men. He wasn't a "homo-thug" either, like some of the magazines and newspapers had been reporting lately. They made it seem like it was a new wave or something—men who appear to be straight from their looks but are really gay and sleeping with other dudes.

It wasn't a fad for Milton. He wasn't technically gay anyway, because he liked women. Just occasionally he would get this insatiable need, and when he got it he had to fulfill it—at whatever cost.

After forty five minutes and two glasses of Hennessy, Milton decided that he needed to make his move. He had been eyeing this one guy all night long. The guy wasn't dressed like everyone else. He wore a black, tightly-fitted nylon stretch shirt. It hugged his chest so tight that Milton could see the ripple of his six pack stomach and his two nipples poking out through the fabric of his shirt. The guy had on a pair of close fitting PaperDenimCloth jeans and a pair of black leather loafers. Milton's interest had been piqued.

Milton knew that he would have to find someone who wanted to "receive" because he was strictly a "giver"—which meant he didn't like being penetrated. Most of the thuggish guys were "givers" as well.

With the Hennessy relaxing his muscles, including his brain, Milton got up enough courage to finally make his move. He walked over to the guy sitting alone at the bar.

"Whatchu drinkin'?" Milton asked.

"I'm not . . . I'm rolling," the guy responded, referring to his use of the drug *Ecstasy*.

"Oh aiight. So wassup for tonight?" Milton asked.

"Whatchu payin'?" the guy responded.

He was a male prostitute. The situation couldn't have turned out better for Milton. Now the guy would have to do whatever Milton paid him to do. Milton got an instant erection just thinking about it.

"What's the price list?" Milton asked, with a serious gaze masking his burning desire. This guy didn't know who he was messing with. He'd be in for a treat.

"A hundred for whatever for one hour . . . wherever you want," the guy said.

"Aiight, let's go," Milton agreed to the bargain.

Milton ordered a shot of tequila, downed it, and jumped from the bar stool heading for the door. The guy followed behind, about ten steps back. Milton was excited about his upcoming encounter; he could get his rocks off without trying to make this guy think he wanted something more. Milton didn't want to know the guy's name or anything about him. His sole intention was to relieve the aching bulge that invaded his loins.

Milton deactivated the alarm on his SUV, and climbed in as his prospect made himself comfortable in the passenger seat. They rode in silence; both anticipating what was to come.

"That first building on ya right," the guy instructed, as Milton navigated his ride. He looked up at the sign that read W.113th Street—they were in Harlem. Milton parked his car outside and they both got out. Other than directions, no words had been exchanged. Milton watched as the guy swayed effeminately toward the building. *Fucking faggot*, Milton thought to himself.

They discretely entered the building. The old fashioned elevator reeked of moth balls and when it reached the third floor Milton was glad to get out.

Milton's date opened the door to apartment 3B and invited Milton in.

"Ok, payment is due now," the guy said, as Milton followed him inside.

Milton dug into his pocket and pulled out his wallet. He searched the back billfold compartment and handed the guy a crisp one hundred dollar bill.

"This way," the guy instructed, satisfied with his prompt payment.

Milton was led into a back room. There was a red light bulb in the ceiling and a red shag carpet on the floor. In the middle of the room, lay a high pile of soft pillows made of colorful patches of satin, chenille, and suede, adorned with assorted red, purple, blue, and orange beads. They looked soft and inviting. Just want Milton had in mind.

Milton thought that the Aladdin/I Dream of Jeanie theme throughout the room was a bit strange. There was a small purple bucket, it could have been blue but with the red light shining in the room, it looked purple, and it was filled to the brim with condoms. In each corner of the room, there were speakers emitting soft jazz tunes. The guy crossed the room and went about lighting candles spread throughout the room, as if he were preparing for a romantic night with his lover.

With the room softly glowing, the guy turned to Milton and asked gently, "What'll you have?"

"Let me show you," Milton responded feeling slightly embarrassed that he was in this room.

"Ok," the guy said agreeably, quickly removing every bit of his clothes, revealing his statuesque body. He was built like a black replica of the statue of David—perfect abs, muscular legs and arms, and a wide, chiseled chest. Milton watched him, growing hotter and hotter by the minute. He noticed the guy's tool, which appeared to be about fourteen inches long. His caramel skin was flawless. Milton wanted to kill him for looking so damn good and kill himself for getting so goddamn turned on by it.

"Come on, big guy . . . time starts ticking when you enter this room," the guy said.

Milton peeled his pants and his boxers halfway off, exposing his swollen member. He could never remember feeling this damn horny for any woman, not even Myra. He moved toward the guy, grabbing his arm and throwing him down on the pile of pillows, positioning himself in back.

"Wait . . . here you go," the guy said, handing Milton a condom. Milton fumbled with the wrapper, anticipation making his hands shake. He was finally able to tear it open and slide it on. The guy assumed the classic doggie style position, on his knees with his ass facing Milton. Milton grabbed his hips, pulling the prostitute toward him. He let a huge glob of saliva leave his mouth, falling between the guy's spread ass cheeks. He held onto his manhood, guiding it in. Immediately, he began moving in and out slowly, but quickly picked up the pace to a fast plow anxious to meet his need. The guy audibly winced in pain from the vigorous pace Milton was setting. The sound infuriated Milton.

Milton grabbed the back of the guy's neck and rammed himself into the guy's ass as hard as he could. He kept a steady pace, banging away. Milton was ramming the stranger so hard that the guy began to fight to get his bearings, attempting to extricate himself from Milton's powerful grip. Milton used all of his 250 pounds of muscle to hold down his victim's thin frame. He moved his hands over the guy's mouth, and grinded his way deeper into the guy's flesh. Deeper and deeper he went, oblivious to the muffled screams. The guy struggled in vain to get away from Milton, crying in pain and fear as Milton took him violently.

"Mmmm Fffffff," the guy tried to scream, fearing that his attacker's dick was going to penetrate his intestines.

"Yeah bitch . . . you wanna fuck men . . . huh . . . huh?" Milton said, as he huffed and puffed for breath. Milton removed his hands from the guy's neck, which he had used for leverage. Milton punched the guy's back, causing him to collapse under him. This turned him on immensely, causing him to orgasm. "Urrrrgggghhh!" Milton screamed and as he released his fluids he continued to punch the guy's limp flesh.

When he was done Milton became overwhelmed with guilt, as he usually did after these types of encounters. He quickly pulled up his pants and stumbled toward the door, leaving the guy sprawled over his beautiful pile of pillows.

Milton rode home in silence. All he wanted to do now was sleep.

Myra paced the floor around the coffee table about fifty times in each direction, staring at the large manila envelope that had been taped to the front door and addressed to Milton. The terrible handwriting in black magic marker on the front read MILTON ROBITS STAR QUATABACK. It looked as if a first grader had scribbled the words. Her curiosity was killing her, but she knew that if she opened it there would be pure hell to pay when Milton returned home—that is, if he came home. It was already quarter past eleven, and still no sign of him.

Myra wondered what could possibly be in the envelope. Nowadays, it seemed that she was more excited about the draft than he was. *Maybe it's something from an agent,* she thought to herself. But careful examination of the handwriting quickly changed that thought. Myra picked it up several times, shaking it, turning it over, examining it to see if any of the seal had come undone so that she could take a peek, but nothing. She couldn't hear anything sliding around inside either. She expected Milton to be home soon anyway, so she gave up and decided to wait and let him share it with her.

Myra took a shower, as she always did before he got home, just in case he wanted to have sex with her. All of her wounds were pretty much healed and she looked forward to the new semester starting. She was tired of being at home all day, with nothing to do but think. She drove herself crazy worrying—first about Vidal, because she hadn't heard from her or seen her since the incident at her apartment, and then about Milton and his unpredictable behaviors as of late. She never complained to Milton though, because she thought that if she did he would think that she was ungrateful; or worse, that she no longer loved him. So she never nagged him, even when he came home late. She couldn't risk losing him, or the chance to become Mrs. Milton Roberts. Plus, she enjoyed the expensive gifts that he gave her whenever he was feeling guilty.

Myra had already acquired a new *Louis Vuitton* bag, a diamond charm bracelet, a heart shaped *IceTek* watch with a diamond bezel, and countless pieces of expensive lingerie from *Frederick's of Hollywood, La Perla and Victoria's Secret.* Milton always gave her these gifts with the promise that there was more to come when he got drafted, so long as she stuck by him and remained loyal to him. Even though Milton wasn't good at expressing his feelings, she felt that he conveyed his love for her in other ways, like showering her with expensive gifts. She never questioned where he got his money or how he managed to pay for such extravagant items.

Myra fell asleep waiting up for Milton. She didn't wake up until she heard him ripping the manila envelope open. Nothing but silence. *Damn should I get up and ask him what it is?* she asked herself. Myra waited another ten minutes to see if he would come running to her with the good news. Still nothing.

Myra threw the comforter back and slid out of the bed, trying her hardest to walk without making any noise. She made her way into the hallway and hoped to peek into the living room without being noticed. Myra tip-toed her way down the hall and peeked into the living room. As she glanced around the corner, she noticed Milton sitting on the couch with his head in his hands. The manila envelope lay at his feet, torn into small pieces, but the contents were no where in sight. *It must be bad news,* she thought to herself. She decided to go back into the bedroom, afraid to find out.

What if he wasn't being drafted?...What if no agent wants him?... What would we do then?...Is he going to break up with me because he thinks he won't have money to make me happy?...Where will I go?. Myra let all of these thoughts invade her mind. She felt like crying. She just wanted to be there for him. Mentally exhausted, she closed her eyes and drifted off to sleep.

Myra didn't awake until later that morning. She got out of bed looking for Milton. She found him asleep on the sofa in the living room. Myra walked over to the couch and kneeled down in front of him, touching him gently on his face.

"Hey," she said softly, almost whispering. Milton jumped out of his sleep like she had thrown a pot of cold water in his face. Myra jumped too, startled by his reaction.

"Oh . . . wassup?" he said, realizing where he was.

"What time did you get home?" she said, still speaking softly.

"I don't know," he replied irritably.

"There was a package here for you. Did you see it?" Myra asked, already knowing the answer. She quickly let her eyes scan the immediate area for the package. She didn't see it.

"Yeah, I got it," he said, leaving it at that. He was not about to elaborate.

"Oh, is everything ok?" she asked hesitantly.

"Yeah. Why you asking me that?" he said, paranoid.

"No, I was just making sure you were ok . . . you didn't come to bed and—" Before she could finish Milton pushed her away from him and stood up from the couch.

Milton walked toward the bathroom, leaving Myra sitting on the floor. She waited five minutes. She decided that she'd had enough of his evasiveness. She was going to confront him right now.

Myra banged on the bathroom door with her fist. Milton opened the door looking at her like she was crazy.

"Look Milton . . . I love you and I just want to be there for you. Please stop leaving me in the dark. All I want to do is show you how much I love you. Please, just let me in to your world. We are so great together. You treat me so well. You've given me everything . . . except for your innermost thoughts. Please stop leaving me out. It's tearing me up inside," Myra pleaded with him, pouring her heart out like she had never done before.

"Are you finished?" he asked bluntly.

"Well, are you going to talk to me?" Myra asked tentatively.

"There's nothing to talk about. Now let me brush my teeth. I got a late practice," he said coldly, turning away from her and slamming the bathroom door shut in her face.

"Well, just remember that I will do anything for you . . . anything to help you get over whatever is bothering you," she said genuinely concerned.

As she turned to walk away, the telephone rang. Milton bolted out of the bathroom, running past her, almost knocking her down.

"Hello," he said, snatching up the receiver.

"Did you get my package?" the voice said menacingly. It was Damien Fuller.

"Yo, Damien. Where you got those pictures from man?" Milton whispered nervously.

"Nigga, I told you that I had some shit on you that would ruin your career but you wanted to fuck around and pay me whenever. So, I decided to show you what I got," Damien said, intimidating.

"Aiight . . . look I'ma have something for you by the end of the week," Milton yielded.

"End of the week! Nigga you crazy, you betta have some shit by tomorrow at 5 p.m. or else those pictures will be all over the papers and no team will want your ass," Damien warned.

"That's impossible, man. You know I don't get no money at this time of month. Besides, I just gave you two payments a couple of weeks ago," Milton negotiated.

"A couple of weeks ago . . . nigga, that was almost two months ago! I'm not gonna be waiting for you to pay when you get ready. This is blackmail nigga; we don't have no payment plans. So have my shit or else. By the way, I see you gotta fine young thang livin' up there with you. I betchu she would want to know about you too . . . hope she not fucking you raw dog," Damien stated cruelly.

"You leave her out of this," Milton said, raising his voice slightly, but hushing it back down to an aggressive whisper so that Myra couldn't overhear.

"Like I said, pay or pray," Damien said, laughing shrilly before he slammed the phone in Milton's ear.

If Milton could only be alone with Damien for one hour, he would torture him and then kill him. He seriously considered getting some of his friends from his old neighborhood to take care of Damien, but each time the thought entered his mind he realized that asking for help would be like admitting to his friends that he wasn't the "star" he made himself out to be.

Milton put the cordless phone back onto the cradle and turned around to find Myra standing behind him. She startled him, making him even angrier.

"Why the fuck is you standing all up on me n' shit!" he yelled, pushing past her again, trying his best to avoid looking her in the face. He stomped back into the bathroom and slammed the door.

Myra watched his little tirade, seriously beginning to think that he was going crazy. Something funny was going on with him and he was beginning to scare her. He wasn't the same well-kept, loving, caring gentleman that she had met when she first started school. He was literally turning into a monster right before her eyes. He was unpredictable, like Dr. Jekyll--Mr. Hyde. The up and down rollercoaster ride was driving her mad; one minute he was loving and gentle, the next minute he was a heartless bastard.

Myra waited a few minutes after he slammed the front door and ran into the living room—searching for the envelope. She just knew that whatever was in that envelope could probably answer several of her questions. She looked under the couch, under the cushions, under the area rug and loveseat. There was nothing. She had no idea what he had done with the package or its contents. Tired from her search, she flopped down onto the floor—emotionally drained.

Milton sat in his vehicle shuffling the pictures one by one, examining them closely. He couldn't believe that Damien had pictures of him actually having sex with a man. He even had close up shots of Milton's face as he reached orgasm. The one thing he couldn't see was the face of the partner. Milton had been so promiscuous with his down-low lifestyle that it could have been a number of men. Without a picture of the guy's face, he didn't have a clue. He put the pictures up to his face to see if he could recognize the hairy legs or the ass in the picture, but no luck.

Milton laid his head on the steering wheel and began to sob out loud. "What did I ever do to anyone to deserve this shit . . . my life is ruined!" he shouted, banging his fists against the dashboard.

After a few minutes of stewing in his own juices, he lifted his head. "No more of this nice guy shit . . . I gotta pay this nigga off . . . that it and that's all. This bitch Myra is about to make me some money or her ass will be back in the p.j.'s getting killed. I don't love these hos!" he exclaimed aloud, sitting up like he had just found a new outlook on life. Milton put the truck into drive and screeched away from the curb.

Chapter 9

RIDE OR DIE

Mr. Shepowitz stared at Myra in shock. He could not believe that such a young girl had endured so much abuse—and at the hands of her own mother too. It was no wonder that Myra had ended up where she was. She never had any real guidance or, for that matter, love. Mr. Shepowitz realized just from speaking with Myra that she would have done anything for love. Never before had one of his clients' stories touched him in such a way.

"Our time is up Ms. Danford. I will be back next week," he stated reluctantly, not really wanting to leave.

"Yeah, next week sounds good because I haven't really even started my story," Myra said with a sigh.

"I'm really sorry that you had to experience such pain so early on in life," Mr. Shepowitz said, genuinely sympathetic.

"Well you haven't heard the half of it . . . but when you come next week I will finish. Don't feel sorry for me. I don't need your pity—I need a defense," she said with feeling.

"Ok, well in the meantime stay out of trouble. Your court date is in a week and we don't want any problems," he instructed.

"Ok," Myra agreed.

Myra returned to her jail dorm and was miserable all night long. She lay on her prison-issued three-and-a-half inch thick mattress besieged with anger. Talking with Mr. Shepowitz about her life had brought back so many issues that she had tried hard to suppress over the years. She wasn't ready to come to terms with them right now. She especially was not ready to deal with her relationship with Milton Roberts. Nonetheless the facts remained.

Myra and Milton sat on the short leather and mahogany wood bench inside *The Cheesecake Factory* waiting for their names to be called. Myra held onto the small square vibrator that the hostess had given her, which would go off as soon as a table was available. They sat in silence, waiting. Myra stared at the glass casing that held all of the different cheesecakes, some with strawberry toppings, some chocolate, and some drizzled with caramel crème. *How many different kinds of cheesecakes can there possibly be?* Myra thought, amused. But being from Brooklyn, she had been spoiled and loved only *Junior's* cheesecakes.

Milton realized all of his surreptitious behavior didn't matter to Myra. The other things that he did for her, like taking her to restaurants and buying her expensive gifts, superceded those ugly moments when his true self came to surface. He knew that, and he used it to his advantage. Milton's time had run out. Myra was definitely ready.

After forty minutes of waiting, they were seated. They both perused the menu trying to decide on an entree. Myra went straight to the seafood options in the menu. She never ordered chicken or steak when she went out because she reasoned that she could make that stuff at home for herself. Milton was not worried about the menu. It was now or never for him.

"I gotta talk to you," Milton blurted out, finally interrupting their silence.

"Ok . . . wassup?" Myra asked, looking up from her menu, concerned by the tone of his voice. She had been waiting for this moment for some time.

"Um . . . my grandmother is sick and I gotta come up with some money for her doctors' bills," he said, full of shit.

"Awww, I'm so sorry . . . is she gonna be alright?" Myra asked, breathing a sigh of relief. *So that's what has been bothering him all this time!*

"I don't know that yet," he said, thrown off by her question.

"How did you find out? I thought you didn't talk to your family anymore?" she asked, remembering something that he had shared with her in the beginning of their relationship.

"Nah, my aunt called the athletics office at the school and told them about it and they told me. So that's why I can't turn my back or else it would look bad when I get drafted. I can't have no bad press," he said, burying himself deeper and deeper in deceit.

Milton knew if he mentioned anything about messing up the draft or his career, he would have Myra's full attention. He knew that his draft possibilities were almost as important to her as it they were to him. He also knew that he had already sold her on the idea of being a rich NFL wife.

"OK, so what can I do to help?" she asked. She was so hyped that he had finally let her into his personal world that she would do anything to help him.

"I just need you to always promise me that you gon' be here for me. Are you prepared to ride or die for me baby?" he asked, luring her in.

"YES baby, of course!" Myra said passionately as she reached across the table and grabbed his face, kissing him on the lips.

"Good. Well I gotta raise some cash, so I'm havin' a gambling party tomorrow night," Milton said, rushing the words out of his mouth.

"Ok. Do you want me to cook something?" she asked.

"Nah, I just want you to chill. But I'm telling you now that there is gonna be a stripper. That way, I can make more paper," he said mendaciously.

"Oh, that's not a problem. I'll just stay in the room when she comes,"

Myra assured him, trying to show Milton that under the circumstances she would be a supportive and understanding girlfriend.

"Aiight, that a girl," he said reaching across the table to caress the back of her hand—knowing damn well that he wasn't hiring a stripper.

"My name is Anne I'll be your server for tonight . . . are you ready to order?" the waitress said, interrupting their conversation.

"Yes, I'll have the Jamaican black pepper shrimp," Myra responded, relieved that Milton's problems would soon be over.

"I'll have the same," Milton said, gloating over his easy victory.

Although Milton had told her not to, Myra had prepared Buffalo wings and fully loaded nachos for his gambling party. She greeted his guests, which were mostly fellow athletes from St. John's. Some were Milton's teammates from the football team and some were from the basketball team. They all seemed to know the drill, like they had been to plenty of these types of parties before. There were several tables set up with different gambling games, including Black jack, Poker, Bid Whist and high-priced Pitty Pat. They also had running bets on the week's college football games. Milton provided the drinks and promised the entertainment. Myra did her part by serving them food. When everyone was served, she retired to the bedroom.

Myra never felt completely comfortable being the only girl in all-guy situations. So she dialed Quanda's cell phone number and listened for the ring. She hadn't spoken to Quanda in a few days—and that was unusual.

"Hello," Quanda answered.

"Wassup? Where you at?" Myra asked.

"Oh, um . . . I'm at the movies with Quil," Quanda lied.

"Oh, aiight, I won't keep you. Hit me back when you get out," Myra said disappointedly.

"Ok," Quanda replied, happy that Myra didn't talk long enough to figure out who she was really with.

Just as Myra pressed the TALK button on the cordless phone to hang it up, Milton came into the room. He looked stressed. She could tell that something was wrong.

"What's the matter, baby?" she asked.

"Yo, that bitch of a stripper cancelled on me," he said petulantly.

"Damn." Myra sympathized, feeling her man's disappointment.

"I gotta do something or else I ain't gonna make nothing. The tables ain't enough and these niggas will never come back if I don't have the stripper . . . that's really what they look forward to," he whined, sounding like a little boy.

"Well, can't you call another service?" she asked, trying to be helpful.

"Nah . . . man look at the time!" he replied, sounding defeated.

"Nothing ever works out for me, man . . . I'ma be the laughing stock of Marillac now," Milton continued, with his academy award winning performance.

"I'm sure they will understand," Myra said, trying to reassure him.

"Look you don't know them . . . aiight!" he barked back.

Myra fell silent. She hated to see Milton under pressure and especially since it was for such a good cause.

"Well, what can I do to help? You want me to try to find you another service?" she asked, with the sincerity of a saint.

"Nah, no one ever wants to help me. I don't have nobody in my corner . . . you know my life story," he continued, laying it on thick.

"I'm here for you, Milton," she said, laying her hand on his forearm.

Myra was used to this type of emotional beating. First anger, then blaming, then the guilt trip. She had endured years of it from her mother.

"Whatchu mean . . . you'll do the job for me?" he asked excitedly, taking the opportunity to quickly slide his ill-intentions into their conversation.

"What?!" Myra squealed, raising her eyebrows. She couldn't believe what she was hearing. *Did he just ask me to strip for his friends*?

"It's no big deal ma ma. I got ya back. Nobody will touch you . . . it's only for like twenty minutes too. We can make a lot of paper baby," he said, enticing her.

"Milton, I'm your girl. Why would you want other men to see my body?" she asked, on the brink of tears.

"Look, it's dancing. It's art. Shit, look at Janet Jackson and Beyoncé n' them singin' chicks. They barely wear clothes when they perform and they make paper," Milton reasoned.

"Don't even compare it . . . it's not the same," Myra said, on the verge of hysteria.

"You know what? Forget it. I knew you wasn't a ride or die bitch. I'll just have to find someone else then. Maybe I'll call my ex over. She would do anything for me; she's not the fuckin' weakest link like you," Milton said cruelly.

Milton knew he was getting in her head. He was a predator, preying on all of the indignities Myra had suffered. He was using her low sense of self-worth, her self-loathing, and affection starvation as to manipulate her.

Myra felt like shit. She wanted to pack her things and leave right that second, but she had no place to go. She knew how vicious Milton could be when he didn't get his way. Myra knew that if she didn't make him happy her life would become a living nightmare. *I told him I would do anything for him, so I have to do this—I'm riding.*

"If I do it, what am I supposed to wear?" she asked. Myra caved in like a sink hole during a torrential rainstorm in a Midwestern state. She couldn't stand for anyone to be mad at her, especially Milton. Vidal had turned her into a people pleaser, which left her vulnerable to exploitation.

"You can wear one of those *Frederick's of Hollywood* joints I bought you," Milton said. He knew that he had just won a major battle. Getting them to do it the first time was the hardest part. Everything after that would be a piece of cake.

"I need a couple of drinks first," Myra said, her nerves already getting the best of her.

"Aiight, I'ma make you a Malibu Seabreeze. Get dressed and I'll be back with it in a sec," he said, bouncing out of the room.

Myra paced the floor back and forth. She went to the bathroom to freshen up. She put her hair up in high ponytail and slipped into a fuchsia and black corset, garter, and g-string set that Milton had given her. Her stomach muscles contracted, making her feel like she would lose her last meal. Everyone she had ever loved, except for Quanda, wanted to use her. Tears flooded her eyes, her heart pounded, and she began sweating profusely. After a few minutes of pacing, she stopped and looked into the mirror that was connected to Milton's dresser. *If your own mother did it to you, what makes you think others wont? At least he is doing it to help his grandmother and not using the money to buy drugs,* Myra rationalized. Standing in front of the full-length mirror, looking at herself all dolled-up, Myra looked beyond her reflection, remembering . . .

"Myra?!" Vidal called out. "Yeah it's me," Myra replied as she walked through the front door of their apartment.

"C'mere I want you to meet some friends of mine," Vidal said.

"Oh boyeee," Myra said to herself as she walked into the living room to find Vidal with three strange men. One was a heavy set Puerto Rican man whom she recognized from the bodega on the corner of Myrtle and Broadway. The other two were black guys whom she had never seen before. One had a bald head and a mustache and reminded her of Gordon from Sesame Street. The other one had long dreads, and he spoke with an accent.

"Myra this is Carlo, Greg, and Jah," Vidal said, introducing them to her. Why the hell do I care? Myra said to herself, continuing to walk toward the kitchen. Vidal followed her close behind.

"Look don't be rude; they gonna give us some money for food," Vidal

whispered.

"What?" Myra asked suspiciously.

"MyMy, all you gotta do is do it quick. They old and they ain't gonna last. Look, I got the money already," Vidal said, showing Myra a small wad of folded cash.

"I ain't doing it. I'm not a little girl no more--I'm thirteen," Myra said, flatly rejecting the idea.

"Well then they gonna kill me Myra. So, I guess you'll be on your own then . . . if they don't kill you too," Vidal threatened, frustrated by her daughter's new-found defiance.

"Kill you for what? Why don't you just give them the money back?" Myra asked, exasperated.

"I can't . . . it don't work like that," Vidal snapped. Myra began to cry. Her mother had been doing this shit so often now that she hated her own body. Vidal worked on Myra's mind for the next fifteen minutes until she caved in and returned to the living room.

"Ok who is going first?" she asked robotically. Myra walked to the bedroom and waited for the first perpetrator to enter.

"Baby, you ready?" Milton asked, slightly out of breath as he ran back into the bedroom. Myra wiped the tears from her cheeks. She took the third drink from his hands and gulped it down in one swallow. The liquor was a lot stronger in this one compared to the last two, but it still did not seem to calm her down. She redid her eyeliner, mascara, and lipstick. The make-up was Milton's idea. He said it would make her look sexier.

"Yeah, I'm ready," she said in a low, barely audible voice.

"It's gonna be aiight, ma . . . I'm here for you. I gotcha back and I love you," Milton said as he grabbed her and hugged her tight. Myra didn't return the embrace. *You love me? You fucking liar*! Myra screamed inside of her head, never uttering a word.

Myra walked slowly down the hallway, feeling like she was walking into impending doom. Her stomach ached with anxiety, a mixture of adrenaline and alcohol, made her feel light-headed. Fine beads of sweat lined up across her forehead right at the hair line. She wanted to run straight for the door and keep running until she couldn't run anymore. Myra could hear all of the guys laughing and talking in great anticipation. They knew that Milton always went all out when it came to adult entertainment; the sky was the limit with his parties.

When she reached the end of the hallway Milton put his hand up, stopping her so that he could start her so called "stage" music.

Peaches and cream . . . girl, you know what I mean . . . Peaches and Cream . . . the 112 song began and that was her cue.

Myra slid into the living room and to her amazement all of the furniture had been moved to one side just for her. She took her place in the middle of the floor nervous at first, but eventually letting the liquor take over her senses.

Ohhhh Peaches and Cream . . . As the music blared, she let the rhythm and bass get right into her skin. She moved seductively across the room, looking each and every guy in the face before closing her eyes and beginning her show. She stuck her tongue out and licked her lips seductively. With a jerk, and in sync with the beat of the music, she bent all the way over touching her toes. This movement exposed her bare ass cheeks. She then moved her g-string to the side exposing her labia. Myra played with herself, fingering her hot box from the back. She had discussed all of this with Milton before the show. Myra got down on the floor and began to gyrate her body up and down, simulating sex; all the while working to remove her corset. She wasn't nervous anymore. All she wanted to do was please Milton.

Myra could feel the liquor taking over her brain completely. She moved as if she were a puppet and someone controlled the strings to her destiny. When her bare breasts were finally exposed the guys went wild. They all moved in closely and surrounded her. They clawed at her, grabbing her thighs, some groping handfuls of breast, and others palmed her ass cheeks. At the same time, they were throwing money.

Fives, tens, and even some twenty dollar bills landed on the floor around her. Some of the guys got down on the floor with her and rubbed themselves on her placing money in the straps that connected her garter to her knee-high stockings. Myra continued to remove what little clothes she had on until all of the pieces were gone. At that point, she felt that it was all or nothing. She lay flat on the floor, and let her legs scissor open wide exposing the inside of her flower. She put her pointer finger into her hole deep and pulled it out slowly sending her audience into a crescendo of frenzy.

This is what he wanted right? He told me to take it all off . . . right?! Myra screamed inside of her head, growing angry at Milton for putting her through this. The anger propelled her actions even further. She continued swinging her body, touching herself, and gyrating to the music for what seemed to be a lifetime.

Finally the music stopped and Myra opened her eyes. She recognized a few faces in the crowd and embarrassment invaded her brain. She quickly picked up the pieces to her lingerie outfit and began running out of the living room.

They all began clapping, whistling and cheering, "Encore, Encore!" Milton sat by and watched the entire show. He was surprised at how well Myra had done. He thought she resembled a professional. Milton had an erection the size of the Empire State Building by the time it was all over. He couldn't figure out if it was from all the money he saw flying around or from the show itself. She was definitely a keeper . . . no doubt about that.

Right after their first meeting, Quanda put her feelers out about

Knowledge. She was very careful about whom she spoke to and whom she asked questions. Quanda had recently buttered up to a guy with Downs syndrome named Cisco. Cisco was one of the wanna-be hustlers in Tompkins. Rumor had it that his father, who he never knew, was one of the biggest hustlers in New York during the eighties, and when he found out that Cisco had Down syndrome, he refused to claim him. Cisco hung around with Budda, Rell and Robbo, wanting so badly to be down with their crew. Knowledge always warned them not to have Cisco around; he didn't trust anybody, even a retard. But the crew waited until Knowledge wasn't around to make use of Cisco's services, having him run all kinds of errands for them. They let him hang with them mostly so that they could rank on him after they smoked enough weed to get the giggles. For the most part, they assumed that because he was mentally challenged he didn't understand what was really going on. They had no clue just how badly Cisco wanted to be like them—so much that he studied and followed their every move. They had seriously underestimated his intelligence.

Cisco knew the ins and outs of their entire operation; their movement patterns, their stashes, their re-up days, and who they got to transport their packages out of town. That worked out well for Quanda. She knew that Cisco had a crush on just about every girl in the projects. She put on the charm, gave him a hug, called him her boyfriend, and he sang like a bird.

Quanda found out from Cisco that Rell's cousin, Saida, was scheduled to drive a couple of pounds of weed and some bricks of coke upstate to Utica, New York and drop it off to a spot that Knowledge had on lock up there. In Utica, Knowledge could sell less for more. He could make a nickel bag half as fat as the ones he sold in the city and sell them for the same price. Quanda also found out from Cisco that Saida would be in a rental car rented for them by a young chick named Pam who lived in Quanda's building. They would pick the car up the night before the scheduled trip, stash the drugs in the grill, and Saida would leave from the corner of Throop and Willoughby Avenues at six o'clock the next morning.

Quanda acted immediately on the information she received. She took a cab to Willoughby and, just like Cisco said, a Hertz rental car was sitting in front of Rell's grandmother's house at 520 Willoughby. Quanda knew that spot real well. She quickly jotted down the plate number, got back in the cab, and returned to her building.

Quanda rushed into the apartment, and grabbed the cordless phone. With her heart racing, she locked herself in the bathroom so that she'd have some privacy. Quanda carefully dialed the numbers and waited for an answer.

"OCCB complaint line—how can I help you?" a female voice on the other end of the phone asked.

"I would like to make an anonymous complaint," Quanda said, whispering and disguising her voice.

"Proceed ma'am," the voice instructed.

Quanda dropped dime. She figured that she would start small and work her way up. Knowledge had no idea that his luck was about to change for the worse.

"YES! YES! YES!" Knowledge screamed as Quanda rode him up and down like a Kentucky Derby jockey. His toes curled and his entire body throbbed with pleasure. *Damn I love this pussy,* Knowledge thought to himself. Knowledge couldn't believe how strong his feelings were for Quanda. She was definitely a different breed of woman. It had only been three weeks since that night at the *40/40* club, and they had spent almost all of their free time together.

Knowledge admitted to himself that his initial intentions with Quanda were not good. He had wanted to wine her and dine her a few times, maybe even get her in the sheets, just so he could find out Myra's status and location. He had a score to settle with Myra and Vidal and he hadn't forgotten. But he didn't anticipate falling for with Quanda. In his eyes, Quanda had a special sophistication about her. He was impressed by the fact that she never asked him any questions about his business, about his whereabouts, and most importantly, she never asked him for any money, which was a common practice among the local street hoochies.

After Knowledge climaxed, he grabbed hold of Quanda and held her close to his chest. She couldn't believe how much she had accomplished in such a short time. *Yeah they play like thugs, but they are really silly putty,* Quanda said to herself, returning his embrace. Quanda collapsed on top of his heaving chest, listening to his heart race.

"Damn girl, you got that gushy stuff," he said, still huffing and puffing.

"Oh yeah? You liked it?" Quanda asked teasingly.

"You damn straight," he replied honestly.

"So what we doing today?" she asked.

"Yo, I got some business to take care of but you can stay here 'til I get back. Then, maybe we can get it on some more and maybe I'll have something nice for you," Knowledge stated enigmatically.

"A surprise? Oh goody," Quanda exclaimed, with the phoniest excited voice she could muster.

She couldn't believe that she was at his house already. *I thought real thugs never took nobody where they rest at,* she thought to herself, feeling a great sense of accomplishment.

"Hold up, ma . . . I gotta pee," Knowledge said, moving Quanda aside as he ran naked into the master bathroom.

Now was Quanda's chance. She needed to look at his two-way as fast as possible. She needed to know what his next business move was. She quickly picked it up from the nightstand. She scrolled through the messages. "MEETING UP TOP AT 6" was the first message. Quanda put that in her mental rolodex. "CALL RELL 911" was the next message. Quanda quickly scrolled to the outgoing messages and read the last message that Knowledge had sent. "THAT SHIP NEEDS TO SAIL TO NEW JERUSE AT 10." When the toilet flushed, Quanda quickly put the two-way pager back in the same spot. She found a position on the bed and struck a sexy pose.

"Yo, I woulda never guessed you was so cool ma," Knowledge said as he approached her, brushing her lips with his. Quanda pulled him down on top of her. He was really feeling her; he still couldn't believe it himself.

"I always had a crush on you," she lied. She really despised him.

Quanda quickly learned that the closer she got to him, the easier it would be to infiltrate his operation. Her mother always told her: "Pussy runs the world. Men are compelled by it—it determines everything they do. They spend nine months trying to get out and the rest of their lives trying to get back in." Quanda decided that using hers was the best way to get what she wanted.

"I wish I didn't have to go," Knowledge said reluctantly, testing her to see if she would ask him any questions.

"I wish you didn't either," Quanda whined, like she was hurting to see him leave. Yes, she knew all about his loyalty tests. Quanda knew that she wouldn't have to ask him anything anyway because he would eventually share it all with her.

Knowledge thumbed through the missed calls on his cell phone, as he got dressed. "Damn," he muttered to himself. He had eight missed calls from Rell and Budda. They knew never disturb him when he was laying up with a chick and they definitely wouldn't be calling his cell either. Speaking about business on a cell phone was always a no-no. Pay phone or no phone was their motto. Something was up.

Knowledge contemplated calling from the house phone—it wasn't in his name anyway. He was anxious to know what was going on, so he picked up the phone and dialed Rell's number. If it was really bad,

Rell would know not to say.

"Yo, what up?" Knowledge said into the receiver.

Quanda could only hear Knowledge's end of the conversation: "The car got a boot put on it!? ... "What?! . . . I'm on my way," he yelled, slamming down the phone.

Knowledge put his clothes on real fast, but played it cool in front of Quanda. Quanda just took it all in. She knew that he was talking in code on the phone, but from the sound of it, her plan had worked.

Chapter 10

UPPING THE ANTE

Bliiinnnng. . . *Bliiinnnng* . . . "Hello," Quanda said, answering the telephone.

"Where the hell you been? I've been calling your phone all day and all night," Ms. Brenda reprimanded her daughter.

"Oh, wassup Ma? Um . . . I was with Chantel," Quanda said, quickly covering her ass.

"Well, have you spoken to Myra lately?" Ms. Brenda asked, calming down.

"Yesterday. Why?" Quanda asked tentatively.

"You need to go see her soon. I just heard that they found Vidal and Jamaica her crack head friend dead with their throats slashed over in Brownsville Houses," Ms. Brenda reported.

"What?!" Quanda yelled, knowing that she would be the person to break the news to Myra. She also knew who had ordered their murders.

"Go see Myra and let her know," Ms. Brenda instructed, softening her tone. She hated to think about how Myra would take the news.

"Aiight," Quanda replied, sadness in her voice.

Quanda was a firm believer in karma. She didn't care so much that Vidal had died the way that she did; after all the shit that she had put Myra through, she deserved it. Quanda was, however, not looking forward to telling her best friend that her mother had died. Even though Myra had suffered some horrific things at the hands of her mother, Quanda knew that deep down Myra still loved her mother and hoped that one day she would get better.

Quanda pulled back the huge down comforter on Knowledge's California king size bed. She stepped onto the expensive Italian marble floor, wincing at the chill it sent to her feet. She went to the bathroom, pushed up the gold-plated faucet handle and hung her head over the HERS sink, splashing water on her face. She looked up at herself in the large mirror that was brightly illuminated by the huge vanity lights above it. "Dammit," she sighed. She realized that she had a long day ahead of her.

When Quanda returned to the bedroom she saw a note on the night stand that Knowledge had left. WENT TO TAKE CARE OF BUSINESS. BE READY AT 9. WEAR SOMETHING SEXY. She crumbled the paper. She would have to call him and cancel their plans for tonight. He was supposed to be taking her to *Peter Luger's Steak House.* He said that he wanted to talk to her about some things. *Damn this could have been my key to getting inside! Fuck it—I have to be there for my girl,* Quanda said to herself. Quanda picked up her cell phone and dialed Milton's house. The phone just rang. "This chick never answers the damn phone. If I was dying, she'd be the last person I'd call," Quanda said out loud. She got dressed and called Knowledge just before she headed out.

"Yo," he answered.

"Hi baby," she said, so convincing with her fake love that she sometimes started to believe it.

"Hey," he replied, softening his tone.

"I gotta cancel for tonight," she said, sounding remorseful.

"Why? What up?" he asked, disappointed. He had become addicted to sex with Quanda.

"My mother just called me and told me to come home right away. My sister is sick," she fabricated on the spot.

"Damn . . . she aiight? What's wrong with her?" he asked, sounding concerned.

"She gon' be aiight I guess. She had a real bad asthma attack," Quanda said, thinking quick on her feet. She wouldn't dare tell Knowledge she was going to see Myra. As far as he was concerned, Quanda hadn't seen Myra since she left Tompkins. And that's what she wanted him to keep thinking.

"Aw shit. You good for cash?" he asked considerately.

"I'm a lil low but I guess it will have to do," Quanda replied truthfully. Even though her main goal in life was to take Knowledge down, she was not going to refuse any of the perks that came along with the job.

"Go in my closet and move my stack of Timberland shoe boxes. Under the carpet is a lil somethin'. Take what you need," he instructed. What lay stashed there was just a small portion of his riches.

"Ok baby . . . thank you. Now gimme a kiss," she ordered.

"I don't know 'bout all that," he said reluctantly.

"Oh, you wit' ya boys now so I'm not good enough for a kiss?" Quanda egged him on.

Smmwwwaaack, Knowledge kissed the receiver.

"That's more like it. Later," she said, smiling as she hung up the phone. He was practically eating out of the palm of her hand. Sometimes it all seemed so unreal, especially given his notorious reputation.

Quanda went into the huge walk-in closet and moved the shoe boxes aside and as instructed pulled back a corner of the carpet. There was a small handle sticking up from the floor. Quanda pulled on it gently revealing a small opening, which resembled a crawl space, filled with cash. Her eyes almost popped out of her head. The cash was separated into stacks that were kept together with thick red rubber bands. Quanda deliberated over whether she should remove an entire stack or just a few bills. She didn't have to think about it for too long. She quickly picked up an entire stack, containing only one hundred dollar bills, and shoved it in her purse. The sight of the money made her nervous. But the fact that Knowledge trusted her enough to allow her access to his stash made her even more nervous. She hastily put everything back in the closet the way it was and called herself a cab.

"Ms. Danford, we are so glad to have you back," Dean Reuben said, patting Myra on her shoulder.

"Thank you . . . I'm glad to be back," she said genuinely.

"Well you know how this works. This is your schedule of classes and your book vouchers," he said handing her a stack of paperwork. "Remember to keep that GPA up," he said encouragingly.

"I will," Myra responded with a smile.

"Oh, one more thing . . . we are offering a work study program. Here is the application. Fill it out if you are interested," the dean pulled out a packet of papers from an envelope, and added to the stack that he had just handed her.

Myra read her schedule and was glad to see that she didn't have any long breaks between her classes. She just wanted to go to her classes and go home. She didn't want to chance running into any of the guys who had been present at her striptease show. Work study, in fact, sounded like a good idea. If she got a job, she could help Milton out with the bills, especially with his grandmother. They would never be so desperate for money that their only option was her stripping.

Myra had made up her mind that nothing would stop her from getting a degree. She just hoped that things with her and Milton would go smoothly from here on out—that they would get married, she would have her career, and he would play professional football. She wasn't angry at him anymore for what had happened. He had been in a bind and she had helped him out—that was all.

Myra walked the campus, perusing her schedule. Lost in her thoughts, she accidentally walked head first into someone.

"Oh, excuse me," she said, startled by the collision.

"That's ok," said a male voice. Myra had to lift her chin high just to see his face.

He was more than six feet tall. She had run right into his chest during their crash. Immediately, she recognized his face. Her heart began to beat fast, and her face became flushed with shame.

"Ok," she said, stepping around the monument of a man, trying to escape.

"Hey . . . wait," he said, following closely on her heels.

Myra picked up her pace until she was almost running. He ran too, trying to catch up to her.

He grabbed her arm and swung her around to meet his chest again. "Listen, you remember me?" he asked.

"No," she said flatly, refusing to look up.

"I was . . . uhhh . . . at the gambling thing," he said hesitantly. Myra remained stoic.

"I was sitting in the corner. I didn't touch you or anything. I just admired your beauty from afar," he said, trying to sound gallant.

Myra couldn't believe her ears. *Is he saying I'm beautiful because he got to look at my tits and ass?!?* She didn't respond.

"Look, I'm sorry. No hard feelings, okay? My name is Brad," he said, sticking out his hand as if he wanted her to shake it.

"Myra . . . none taken," she said flatly ignoring his request for a handshake.

Myra craned her neck to look up at "Brad." She immediately recognized him as the star of the Red Storm men's basketball team. Myra was slightly taken aback by his appearance—he was gorgeous. He had a deep mahogany complexion, with a small scar on his right cheek which made him look ruggedly sexy. He had a clean-shaven bald head, a perfectly aligned goatee, and his eyes were chestnut brown.

He wore an oversized *North Face* snorkel coat which hung open to expose an off-white *Sean Jean* knitted sweater. His jeans were just right—not too baggy and not too tight. And, of course, he had on an obviously new pair of Timberland boots.

"So where you headed...to class?" he asked. Myra moved her gaze back to his chest to keep herself from staring.

"Yeah," she replied.

"Maybe we can hang out sometimes?" he asked sheepishly.

"I don't think so. Milton is my boyfriend," she said, looking at him as if he should have already known that.

"He is?" Brad asked, raising his eyebrows as if he was genuinely stunned by the news.

"Yup," she replied, through pursed lips, and walked away.

All the way to her class she wondered why this guy Brad had seemed so shocked at the fact that she and Milton were a couple. She wondered if it was because Milton had had a lot of other girlfriends in the past or if it was because he couldn't believe that any man would let his girlfriend strip for a bunch of guys.

Myra went to all of her classes but she hadn't learned a thing all day. She didn't have the same fervor about school that she had when she first started in the fall. Her spirit had been broken.

After class she went to the football field to see if Milton was ready to take her home. As she approached, she could see that there were only two people on the field—a guy and a girl. *Hmmm, practice must be over already,* Myra thought to herself. As she turned to leave the field, she noticed that the man had looked in her direction. She realized then that it was Milton on the field, standing in close proximity to the strange woman.

Myra's heart jerked in her chest partly due to jealousy, but mostly due to fear. She didn't know what to do. Should she approach him and ask what was going on or should she just remain silent and make her presence clearly known? She decided to approach the two.

"Hey," Myra said, walking right up to Milton.

"Yo," he said, acting as if she was just one of his friends.

The girl looked from Myra to Milton and back again. She was obviously trying to sum up the situation.

"Are you taking me home?" Myra asked innocently.

"Nah, take the car service," Milton responded, refusing to look Myra in the eye.

"What time are you coming home?" she asked, trying to let the girl know that she and Milton lived together.

"Yo, go 'head man, I'll get there!" he said, annoyed and still acting as if Myra was a stranger to him.

You'll get there . . . you bastard, Myra screamed inside of her head. But as usual when she felt hurt or in trouble she remained silent. She was boiling over with anger as she stomped away from Milton and his female friend. Myra went to the athletic office and called the Jewel car service to take her home. She cried for the entire ten minute cab ride home. When the cab pulled up to the gate, Myra got out and thanked the driver.

Myra fiddled around in her pocketbook searching for her pass to the gate; there were new security guards on post who had not yet become familiar with all of the residents. Before Myra could locate her pass, someone touched her on the shoulder. She jumped, startled by the contact. Myra hadn't even noticed Quanda sitting on the bricks in front of the building.

"Girl don't scare me like that," Myra said, scolding her friend.

"Hey, calm down. What's wrong wit you? You been crying?" Quanda asked, perceptively, noticing her friend's red rimmed eyes. *Had someone already told her about Vidal?*

"Girl it's a long story. Come upstairs and I'll tell you," Myra said, choking on her words.

"Ok," Quanda agreed, thinking that maybe Myra didn't know after all.

They both walked to the building in silence. Myra was contemplating whether or not she should tell Quanda about all of the things Milton was doing. She knew that her best friend was very protective of her. Myra always felt that Quanda would kill for her if she had to; she felt the same way for Quanda. Quanda was silent as she thought about her task at hand.

As they entered the apartment complex, Quanda made an effort at small talk in order to break up the monotony.

"So how is it being back in school?" she asked.

"Today was my first day back," Myra replied in monotone.

"Oh, ok . . . where's ya boo at?" Quanda asked.

"He had a late practice," Myra lied, deciding to hold off on telling Quanda *everything* until they got comfortable. She had to figure out what kind of mood Quanda was in first.

"Oh," Quanda said, not knowing what else to say.

"I miss you so much," Myra said, grabbing Quanda and hugging her tightly.

"Oh baby girl, I miss you too," Quanda said, with tears in her eyes as she returned the embrace.

Quanda pulled away from Myra first and held her hand. She decided to just tell her, fearing that Myra would be upset if she knew that she had prolonged telling her something this important.

"Listen MyMy, I came by to talk to you about something important . . . let's sit down" she said, gearing up for what was to come.

"What is it?" Myra asked, a feeling of dread washing over her body.

"I don't even know how or where to start," Quanda began nervously.

"Just start," Myra said, growing concerned.

"Ok . . . look, MyMy, Vidal is gone," Quanda let the words roll off her tongue; she didn't know any other way to say it. Myra stared at her friend. *What does she mean "gone"?* Myra thought to herself. She couldn't even open her mouth.

"MyMy it's ok, I'm here for you," Quanda said, tightening her grip on Myra's hand.

"NOOOOOOO!" Myra began to scream, realizing what Quanda was trying to tell her. Quanda was slightly startled by Myra's strong, emotional reaction to the news.

"C'mere . . . I know I know . . .shhhhh," Quanda said, opening her arms wide, offering her comfort.

"What happened?!? How do you know?" Myra asked, yelling and crying at the same time.

"They said that she was found wit her throat cut . . . out in Brownsville Houses . . . her and Jamaica," Quanda explained.

"OOOHHHHH GOD . . . NOOOOOO!!!" Myra yelled, rocking back and forth as if she were in a great deal of pain. "She was my mother . . . she was all I had!" She sobbed loudly.

Quanda began to cry in response to her friend's obvious distress. She knew that Myra always held a small piece of hope that one day Vidal would get better.

Myra continued to weep for the next hour. Quanda comforted her as best she could and decided to spend the night with her. She would make sure that Myra ate well and got a lot of rest. She wasn't going to abandon her in her time of need.

Everything that Myra had to tell Quanda was forgotten. The incident with Milton and the girl was quickly erased from her mind. All she could think about was her mother and how she didn't even get a chance to say goodbye to her—that she hadn't been able to save Vidal from the captivity of her addiction. Myra was haunted by feelings of guilt—it was all her fault that her mother was dead. She felt should have tried harder to save Vidal.

Quanda went to Rite Aid to purchase a bottle of Tylenol P.M. for Myra. She knew that Myra would never be able to sleep without something to make her drowsy. Around midnight, Myra surrendered to the medication. Quanda hadn't paid attention to the fact that Milton was not home yet. She was too busy planning how to get the next phase of her plan off the ground. Quanda tip-toed away from her sleeping friend and headed toward the kitchen, cell phone in hand. She quietly dialed the digits and, just as planned, the pay-phone rang.

"Yeah?" the voice answered at the other end.

"My plans got messed up . . . you heard about Vidal, right?" Quanda asked, whispering into the phone.

"Yeah, mommy told me," the voice answered. It was her brother Quame.

"So, did you tell Vell the information I gave you?" she asked.

"Hell yeah. It's going down tomorrow," he informed.

"Look, make sure you don't go. Them niggas is professionals. Just let Vell handle everything," she instructed.

"Nah I'm going too. I got just as much hatred for that nigga Knowledge as you do," he said with venom in his voice.

"Quame!" Quanda barked his name, immediately realizing that she was yelling. Not wanting to wake Myra, she lowered her voice to an angry whisper.

"Quame, you betta not go. They be packing mad heat—it's too dangerous. Vell is an old timer, he can handle his and plus he is probably gonna send in his hit men. So you just fall back and reap the benefits," she continued.

"Yeah aiight. But when shit goes down, I'ma be somewhere watching," he assured her.

"Whateva . . . just make sure you don't go up in that spot," Quanda cautioned.

"Yeah aiight . . . later," Quame agreed.

"Listen Quame, this is all for pops so let this shit ride out the way it's supposed to. I love you . . . see you tomorrow," Quanda said right before she hung up the phone.

Quanda sat on the low window sill in Milton's kitchen, thinking about all of the lies, the scheming, not to mention the danger she had put herself in and now her brother. She wondered if revenge was really worth all of this. Quanda knew that her brother Quame had become a runner for Vell, his godfather, and an old timer in the drug game. An O.G. is what they are called in the hood. She also knew that during his spare time he was a great stick up kid, robbing younger drug dealers from the surrounding projects like Sumner, Roosevelt and Lafayette Gardens.

So when she found out that Knowledge had his re-up packages delivered on Friday mornings at 4 a.m. to building 99 on Tompkins Avenue, she decided to make that next on her agenda of destruction. Quanda, of course, immediately shared this information with her little brother, who was well aware of the fact that Knowledge played an integral role in their father's death. He too had a score to settle with Knowledge. Quame took the information and ran with it. He let Vell in on the tip and they formulated a plan of attack. Vell's hatred for Knowledge ran deep as well. Vell always thought that he would be next in line to run Tompkins after his partner Akbar was murdered. When he tried to take over the corners and buildings in Tompkins, Knowledge declared war. He ordered that Vell's workers be murdered, anytime of day or night, and then he'd take over whatever corner or building they had. Vell attempted to take back what was his, using his own strong arm tactics, but after he lost about five of his crew members—and Knowledge about three—Vell decided that the human bloodshed wasn't worth it. Besides, he had spots throughout the five boroughs. Vell finally gave up and relinquished Tompkins to Knowledge.

In Quanda's eyes, she was killing two birds with one stone—revenge for her father's murder and Myra's assault.

All Quanda had to do was sit and wait and hope that when Knowledge was brought to his knees, she would have a front row seat.

"Yo, she was just a friend. You made a fool of yourself," Milton practiced the words he would say to Myra when she brought up the fact that she had caught him with another girl. His plan was to flip the script on her and make her feel guilty, even though he knew he was dead wrong. He continued to practice until he reached the door to his apartment. It was six o'clock in the morning and Milton was just returning from one of his "night-outs."

As the door slid open, Milton could tell that something was different. All of the lights and T.V.'s were off. Myra never stayed in the house alone without having every light on, and at least one T.V. on. Milton crept slowly into the apartment.

Maybe she ain't here, he said to himself.

Suddenly the toilet flushed and the bathroom door swung opened. Milton braced himself. Quanda emerged and came face to face with Milton.

"Ahhhh . . . shit, Milton. You scared me!" Quanda said, looking like a deer caught in headlights.

"You scared me too," Milton said, chuckling nervously.

"Wassup? Listen, let me holla at you in the living room," Quanda said, motioning for him to go into the other room.

Milton immediately became nervous. *Did Myra tell her everything? Is she gonna beef with me or wanna fight? Did she come to take Myra away?* As he walked slowly toward the living room, he let all of these questions run rampant through his brain.

"Wassup?" he asked, trying to sound casual.

"Myra is going through some shit right now. I'm here because they found her mother dead with her throat slashed open," Quanda said without beating around the bush.

"Damn," Milton replied, trying to appear upset. In all actuality, the first thought that came into his mind was *now she definitely can't go nowhere.*

"She's gonna need all of the love and support she can get. You and me is all she got left," Quanda continued.

"You know I'm here for her," he responded, as expected.

"As long as you step up . . . we'll be cool. Don't stress her—just love her. I don't know if you know, but she loved her mother even after all of the ill shit Vidal did to Myra. The lady was her mother," Quanda said, not realizing that Myra had not shared everything about her childhood with Milton.

"Nah, I'm feelin' her or else she wouldn't be here. I'ma be here for good," he said, wanting to let out a big Kool-aid smile, but somehow managing to keep his melancholy face on.

"Good. Don't make me hafta kill ya ass," Quanda said jokingly, but meaning every word she said.

"C'mon now," Milton said uncomfortably.

"I'm just saying," Quanda responded, ending their conversation there. There was so much going on, between Myra and the Knowledge thing that Quanda never thought to question Milton about the time he finally decided to come home.

Milton went into the bedroom and Quanda lay down on the couch. Neither fell asleep. Both wanted to be awake when Myra came to in the morning.

"From now on, Rayon, you take care of the drops and the cash collection cuz for the last month shit has been either short or coming up missing, and some kind of way 5-0 is findin' shit out. Certain movements is getting hotted up," Knowledge said, speaking to his subordinates during one of their weekly meetings.

This nigga musta forgot who helped him build this empire . . . he gon' ask me of all people to carry, Rayon thought to himself. He wasn't happy about having to do street work anymore. He felt that he had proven himself worthy enough to be past that stage in the game. He knew that Knowledge wouldn't dare take the risk of even walking from his car to the building with drugs or money on him—much less dropping off the weight for re-ups. Nevertheless, Rayon agreed.

"Rell, you hot right now. You gon' hafta lay low for a while. I hope you been stashing like I taught you," Knowledge continued.

"Nah man, I gotta eat" Rell replied, knowing that he hadn't saved a dollar since he started hustling. All of his cash went to clothes, jewelry, and women. He lived by the money, hoes, and clothes creed, made famous in the 90's by the Brooklyn Lo-Lives.

"Look nigga, you cost me $450,000 worth of shit off the top and that don't include what the street value was. You lucky I don't body you and ya bitch ass cousin Saida. I still don't know who dropped dime. There's just no fuckin' way 5-0 coulda known about that shit . . . no way. That shit was air tight," Knowledge barked in response.

First he stole my girl now this nigga fucking with my paper . . . he bugging for real, Rell said to himself. Rell fell silent, knowing that there was no winning with Knowledge. It was either put up or shut up.

Robbo and Budda were quiet throughout the entire meeting as well. They were afraid that if they even uttered a word they might be in the same position as Rell; and they needed their jobs.

"Anybody else got anything to say?" Knowledge asked with hostility. When no one responded, he flatly dismissed his underlings.

Knowledge secretly couldn't wait for the meeting to be over. He wanted to call Quanda so bad. He dialed her cell phone number, but it went straight to voicemail. "You called the right numba but at the wrong time . . . so do ya thing at the beep," Knowledge listened to Quanda's voice.

"Yo, you know who this is . . . hit me. I miss you and that kitty-cat like crazy," he said, hitting the pound key to send his message.

Knowledge couldn't believe how he was feeling. Usually when he couldn't find one of his chicks, he just moved on to the next and so on. For some reason, he felt that if he couldn't have Quanda by his side, he didn't want anyone.

Knowledge climbed into his Mercedes-Benz G Wagon (the car of the day), turned up the volume on Jay-Z's Black album . . . *If you feelin' like a pimp nigga gon' brush ya shoulders off . . . ladies is pimps too gon' brush ya shoulders off.* The lyrics relaxed him as he headed home, anxiously awaiting Quanda's call.

"Quanda, Milton, how am I ever going to repay you?" Myra asked, tears welling up in her eyes.

"Listen, don't worry about that. Just have your mother cremated and we'll get past this thing together," Quanda replied, as she and Milton handed a wad of bills to Myra.

"Thank you . . . I love both of you," Myra said, bursting into tears. Milton stared out the window, emotionless.

They all rode in silence on the way to the crematorium where Vidal's remains would be cremated. Vidal didn't have any life insurance; so to prevent her from being buried in Potter's Field, where they bury indigent people, Milton and Quanda had gone Dutch and gave Myra the money to have her mother cremated. It was much cheaper than having a traditional burial.

Quanda thought that it was the least she could do for her friend. Besides, the money she'd given Myra had come from Knowledge's stash. Quanda felt that that bastard Knowledge owed it to her friend anyway for what he did to her. Milton had a little cash left over from his last gambling party; he gave it up reluctantly just to save face in front of Quanda. Vidal's remains were cremated and given to Myra in a small black urn. Myra felt a sense of relief and closure, knowing that her mother was in a better place. She clung tightly to both Milton and Quanda. They were the only family she had left.

Back at Milton's apartment, Quanda looked at the clock on her cell phone. She knew it was time for her to go, she had things to do.

"MyMy, you sure you gonna be aiight if I leave today?" Quanda asked, concerned. She had to be there with Knowledge to see the look on his face when the next dastardly deed went down.

"I'm sure . . . Milton said he was staying in with me," Myra responded weakly.

"Well if you need me, I'm a phone call away," Quanda assured her.

"I know," Myra said softly, hugging her friend at the door as she left.

"I'll call you tomorrow," Quanda said, returning her friend's embrace before turning to leave.

Seeing Myra so emotional over Vidal's death incensed Milton. He had never felt love like that for his mother or his grandmother. He sat on the bed and began thinking about why that was.

"Maw . . . Maaaaaaaaaaw!" Milton called out to Bertha in the darkness, shaking her awake.

"What da fuck you want boy!" Bertha yelled, jumping up out of her sleep, reaching over and clicking on the lamp on her nightstand.

"Maw I gotta tell you something," Milton said, shaking and nervous.

"What is it boy . . . it bets ta be damn good or else I'ma kick ya ass fa waking me up!" Bertha yelled, with spit flying out of her mouth, and landing on Milton's face.

"Scriggy . . . he . . . he . . . he . . ." Milton stuttered, unable to get the words out of his mouth. He began hyperventilating.

"What is you tryin' to say you monkey-face skine?" she yelled.

"He . . . he . . . doing nasty stuff to me in my butt and in my mouth," Milton blurted out, finally able to find the words.

"NIGGA, I KNOW YOU AIN'T TRYIN' TA SAY SCRIGGY IS NO FAGGOT!" Bertha shouted, jumping out of her bed at the same time.

Milton was terrified, he felt like he had just made the worst mistake of his young life. He was mistaken to think that Bertha would ever love him, much less believe him or protect him.

"OH YA ASS IS MINE, NIGGA. YOUR ASS IS ALL MINE TONIGHT. YOU WANNA BE A FAGGOT AND CALL SOMEBODY ELSE A FAGGOT!" she yelled, scrambling to her feet in search of her cowhide belt.

Milton stood there, frozen with fear, regretting what he had just confessed. Bertha finally found her belt, by this time she had woken Scriggy. She made Milton undress, and they took turns beating him mercilessly for the rest of the night.

Milton ran his fingers over the raised keloid scars that Bertha and Scriggy had left on his arms that night. Those were scars he would never forget. They were proof that nobody in the world loved him.

As soon as the apartment door slammed shut, Myra put in the code to lock it and Milton emerged from the bedroom. He stood up against the wall between the living room and the hallway leading to the bedroom. He had a dark look in his eyes, one that Myra had never seen before. Myra was tired and she just wanted to lie down. She ignored him and walked toward the hallway. Before she could move past him, Milton grabbed her upper arm.

"C'mere. We need to talk," he said through clinched teeth, practically throwing her back into the living room. He was jealous that Myra had people around her who loved her, whereas he had no one. His nostrils flared, and his chest heaved in and out.

"Why you grabbing me like that? What's your damn problem?" Myra asked, rubbing her arms to soothe the pain.

"Shut up!" he commanded.

"What the hell is your problem?" she asked again, becoming afraid. She had never seen Milton look so scary before. He was sweating and it looked as if he had been crying. *Was I in here with Quanda that long?* Myra asked herself silently.

"You supposed to be my girl but you don't even care about me! You are just like my fucking grandmother and my mother!" Milton yelled.

Myra stayed quiet. She was terrified and couldn't figure out where this deranged behavior was coming from.

"You better prove to me that you love me! PROVE IT RIGHT NOW!" He continued to rant and rave. A large vein was pulsing strongly against his temple.

"What do you want me to do to prove it?" Myra asked, in the softest tone she could muster, trying to calm him down.

"Take off ya clothes for me like you did for those niggas. You like that shit, don't you?!" Milton retorted, moving closer to her.

Myra was frozen. She wouldn't dare move. This wasn't the person she knew. She looked into his eyes as he moved closer to her. She knew from all of her years of being exposed to drug addicts that he was high off of something. He grabbed her again and clawed at the button of her jeans. She remained stock still.

He was finally able to get her jeans off. When he did, he proceeded to penetrate her dry vagina forcefully. Myra held in her screams, but tears streamed down her eyes. He banged at her flesh over and over again, grunting and snorting like an animal in heat. She didn't know if what Milton was doing to her right now would be considered rape since she was his girl, but she felt violated like she was being raped by a stranger. Myra laid there for the next hour while this stranger had his way with her. She had no idea that he was about to up the ante on her—that the rest of her life, as she knew it, would quickly spiral out of control.

"I still can't believe I'm doing drops," Rayon complained.

"Word, son. That nigga Knowledge is tripping right now," Budda replied. He was Rayon's security for the night.

"He better get his head outta that bitch Quanda's pussy and start thinking straight," Rayon persisted.

"For real, son . . . that nigga Rell is tight over that shit too," Budda said.

"I would be too. How he gonna be all in love with somebody else's bitch . . . and that bitch hang out with Myra who just disappeared owing that nigga money? I know that bitch Quanda be frontin'. She know where Myra at," Rayon insisted.

"That nigga think he's God. He wants everything for himself, even our women. That shit ain't right," Budda continued, realizing that he'd never be able to say these things to Knowledge's face.

Both Rayon and Budda continued to ramble on about the power trip Knowledge was on as they pulled up in front of 99 Tompkins Avenue. As usual, there wasn't a soul outside. They didn't even bother to take out their guns; besides, this drop had been going down like clock work for the longest time. It was well known that no one was stupid enough to mess with Knowledge and his drugs or money.

Budda stepped out of the black Suburban first. He was supposed to have his burner in hand while Rayon retrieved the duffel bags from the back. They were too busy talking it up to pay attention to their surroundings.

"Yo, you saw her titties? Son, she is a bad ass bitch," Budda quipped.

"Nah, her friend is even hotter and I heard her head game is right," Rayon replied. Rayon entered the building first, although he wasn't supposed to.

Budda was less than a second behind him. Both men got on the dark elevator, even though they were instructed to always take the stairs. Knowledge had warned them that being in an elevator was the perfect trap for a stick up.

"Damn these fucking lights always out," Rayon complained, as he pressed the button for their destination and the elevator doors came to a close.

The dark elevator began its ascent. CLANG! The elevator jolted to a stop. Rayon prepared to search in the darkness for the ALARM and the EMERGENCY STOP buttons, because pressing them simultaneously would usually give it a jump and get the faulty elevators moving again. But before he could even feel for the buttons, they heard a noise in the dark, right above them.

"What the fu—" Budda started to say, but before the words could even finish making their way out of his mouth . . . *PIP, PIP, PIP,PIP, PIP, PIP, PIP, PIP, PIP, PIP, PIP.*

Muffled shots rang out from a Desert Eagle masked by a home made silencer. The hollow point bullets rained down on Budda and Rayon from the escape opening in the top of the elevator, burning their way through their flesh and exploding on contact. In the projects, riding on the tops of elevators was like a well crafted sport; one that the assailants had mastered.

Rayon and Budda never knew what hit them, and they damn sure didn't have enough time to pull out their burners and return fire. No one in the building heard a thing. The assailants, dressed in an all black with their faces covered; jumped down into the blood bath and retrieved the two duffel bags Rayon had been carrying. One contained the drugs and the other the money.

One of the men peeled back the heavy elevator doors. To escape, the assailants had to wedge themselves between the doors, being careful not to slip into the elevator shaft as they jumped down to the lobby floor. That was another project skill that was essential to learn. In project buildings, elevators often got stuck between floors; making an escape plan a crucial part of survival, especially because waiting for the fire department or NYPD to come could take several hours. The masked men escaped just as easily as they had killed.

Robbo and several of the females who were employed by Knowledge to cut and bag the drugs were in the apartment awaiting Rayon and Budda's arrival. The kitchen table held all of the necessary products: a scale, baking soda, pots, boric acid, caps, and small plastic baggies. All they had to do was wait for the product to arrive. While waiting, Robbo had smoked two blunts of weed and drank so much Hennessy that he passed out without even noticing that his co-workers were late with the drop off.

BANG, BANG, BANG! Robbo was startled out of his sleep by the pounding on the apartment door. When he looked around and finally got his bearings, he noticed that the sun was blazing brightly through the window.

"Oh shit! It's broad daylight . . . must be those niggas coming late," he mumbled to himself, stumbling to the door. Before he yelled to see who it was he quietly looked through the peep hole. He saw two police officers standing on the other side of the door.

"Oh fuck!" he said to himself. His heart began pounding against his sternum. He tip-toed away from the door back into the apartment and decided not to answer. He walked into one of the bedrooms where two of the female employees slept.

"Cheryl . . . Cheryl! Yo, wake up" he said, shaking one of them violently.

"Hmmmm," she responded, moaning and waving him away.

"Yo, bitch! I said wake the fuck up!" Robbo rasped through clinched teeth, grabbing a handful of her micro-braids.

"WHAT?!" she jumped up, exposing her skeletal frame. Crack had gotten the best of her. She got a few free hits for allowing them to use her apartment to prepare and stash their supply. She wouldn't have dared to steal from Knowledge; she knew the penalty–death.

"Yo, 5-0 was at ya door. Go look out the window. Find out wassup with that," he ordered.

Cheryl climbed out of the bed, rubbing the sore spot on her scalp, as she walked to the front of the apartment to look out the window.

There had to be about fifty police vehicles in front of her building, and every major news van, including Channel 7, Channel 4, NY 1, WB 11 and UPN 9. She turned around to go back into the room to report her findings, but was startled to find Robbo standing directly behind her.

"Oh shit. You scared me . . . damn," she said, feeling a sudden rush of adrenaline.

"Wassup?" he asked.

"I don't know, but 5-0 is all over out there and so is the news," she reported.

"Yo, Ray and Budda never came?" he asked, already knowing the answer.

"Nah, and I broke day waiting on them niggas," she replied.

"Aiight. Go downstairs and find out what the deal is and come back and plug me," Robbo instructed.

"Aiight," she agreed, slipping on her clothes and not bothering to wash her face or brush her teeth.

Cheryl left the apartment and as soon as she closed the door behind her she noticed that there were police officers and detectives all over the building. They had the elevator doors pulled back. They held flashlights into the shaft, trying to brighten their way. She decided to play the concerned citizen. She approached one of the uniformed officers that she encountered in the stairway as he was coming up and she was going down.

"Excuse me officer. I live in the building and I have children. Can you tell me what is going on?" trying to be as grammatically correct as possible.

"Yes ma'am. There is an ongoing investigation into two homicides that occurred in your building overnight. We are advising that everyone stay inside until the entire crime scene has been reviewed and all evidence has been collected. It shouldn't be much longer," the officer informed her. She could tell that he was a rooky; a veteran officer would have never spoken to her so politely, much less given her that much information.

"Oh my goodness . . . a double homicide..." Cheryl said, placing her hand over her chest in a clutch the pearls motion, like she had never heard of such a thing.

"Yes ma'am. Now we ask that you return to your apartment," the officer said, a bit more forcefully.

"One more question, sir . . . do you know who was murdered?" she asked innocently.

"All I can tell you right now is that the victims were two male blacks. We'll know more once the investigation gets underway," he responded vaguely.

"Oh thank you. I'll be sure to keep my children inside until I get further instructions," she said, turning on her heels and heading up the stairs to her apartment.

When Quanda was finally comfortable leaving Myra alone, she immediately called Knowledge. He told her to come right over. Quanda quickly packed and overnight bag and waited for Knowledge to pick her up around the corner from her building. Knowledge was so happy to hear from her. He hadn't even bothered to check his stash to see how much money Quanda had taken. He honestly didn't care.

"Hey you," he said, leaning over to kiss Quanda's cheek.

"Hey," she said in a voice still groggy with sleep.

"We got a big day ahead of us, so wake up," Knowledge said. His whole demeanor changed when he was around her, and he didn't mind it at all.

"What you got planned?" she asked, turning over and letting the comforter fall away from her bare breast.

"Remember, I told you I wanted to talk to you," he said seriously.

"Oh yeah," she said, giggling when he reached for her breast.

Knowledge and Quanda had breakfast at a small café in downtown Brooklyn, near the promenade. After that, they headed into the city. Knowledge drove his baby blue BMW 745. It had a tan leather interior with baby blue trim. Of his collection, it was Quanda's favorite.

They listened to the entire *Anthony Hamilton* CD as they drove. The atmosphere was calm and relaxed. When they pulled up in front of the stores on 5th Avenue, Quanda's eyes grew wide.

"See baby girl, I told you I could give you the best of the best . . . no more hood shopping for you," Knowledge said proudly.

"You can afford this place?" Quanda asked incredulously, looking out the window at all of the high-priced boutiques that she had heard about but never actually seen.

"What I wanted to talk to you about is this, ma. I want you for myself . . . for you to be my Bonnie and I will be your Clyde. If you can accept this, then it's all yours," Knowledge said, opening his arms wide.

"I don't even know what to say," Quanda said stunned by his statement. Thoughts of Gucci, Prada, Chanel and Saks were making it hard for her to stay on track—to keep her focus.

"Say yes," Knowledge pleaded.

"Yes," Quanda said, ignorant to what she had just agreed to.

After a whirlwind shopping spree, Knowledge and Quanda were exhausted. They had hit every store on 5th and Madison Avenues.

Quanda stared at her new *Cartier* diamond bezel watch all the way home. She hadn't even noticed that they were back in Brooklyn until Knowledge started to complain about the parking conditions in his posh Park Slope neighborhood.

"It ain't never no damn parking around here. I paid all of this money for a fucking brownstone and still gotta pay mad money for a private garage to park my cars," he protested.

"How far is the garage?" Quanda asked.

"I usually never tell nobody where I park up my rides, but fuck it, ma, let's go," he said.

Knowledge drove to a private lot, not too far from his house. He used his pass to enter the underground garage and he drove to his private spot. Quanda noticed several luxury cars lined up in the same row. She figured that had to be his collection. After they parked the car, they took all of the bags out of the trunk and walked to his house. They both remained quiet on their walk back. Quanda made mental notes of her location and where they had been.

"Go get comfortable and let me check on some stuff. Then . . . it's us in the shower . . . in the bed . . . and then I'll tell you something else," Knowledge said teasingly, as they entered the apartment. Quanda smiled back.

Knowledge took out his two- way pager and his cell phone. He hadn't looked at them all day. He waited until Quanda had left the room before he started checking his voicemails. He didn't want her overhearing anything, just in case one of his scorned exes had left any sinister messages for him. He opened his two-way and his INBOX had 15 new messages.

"Damn," he said to himself. He started retrieving his messages. YO HIT ROBBO 911. THE BEAST IS SWARMING. YO CALL ROBBO 911. All of the messages were the same, asking for his immediate attention. "What the fuck done happened now?" he mumbled. Things within his operation were going awry and he couldn't figure it out. He picked up his cell phone and scrolled through the phonebook for Robbo's cell number. He found it and pressed TALK. Robbo answered on the second ring. His voice was shaking.

"Can I be easy on this wire?" Robbo asked.

"Nah, son. Wassup?" Knowledge asked. Robbo began to break down; he couldn't hold it in any longer. He couldn't wait for Knowledge to get to another phone to call him back.

"Yo man, somebody got Ray and Budda, man," Robbo whined through his tears. Knowledge had never heard a grown man cry so hard.

"Whatchu talking about, son?" Knowledge asked, not wanting to comprehend what he was being told.

"They dead man... and 5-0 is swarming all over, the operation is shut down," Robbo continued through his sobs.

"WHAT THE FUCK YOU SAYING SON?!" Knowledge yelled. His head was spinning. He couldn't be hearing Robbo correctly. Rayon had been his best friend since they both dropped out of school in the fifth grade. He couldn't be dead.

When the news finally sunk in, Knowledge threw his cell phone up against the wall smashing it into six pieces. Quanda peeked out of the bedroom. The noise had startled her and she wanted to make sure he was alright. When she saw his face, she knew that the deed had been done. But she didn't know that murder was involved.

"Baby, you ok?" she asked, approaching Knowledge as he sat on his black butter soft leather sofa flicking through the channels on his 50 inch flat screen plasma TV, trying to find the news channel. He didn't respond. Quanda looked at his glassy eyes and flaring nostrils. The vein in his neck pulsed fiercely against his skin.

"Talk to me baby . . . please," she coaxed, sitting down next to him.

Just as she took her place on the sofa, Knowledge flicked the channel to the news on NY1:

"In breaking news today two men were found shot to death in an elevator located at 99 Tompkins Avenue in the Tompkins housing projects in Brooklyn. One of the men has been identified as Rayon Wilson. The second man's name was not released due to his age. Police say Mr. Wilson was a known member of the reputed Criminal Minded crew, an alleged drug gang operating here in the Bedford Stuyvesant section of Brooklyn. Police say that they believe that the shootings may be drug related, as both victims had large sums of cash on their persons and both carried firearms. Detectives from Brooklyn North Homicide state that the investigation is ongoing and there are no suspects at this

time but again the shootings appear to be drug related. Reporting live in Brooklyn, I'm Samantha Baylor, New York One news."

A cold chill came over Quanda's entire body. She was responsible for Rayon and Budda's murder. *It wasn't supposed to happen that way. They were only supposed to be robbed,* she thought to herself. Her intentions were just to have the drugs and money stolen. She didn't want anyone to die that was not directly involved.

"You gotta leave . . . I need to be alone," Knowledge said, getting up from the couch, leaving her sitting alone.

For days after the shootings, Quanda was spooked. She knew that she would eventually have to meet with Vell to collect her share of the crime profits. Even though Quame was her brother, she didn't trust him with her cash. Each time her cell phone rang, she was shook. She really did feel bad about what had happened.

On the day that she went to meet up with Vell, she was very careful to look in front and behind her when she left her building. Knowledge hadn't called her in days, and she had to be sure that none of his little workers saw her meeting with Vell—Knowledge's arch enemy. Quanda was almost certain that no one had seen her.

Chapter 11

YOU ASKED FOR IT

The next few days seemed to drag by for Myra. She hadn't really been speaking to Quanda all that much because she was afraid that if she did she would have the urge to tell her everything that was going on at home. Myra was missing more and more days of school. She felt herself changing inside. She was beginning to feel angry and ruthless.

Myra felt like she had nothing in life to look forward to. And then she got word that she was being summoned to the dean's office. Her hands shook as she walked slowly through Bent Hall to the dean's office. She couldn't imagine why she was being asked to report there. She walked in expecting to be chastised for her recent school performance, but instead heard something that, in her mind, had the potential to reverse all of her bad luck.

"Congratulations, Ms. Danford. You were selected for the work study program. You have been chosen to work with the N.Y.P.D.," Dean Reuben said proudly.

"Really? Thank you," Myra responded incredulously and gratefully.

"Here is the personnel package. Fill it out and take it with you to the job site listed below. They will be expecting you. Good luck," he continued with a smile.

Myra was surprised that she had been accepted for the work study program. After all, her grades had been suffering recently due to lack of sleep and stress from home. She grabbed the paperwork and practically ran from the office. She was so excited to get a real job that she didn't even read up on all the details. She sped across the campus from Bent Hall to Alumni Hall to find Milton. She had to share the good news with him.

In Myra's mind, this opportunity was a godsend. Since the first "gambling party," Myra had let Milton talk her into three more, each time resulting in a striptease show where she had to bare it all for a crowd of men. Milton always promised after each one that it would be the last. Myra had forgiven Milton for what he made her do, but this paper in her hand was the guarantee she needed to ensure that it would never happen again.

When Myra entered the Athletics office, she could hear voices. The carpet allowed her footsteps to go unheard as she continued down the hall. She could hear two male voices arguing.

"Look Milton, you are fucking up in practices. We can't buy a win right now and I don't think you are ready to enter the draft. Maybe you should go injured, use your one year waiver and wait until next year," the coach said seriously in a loud voice.

"Fuck you and this team! I'm the star and I'm going in the draft this year!" Milton yelled back.

"Well, you better not sign with an agent because if you do you won't be able to come back here," the coach continued.

"Ya'll ain't trying to help a nigga out. So don't tell me what I should or shouldn't do," Milton said angrily.

"Look kid, I'm trying to help you out here. You're skating on very thin ice. Whatever problems you got going on that are distracting you, you better handle them and quickly," the coach strongly advised before storming out of the room.

Myra didn't know what to do. She knew how terrible Milton's temper could be. Her stomach began to knot up. She felt like winged bats were flying around in her gut. Myra stood in the hall feeling like she was suspended in time, wanting to move but unable to pull herself away.

What was the coach saying? Milton wasn't getting drafted? Myra wondered what impact that would have on their future. She had been banking on the draft to make things better for their relationship. She wanted so desperately to ease Milton's hardships. She felt the same way about him that she had about Vidal—she had to save him from the harsh world that he lived in. As she came to her senses, she quickly ran out of the office before Milton spotted her. She didn't want him to know that she knew what was going on.

Myra walked rapidly to the library. She wanted some place quiet to clear her mind. She felt the urgent need to pray. Myra remembered how she'd learned all about God and prayer. As a child Myra attended the Yogi Bear Church. A school bus would come to the poor neighborhoods and pick up disadvantaged kids and take them to a warehouse where a group of white evangelists would conduct a fun church sermon. She could hear them singing now:

I got the joy, joy, joy, joy down in my heart, YEAH! Down in my heart, YEAH! Down in my heart, YEAH! And if the devil doesn't like it, he can sit on a tack, OUCH! Sit on a tack, OUCH! Sit on a tack! And I'm so happy . . . so very happy. I've got the love of Jesus in my heart. Yes, I'm so happy.

That was how simple white people thought children in the hood were. They thought hood kids were so stupid that they could lure them to church by naming their church after a cartoon character. Little did they know Myra was an exception to the rule. In fact, there were many kids in the projects that received religious teachings right at home.

Myra entered the St. John's University library and found a quiet corner behind a back bookshelf. She began her prayer in earnest:

Dear God. I know that I haven't prayed since the days of Yogi Bear but I just want to ask for your forgiveness for anything I've done to deserve all of these things that are happening to me. I know you wouldn't give me too much to bear, but sometimes I feel like I might lose my mind. I know that Milton has issues but if you just stick by us and see us through to the draft, I know things will get better. He will become a better man to me and I will be the woman that he wants me to be. Please forgive him too . . . he doesn't mean the things that he does to me. He is hurting himself. If you love us please make things better. In Jesus name, Amen.

Myra stayed in the library until it closed. As she left the library someone tapped her on the shoulder. Startled, Myra whirled around on her heels.

"Sorry I didn't mean to scare you," the guy standing in front of her said, holding up his hands in a halting motion.

"Well touching someone like that would scare them!" Myra scolded.

"Don't you remember me? Brad . . . Brad Holson? I introduced myself to you before," he reminded her.

"Yeah, I remember you. I apologize for yelling at you, but you can't just come up behind someone like that when it's dark outside," Myra said apologetically.

"That's Ok. I accept your apology. Where you headed? I'll give you a ride," Brad offered.

"I'm good. I'll just take the car service," Myra replied.

"You look like you've been crying. Don't let a man stress you. There are a lot of fish in the sea," Brad said suggestively.

"What makes you think a man has me stressed? I'm in love for your information, Mr. Brad," Myra said indignantly as she stormed away from him.

"I didn't mean to offend you. I just think you're too beautiful to be stressed!" Brad yelled, talking to Myra's back, as she sped away. *I won't give up on you. I'll have you for myself one day,* he mumbled to himself, as he walked in the opposite direction.

Myra thought about Brad's words on the ride from St. John's to Dara Gardens. She wondered why Milton couldn't be like Brad, telling her how beautiful she was, and that she didn't deserve to cry.

Myra dreaded going home to face Milton. Tonight was the one night she wished that he would pull one of his disappearing acts.

Myra could hear muffled noises coming from inside of the apartment as she approached the door. *Damn he is home,* she said to herself swiping the card key. As she entered the apartment, she was assailed by the smell of weed smoke and burning cocaine. She was an expert at detecting drugs, after all of those years living with Vidal. Several men were lounging around the apartment, some were smoking weed, some were smoking cigars laced with cocaine, and others were sniffing lines of cocaine off of a mirror that lay on the small wooden dinette table. The atmosphere reminded her of her old life, an apartment filled with people getting high.

This wasn't the usual gambling party crowd. Myra noticed that most of the party-goers were in business attire. Some wore ties that had been pulled slightly opened and away from their necks and some still had on their suit jackets. Others wore just their dress shirts with expensive cuff links and slacks. *Maybe these were some of Milton's business associates or people trying to help him with his career?* Myra thought to herself. Almost everyone present was Caucasian.

As Myra continued to scan the faces in the crowd, she spotted a few African-American faces and realized that she recognized a few of them. There was more than one notable sports figure there, a few current and retired NBA players, and a few NFL players. Her knowledge of sports afforded her the ability to figure out that most of these athletes were from New York home teams like the *Knicks*, *Nets*, and *Giants*. She was a little star-struck, but quickly came to her senses and started to seek out Milton in the crowd. The party-goers hadn't even noticed her there.

As she made her way further into the apartment, she noticed that a porno movie was playing on the television in the living room. *What kind of freak show shit is this?* Myra thought as she spotted Milton in the corner.

"Yo, Myra," Milton said rushing toward her with a smile glued to his face. She looked at him, her eyebrows furrowed with confusion.

"Hurry up and come in the room," he said, practically dragging her down the hallway into the bedroom.

"This is our night to make some big cash. These guys are major players and they just want a short show," he started abruptly.

"Milton, I'm not doing that anymore," Myra said, finally putting her foot down.

"What?" he asked disbelievingly.

"I got a job today, Milton. We don't need to do this anymore. Between your stipend and my job, it will be enough to help your grandmother out. I mean, you haven't even gone to visit her or anything. You still haven't told me where all of the money from the other parties went," she said, finally confronting him.

"You think a little work study job can help us out around here, huh? You got the fucking nerve to question what I do with the money?! Look at ya fucking wrist—the clothes you wear . . . the shoes. You think my stipend buys you Prada sneakers or fucking Gucci bags? You fucking ingrate!" he yelled, making reference to all of the guilt gifts he had given her.

As he let a barrage of vituperative words roll off of his hissing tongue, Milton moved closer and closer to Myra's face, grabbing it forcefully with his hands.

"You're hurting me, Milton," Myra said in pain, trying to pry his hand from her cheeks. He continued his tirade.

"If you can't do shit for me, ya ass gotta go. I'm here busting my ass for this draft trying to feed you—keep a roof over ya head n' shit—and you telling me what you ain't gonna do no more. I know your kind. You want a fucking hustler, right? Somebody that will put your fucking life at risk every day? If you can't ride you gotta go. I never met a bitch as weak as you, you're dumb and who the fuck do you think will want you!! You better remember ya ass ain't got no where to go!! Those niggas in Tompkins will kill ya ass!!" he roared, finally releasing her with a hard shove to the face, sending her sailing to the floor.

Myra couldn't believe her ears, or Milton's behavior. Milton knew that she had no where to go. She couldn't figure out why he was saying these hurtful things. Her heart was broken. She felt sharp pains in her chest, like her arteries were constricting. He had shot her down so many times—made her feel guilty so many times. A knot formed in her throat. She felt as if she had swallowed a hand ball. She began to cry. She couldn't hold it in anymore.

"Don't fucking cry—just pack!" he shouted, standing over her bent figure.

"Milton, pleeease. I love you, but I can't do this anymore. There is a better way . . . I know a better way," she said, choking through her sobs.

After the first time Milton had Myra perform those lewd acts, she had come up with several other ways that she could earn money for them both. She was just never given a chance to share them.

"Yo, pack ya shit and get da fuck out now!" he said firmly, turning his back on her. If she couldn't make him any money for him, he had absolutely no use for her.

Myra thought about her choices and came to a conclusion—she didn't have any to even consider.

"If I do this you have to promise me this will be the last time. If you need money after this, I'll give you my whole check from the job. There is a better way . . . I'll come up with a better way," she swore.

She felt trapped; she knew that if she refused she would have to return to the projects and most probably someone would try to kill her. She had no choice; she had to do it or die.

"Yeah yeah . . . this will be the last time," Milton said hastily.

"Promise?" Myra insisted.

"Are you down or are you leaving?" Milton said, being a real bastard.

"I'm down," Myra conceded. She had no idea what she was in for.

"Aiight, get dressed and ready. Take this, since you are so stressed," Milton said, handing Myra two small round tablets. In her frazzled state, Myra threw them down her throat and swallowed hard, not questioning the content.

Myra emerged from the bedroom wearing a sheer red, crotchless body suit. As she made her entry intro the crowded living room, she could feel the Ecstasy pills taking effect. Myra didn't ever remember feeling this good about herself. Even when she looked at herself in the mirror, she saw a different image than what really appeared. She saw a princess, a Cinderella type figure staring back at her. She never noticed that her entire body was exposed, making her look like a street walking whore. When she entered the living room, the crowd of hungry, drugged-up predators immediately encircled her. She never noticed the other female until she was right up on her.

The drugs made Myra oblivious to the other girl; in fact, she thought nothing of it. Myra began to move her body to the music like she did at the other parties. The other female, a small Pamela Anderson looking white girl with large breast implants did the same. The girl flung her head around and around in a circular motion throwing her blonde hair weave with it, at the same time moving toward Myra. Myra was feeling too good to protest. The white female got down on her knees in front of Myra and out of no where she grabbed onto Myra's ass pulling Myra toward her face. Myra let the Ecstasy propel her right into the girl's face. The girl opened her mouth and dived right into Myra's love triangle. The men went wild. They began throwing large bills toward the girls as they continued with their lesbian freak show.

Myra was lost in her own mind. She closed her eyes, and pretended she was a princess. Her mind was operating at a higher level of consciousness. It seemed as though her mind and body were in complete separate worlds. The girl devoured her all the while.

Myra was down on the floor and she and the girl were engaged in some serious lesbian action. The crowd of white businessmen and professional athletes were chanting, "Ass action! Ass action!" Myra opened her eyes for a few seconds and everything around her was a blur. All of the faces were distorted, like she was at a carnival looking at them through a fun mirror. The next thing Myra knew, she was being lifted up and passed around the crowd. Before she knew it, her entire body suit had been ripped from her body. It lay scattered in pieces all over the floor.

Myra's skin felt sensitive to every touch. Although they did all sorts of things to her body, every touch felt good. The drugs were in full effect now. Myra kept her eyes closed because opening them made her feel dizzy. She never noticed that the girl had strapped on a huge dildo but she did hear the shouts grow louder and louder. She could tell that something had excited them. She laughed involuntarily at their cheers. They put her back on the floor, stark naked in the middle of their circle. Her ears began to ring. The next thing she felt was a sharp pain invading her anus. The girl had penetrated her forcefully from behind.

"Aaaaaaahhhhhhh!" Myra screamed out in agony. The feeling was sharp and intense. She tried to crawl away, but there was nowhere for her to go.

The men surrounded her. "RAM! RAM! RAM!" they chanted.

Myra clawed ferociously at the carpet to no avail. She finally passed out, but her abuse was far from over. In her unconscious state, Milton allowed several of the men to have their way with her limp body—for a fee. He didn't even care if they wore a condom or not. They paid Milton big money to do what they pleased with her body—things that their wives would have never done. This was, by far, one of Milton's most lucrative nights.

Myra awoke the next afternoon with a serious need to urinate. She had slept through her morning classes again. She felt as if a 500-pound man was sitting on her stomach. She threw back the comforter, noticing that she was still butt-naked. When she stood up to walk to the bathroom, her legs buckled under her. She had never felt this bad before. She could hardly stand, a fierce pulling sensation shot through her lower abdomen. Her vagina and anus were throbbing and each step caused the aches to worsen.

"Uggghhhh," she moaned, as she moved very slowly across the room. She felt like she would pee on herself if she didn't move any faster. Myra dragged her feet as she moved, afraid that if she lifted them her insides would fall out. She was finally able to make it to the toilet, and when she sat down the pain got even worse. She bent over as the urine escaped her bladder. It burned so badly. Myra felt as if someone was holding a torch to her vagina. The urine trickled out slowly, prolonging her agony.

Myra knew something was wrong. When she wiped herself from front to back, she noticed blood on the tissue. She decided that talking to Milton about her problem would be a waste of time, so she called Quanda.

"Hello," Quanda answered.

"Hey," Myra replied, immediately beginning to cry.

"What's the matter MyMy"? Quanda asked, genuine concern in her voice.

"I think I need to go to the hospital," Myra moaned, barely audible.

"Why?" Quanda asked fearfully.

"I can't walk . . . my stomach is killing me and my pee is burning," Myra explained.

"Aw shit. Ok get dressed. I'll be over there as soon as I can," Quanda said. She had free time on her hands since Knowledge had decided to be alone. She had money to spend too, since Vell had given her her share of the crime profits.

Quanda caught a cab to Queens and picked Myra up. When they got close enough to each other, both girls secretly examined one another. Each noticed the new and expensive clothes, watches, shoes and pocketbooks. Both wondered how the other had acquired such expensive items, but neither said a word.

Together they went to the emergency room at Mary Immaculate Hospital. Myra was taken in right away because she had a fever. Quanda fell asleep in the waiting room, waiting to hear from the doctors about her friend's diagnosis.

"Quan," Myra said, shaking Quanda awake.

"Hmmm," Quanda responded, disoriented.

"I'm done," Myra said.

"Huh . . . what? Damn, what time is it? What did they say?" Quanda asked, finally getting her bearings.

"It's 8 o'clock. They had to give me an emergency IV with antibiotics. They said that I have a urinary tract infection . . . and," Myra hesitated.

"And what?" Quanda asked anxiously.

"I'm pregnant," Myra said unenthusiastically.

"Get outta here! Oh girl, I'm so happy fa ya'll!" Quanda responded, jumping up and hugging her friend. "Wait how far are you?" Quanda asked.

"Four and a half months," Myra said, on the brink of tears.

"And you didn't know all of this time?!" Quanda exclaimed.

"I was too busy to even miss my period," Myra said. She was just as shocked by the news as Quanda.

Myra didn't tell Quanda that the doctors had informed her that she had Trichomoniasis, a sexually transmitted disease; nor did she tell

Quanda about the trauma she had suffered to her vagina or about the tears in her anal tissues. She was horrified and decided right then and there that she would never do another gambling party again—and this time she meant it. She had a serious bone to pick with Milton.

Quanda had no clue about what was going on in Myra's life. She sure didn't know what Milton had been making her do, so to her the baby was good news. Myra didn't know how to feel. She would decide what to do after she told Milton. Quanda and Myra hopped a cab back to Dara Gardens. On the way, Quanda filled Myra in about all of the things that were going down in Tompkins.

"Yes, girl. Rayon and Budda dead in the elevators. The block is hot; 5-0 done shut shit down," Quanda rambled on.

"Dag, I hate to see anybody die like that, but you know what they say, this world is 360 degrees round . . . karma is a bitch and what goes around comes around," Myra said.

"Fo' sho. You know, that's my motto about life," Quanda agreed, laughing. She had stopped racking herself with guilt over the murders. She reasoned that Rayon also probably had something to do with what happened to Myra and that God was giving him his just deserves.

"When is the funeral and stuff?" Myra asked.

"I don't know exactly, but I heard it was gonna be right at Woodward on Troy. I might go, just to be nosey. You know the hood is gonna turn out; they always do," Quanda said.

"Damn, wish I could go" Myra said forlornly.

Myra realized how much she missed Quanda. Quanda had taken Myra's mind off of her problems, just as she always did. Myra didn't have time between all of the stories and laughs to think about how she was going to tell Milton the news. She also didn't think about how long she would be able to work and go to school before her stomach grew too big. She had already decided that she was going to keep the baby, and that meant that there would be no more stripping or sex for money.

"Milton!" the coached yelled, waving Milton toward the sidelines.

"What?!" Milton asked, running toward the coach.

"You're out! Philips you're in," the coach said flatly, waving toward the back up quarterback on the bench who was anxiously awaiting his time to shine.

"What the fuck you doin'?!" Milton asked angrily, approaching the sidelines.

"I'm coaching. And since you're not playing, your ass is sitting on the bench for the rest of the game," the coach chewed him out.

"Yo, the fucking scouts are here to see me, coach!" Milton yelled, getting right up in the coach's face, drawing attention from the crowd and the NFL scouts.

"Too fucking bad! We need this win and you're playing like a fucking sissy! We can't afford another interception. Now sit the fuck down!" the coach growled back.

Milton took off his helmet and threw it on the ground, sending it rolling down the grass in the coach's direction. A loud OHHHH resonated from the crowd as they witnessed Milton's outburst. He sat down and looked up just in time to see scouts from the *Miami Dolphins* and the *New York Jets* exiting the stadium. They had seen enough. Milton's lifestyle was ruining his career. He had to do something to get Damien out of his life so that he could try to salvage what was left of his reputation. Milton was desperate, but he knew that if he asked Myra to perform again, she would surely leave.

St. John's lost the game. The men's locker room was dead silent after the game. Milton's teammates didn't want anything to do with him. His behavior had become so erratic and bizarre lately.

Milton stood under the shower head, allowing the water to run over his entire body, trying to calm down. He was stressed and he knew only one way of getting rid of it. Milton was preoccupied with thoughts of deviant sex. He finished showering, put his equipment away, and then sat on the short wooden plank in front of his locker putting on his sneakers. He heard a noise come from the second row of lockers located behind him. Everyone else had already cleared out of the locker rooms. Milton looked around suspiciously. He didn't see anyone, so he continued to get dressed.

When Milton was finally done, he got up from the bench, grabbed his gym bag and headed toward the door. He walked slowly down the narrow space between the lockers and the benches in front of them. When he reached the end of the row, he was startled by another loud noise; it sounded as if someone had banged on one of the metal lockers. Milton stopped in his tracks and surveyed the area behind him. He saw nothing. He picked up his pace, heading for the door. Suddenly, Milton felt someone grab him from behind, his arms twisted painfully around his back.

Damien appeared in front of him, and he was with someone else, but Milton was unable to see who the person was because the person held him in an unbreakable arm lock.

"Ay man wassup?" Milton asked, a nervous smile spread across his face.

"This is wassup, nigga!" Damien said, as he punched Milton so hard in his stomach it made him throw up.

"I told you that I wanted my money on time . . . but you had to go and play," Damien continued, this time lifting Milton's down-turned head and punching him across his face.

"Yo, Damien, man . . . I'ma get ya money, man . . . please," Milton pleaded, barely able to lift his head.

"This is your last warning," Damien warned, simultaneously cocking the hammer of a black .357 Sig Sauer, placing it at Milton's head, pulling the trigger. As the gun clicked . . .

"BANG!" Damien yelled, laughing shrilly. Milton flinched, closing his eyes expecting to die on the spot. He couldn't control his bladder; hot urine ran down his pant's leg.

The other man released Milton with a violent push, letting him fall to the floor.

"You got two days to bring me all of the payments you owe me. Next time, it will be loaded," Damien said, stepping over Milton like he was a pile of garbage.

Milton pulled himself together and got up from the floor. Visibly shaken and desperate, he drove straight to his friend and teammate Craig's house.

"Yo man, why you banging like that?!" Craig complained loudly, but quickly changed his tone once he saw the condition that Milton was in.

"Craig man, I need ya help" Milton said, sounding defeated.

"Wassup?" Craig asked, concerned.

"I need a gun," Milton said straightforwardly, knowing that Craig's father was a gun dealer.

"For what?" Craig asked warily.

"Look man, can you help me or not?" Milton asked impatiently.

"That depends . . ." Craig hesitated.

"On what?" Milton asked.

"Milton, man, you looked tossed right now. You come here looking like shit, talking all fast and crazy, asking me for a gun, and I'm not supposed to ask you what it's for?" Craig questioned.

"I can't trust nobody right now, man. I'll pay for it . . . just get it for me," Milton demanded.

"What kind of gun?" Craig asked, acquiescing.

"Something that I can carry on me without being noticed, but something powerful," Milton instructed.

"Like a .45 or a 9mm glock?" Craig asked.

"Yeah, either one sounds good," Milton said, not caring what kind of gun it was, so long as it had bullets.

"Aiight, hold up" Craig said, disappearing into his bedroom. He returned with a nickel plated .45 caliber Heckler and Koch handgun. He held it out in front of Milton, and as Milton reached for it, Craig snatched it back.

"Yo man, this is strictly for your protection. Don't do no dumb shit with it," Craig cautioned, remembering Milton's recent string of bizarre behavior.

"Yeah, aiight man. It's just for my protection," Milton said, repeating it back like a dope fiend waiting for a hit.

"Don't fuck me over, Milton," Craig warned.

"Nah son . . . I won't," Milton agreed, snatching the gun from Craig's hand.

Quanda had left and Myra was alone again. She stood in front of the mirror for hours looking at the side profile of her stomach. She was overwhelmed with thoughts of the miracle that was taking place in her body. *It's not big at all. I can't be any damn four and a half months. A mother—me. I can't believe it,* she said to herself. This wouldn't be the first time that Myra had experienced pregnancy. She thought back . . .

Myra stood over the toilet bowl gagging as the acid from her stomach crept up her esophagus. She did this over and over again until the small amount of food left from the day before retched its way out of her body. She splashed cold water on her face in a futile attempt to make herself feel better. She had school and she felt like shit. Myra had no idea what was wrong with her. That morning she dragged herself over to Quanda's house to eat breakfast and walk to school with her. Vidal was missing in action of course. Quanda opened the door and immediately knew something was wrong with her friend—their bond was that strong.

"What's the matter Myra? You look sick," Quanda stated observantly.

"I'm sick . . . I been throwing up every morning for like a week now," Myra informed her.

"Whatchu been eating?" Quanda asked suspiciously.

"Well, I eat over here mostly . . . so nothing strange. Oh, Ms. Madi gave me some rice and beans with chicken two days ago, but that's 'bout it," Myra reported.

"Maybe you got food poisoning? I'ma talk to my mother," Quanda said. After Quanda told her mother about Myra's symptoms, Ms. Brenda immediately grew suspicious. It wasn't a secret what Vidal had been doing to Myra. The only reason she hadn't called Social Services on Vidal yet, was because she feared that Myra would be put into a foster home far away, which would destroy both Myra and Quanda.

"Myra, did you have your period yet?" Ms. Brenda asked.

"I think so," Myra responded uncertain. At twelve years old, no one had explained to her anything about her body and the changes it goes through.

"Do you have blood on your panties sometimes?" Ms. Brenda continued with her line of questioning.

"Yeah, one time I did and my mother said I couldn't go to school that day," Myra answered.

"When was that?" Ms. Brenda asked.

"When we had our play in school," Myra replied after thinking back for a moment.

"Ok, so that was two months ago," Ms. Brenda calculated using her fingers to figure the amount of time.

"Yeah, I guess" Myra said.

"Listen Myra, do you feel well enough to go to school?" Ms. Brenda asked, on the brink of tears. She knew what was wrong with Myra; she just didn't know how to tell her or how to deal with the situation.

"Not really," Myra said.

"Ok girls, stay home today. I'll take you to the health station in Sum-

ner," Ms. Brenda said.

After leaving the clinic, they all walked home in silence. Quanda and Myra were confused and Ms. Brenda was disgusted. She had just found out that Myra was pregnant, by God knows who, at twelve years old. Ms. Brenda explained to Myra that the doctors were going to take the baby out because little girls are not supposed to have babies. Myra was sad. She had always taken very good care of her dolls; she didn't understand why she couldn't have a baby.

The day that she came home from Choices, the abortion clinic, her stomach hurt and she bled and bled for days. Ms. Brenda nursed her back to health, and showed her how to keep herself clean when she bled.

Myra stayed at Quanda's house for an entire month, but after a while she felt like she had worn out her welcome and so she went back home to Vidal. Vidal was angry at Myra because of the ass-whooping she had received from Ms. Brenda. Ms. Brenda reasoned that if she couldn't get help from Social Services, she would take matters into her own hands, and that is just what she did.

When Myra grew tired of touching her stomach, she decided to go to bed. Milton hadn't come home yet and she wasn't really looking forward to seeing him anyway. She had no idea how he was going to react to the news, but given his recent behavior she could only imagine.

Myra took a shower and crawled into the warm bed. She was due to start work the next day, and she needed as much rest as she could get. She thought about how nice it was seeing Quanda. She wished she could see her every day. She closed her eyes and thought of all the good times that they had shared as friends. Her warm memories lulled her to sleep.

Myra was awoken by a sudden jolt of the bed. She jumped up, her heart racing. Milton was kneeling over her and onto the bed, with a silver gun pointed at her.

"What the fuck are you doing?!" Myra screamed. She was too

shocked to be afraid; the adrenaline that raced through her body was clouding her judgment.

"Shut the fuck up," Milton said harshly. Myra stared wide-eyed into the barrel of the gun, but remained silent. She was suddenly on reality's page.

"I need some money, and I need it now," Milton said, continuing to point the gun in Myra's face. His sanity was slipping just as fast as his career; and it seemed as if he had lost grip on both.

"Milton, I don't have anything, you know that," she said softly, being careful not to raise her voice.

"Well, you better think fast about how to get some," he said, sounding deranged.

"Milton, I love you. Why are you doing this? What is going on with you?" Myra said, tears cascading over her cheeks.

"Shut the fuck up . . . talking that love shit right now. Think of how we can get some money or your ass is gonna be out on the streets!" Milton yelled, letting all of the alcohol and cocaine he consumed just hours before muddle his senses.

"Milton, I'm pregnant. I can't do this anymore," Myra blurted out. Her mind was racing. That was not the way she had planned to tell him, but she thought that, in this case, it might just save her life.

"Pregnant"? Milton repeated, like he hadn't heard her correctly.

"Yes, I'm pregnant with our baby. I'm four and a half months," Myra said.

Milton felt as if someone had stabbed him in the chest. He moved the gun from her face and flopped down on the bed like a heavy weight had been dropped on him. A million thoughts ran through his head, each pulling him in a different directions—his secret lifestyle, his fading career, owing Damien money, and now THIS. He suddenly became even more enraged than he had been before.

"When you got pregnant?" he asked, grinding his teeth so hard that his jaw ached.

Myra couldn't see his face. She had slowly gotten off of the bed when he took the gun from her face. With his back turned to her, she slowly began putting on her clothes. She knew that she had to get out of there tonight. *Maybe when the alcohol wears off he will be ok,* she thought.

Suddenly, Milton jumped up and rushed toward her.

"I said, when did you get pregnant?! How you know it's mine?" he asked. His sudden burst of motion caught her off-guard. She was frozen with fear, but somehow managed to answer.

"Milton I haven't slept with anyone else," Myra said truthfully. She had been loyal to Milton from the very beginning. She didn't remember having been raped or sodomized just a few days earlier. In his heart Milton knew that it was his baby. A part of him was growing inside of the one person who, no matter how bad he treated her, never left his side. He grabbed her and hugged her tightly, the gun still clenched tightly in his hand. He didn't know what else to do. She was the only person in his corner at this point. Milton did a good job of masking his anger; he realized that he could get more bees with honey than he could with shit.

"Look baby, I'm in a lot of trouble. I can't tell you about it right now, but I need some money fast. If I don't get it, I won't be drafted and we won't have all of the things we've been dreaming about—no house, no wedding, no car, nothing. You gotta help me," Milton pleaded, starting to cry. He had changed his mood like night and day. He wanted to tell Myra everything—to purge himself of all the demons that haunted his life, but he just couldn't bring himself to do it. He was still holding onto hope that he could finance his dreams. He knew that if he told her that his career and their future was on the line she would definitely help him out. Milton knew that he was all Myra had right now and he played on that every chance he got.

Myra had grown tired of Milton's empty promises, but her heart was torn. He looked so vulnerable right now. This was the Milton she remembered, the sensitive and loving man that could talk to her about anything. Myra still held onto those few precious memories from the very beginning of their relationship, when things were going good.

"What's the matter? What kind of trouble are you in?" Myra asked, now fully returning his embrace.

"I can't tell you that right now," he answered vaguely.

"Milton I can't dance or do that other stuff . . . I'm pregnant now," Myra reiterated, with regret in her tone. She felt selfish telling him that she couldn't help him anymore because that was what she had been telling herself she was doing all of those times that she performed at the gambling parties. In fact, she repeated it to herself so often that she really believed it. Myra felt guilty about not being able to help him, just as she had felt when Vidal died. She didn't want anything like what had happened to her mother to happen to Milton.

"I know, baby," Milton said understandingly.

"I do know one way that we might be able to get some money," Myra said, thinking fast, desperate to help him and relieve some of her guilt.

"How?" Milton asked, pulling himself out from her arms and looking at her face. Myra hesitated before she spoke; she had to choose her words carefully.

"I know an old man who keeps a lot of money in his house, and he lives alone. He trusts me and would let me in if I went there. You could just stand back and when he opens the door we could go in real fast, take the money and leave. Nobody will get hurt," she said.

It was something Myra had always thought about—robbing Quincy. She knew where he kept all of his money because of all the times her mother had sold her body to him. She had always secretly watched him go to his stash to pay Vidal with either drugs or money. Myra could picture it like it was happening.

Quincy bent down and dug into his raggedy, rubber-soled black loafer and retrieved a key. Myra stood behind him crying hysterically as Vidal stood nonchalantly to the side of the room.

"MOOOOMMMYYY PLEASE, PLEASE don't leave me here again! PLEEEEASE! Myra pleaded, tugging wildly at Vidal's arm.

"Shut her da fuck up," Quincy snapped, as he sat down on the stained, old dirty mattress with his Colt in one hand, while the other hand opened the gold-trimmed black trunk that sat on the floor at the end of the mattress.

"Be quiet, Myra. Dammit. I'm not leaving you. But if you don't shut up, I will," Vidal said, trembling with nervousness, giving Myra false hopes. She immediately shut her mouth. They both watched even though Quincy tried to block their view as he dug into the trunk to pay Vidal. But Vidal didn't want cash; she wanted some of the EWW WEE dope he was famous for. He sold the best dope in town.

Myra peeked around Vidal's gaunt body. She couldn't believe all of the stacks of money Quincy had in that black trunk. He handed Vidal her bundle. Myra clutched onto Vidal, but she quickly pushed her away.

"NOOO MOMMY . . . YOU LIED TO ME!" Myra cried indignantly. With tears streaming down her face, Vidal violently pushed her daughter to the filthy floor, leaving Myra behind.

Myra had always wanted revenge but she had never had the guts to go there and try to rob Quincy alone. She knew that he could barely walk now. He had gotten even bigger and sloppier over the years, and she knew that he damn sure couldn't take on Milton, 'star quarterback'.

The man who she loved was in trouble, and this would be an easy way to get the money to help him and to exact a little revenge on her behalf. Besides, Quincy was getting old sitting in that dirty, run down house with all of that money just rotting away. Myra thought about all of the possibilities that the money could bring. It would help Milton take care of whatever he had to take care of, get him refocused on his career and their future. Or maybe she would take some of it and leave Milton and find her own secret apartment somewhere.

"Where does he live?" Milton asked, all ears now. Although he had promised himself years ago that he wouldn't commit crimes, he was desperate. It was either this, or let Damien ruin him.

"He lives in the Stuy," Myra replied.

"Well, tell me more about this plan," Milton said, now pacing the floor and biting his nails, his nerves getting the best of him.

"All we gotta do is go to the house. I'll knock and you can stand behind me. When he opens the door, you push in and we go in to take the money and get out fast. He can barely walk, but he has guns and huge vicious dogs up there. So we gotta be careful that he doesn't get to the room that he keeps them in," Myra instructed.

"How you know where he keeps his money?" Milton asked curiously.

"I used to go there with my mother. One time I peeped where he kept his stuff," Myra lied.

"Go there with your mother for what?" Milton asked suspiciously.

"She used to cop from him," Myra said, leaving it at that.

"Oh aiight, so he is a dope dealer then," Milton clarified, immediately growing excited about his prospects.

"Yeah, and I hate his ass," Myra said, unable to conceal her real feelings anymore.

"Can we go tonight?" Milton asked eagerly.

"I gotta start my new job in the morning," Myra said reluctantly.

"I thought you said you wanted to help me. Who gives a fuck about that bullshit job?! Working for the beast ain't cool anyway," Milton said.

"It doesn't matter what you think. It's a good job and right now I need an income," Myra said, growing angry and tired of the way Milton spoke to her. She didn't know if it was the pregnancy and the hormones, but she was fed up with his abusive ways. She had promised herself that she wasn't taking anymore shit off of him, draft or no draft.

Myra had something planned for everyone in her life who had ever done her dirty. She was a true believer in something that Ms. Madi always told her: *"Mami este mundo (the world) 360 degrees round. Everything you do it comes back to you—good or bad. Mami. what goes around comes around . . . esta karma. Remember, ok?"*

Myra was done with being a stepping stone. She felt good about what she had planned for Quincy. In her mind, she would get Quincy back for all of the heinous and cruel things that he had done to her.

"I'm sorry baby," Milton said, realizing from her tone that he was treading on very thin ice.

"If we're gonna do it tonight, we gotta go now before the sun comes up," Myra said, not feeling the least bit nervous. It was about surviving or dying, just as it had always been for Myra. The difference was that now her heart had grown cold.

Chapter 12

REVENGE IS BITTERSWEET

Myra knocked three times on the old wooden plank that served as a door. She looked around suspiciously to see if anyone was walking by, and then she hit the makeshift door again with all of her might. She knew that three hard knocks was the code; it let Quincy know that someone he knew was at the door.

Milton stood to the far left of the door opening, hiding in the shadows just in case Quincy decided to look out of the side window before he opened the door.

"Yo, I thought you said this cat had money? This house is all fucked up," Milton whispered uncertainly.

"Looks can be very deceiving," Myra whispered back.

"WHO IS IT?!" Quincy yelled, startling both Myra and Milton.

"It's Myra, Quincy," she yelled back, moving her face closer to the wooden plank.

"Myra?" he quizzed.

"Yeah, Vidal's daughter. Look, I need to see you about something important," Myra said, staying as calm as she possibly could given the task at hand.

Quincy slowly cracked the door to make sure it was who he thought it was. Sure enough, it was the Myra that he had remembered. Immediately, he put his *Colt* down on the old radiator that sat behind the door. He was excited; his first thought was that she had come to him because she'd become a dope-fiend like her mother. Quincy hoped she had come to give him some special attention in exchange for some of the pure dope he hoarded.

"Whatchu doin' here, gal? I ain't seen you in years!" Quincy asked, speaking to Myra like she was an old friend coming to visit.

"Are you going to let me in to explain?" Myra asked impatiently, still talking to him through the crack of the door.

"Oh, hell yeah. Shit girl, I missed you. Whatchu got for daddy?" Quincy said, chuckling as he pulled back the door to let Myra in.

His comments sickened Myra, and infuriated Milton. For a minute, Milton was taken back to the past . . . remembering his cousin Scriggy saying those same words: *"Yo little cuz, you home from school early. Ya grandma ain't here . . . so whatchu got for daddy?"*

As soon as Quincy opened the door wide enough, Myra stepped in and Milton bolted from behind her, gun in hand. He rushed Quincy, tackling him down to the floor. Quincy rolled and rolled, reminding Myra of a *Weeble Wobble* toy. Myra quickly shut the door behind them; she wasn't expecting Milton's sudden violent action.

Quincy scrambled in the dark trying to get up, his obese body preventing him from being able to get enough leverage to pull himself up off the floor. He scolded himself for trusting Myra and putting his gun down.

"WHAT THE FUCK IS YA'LL DOIN' ?!" Quincy spat angrily, wheezing and gasping like he was having an asthma attack.

"Shut the fuck up and getcha fat ass up!" Milton ordered, holding the gun to Quincy's forehead. Flashes of Scriggy's face pervaded Milton's psyche. Myra remained silent, struggling to deal with her own demons. The odors, the hallway, Quincy's dirty body, all brought back painful memories for her. *Lick it . . . suck it . . . open ya legs . . . shut up . . . stop crying . . . get on ya knees . . . take off ya clothes . . .* Quincy's commands from the past flooded her ears. She felt like she was dreaming.

The drafty hallway caused her teeth to chatter loudly. Myra had imagined this day for years—today was the day she would exact her bittersweet revenge on Quincy.

"Stand the fuck up and take me to the money!" Milton yelled, gun-butting Quincy on the side of the head to let him know they meant business.

"Agghhhh . . . ok ok," Quincy whined in pain, finally pulling himself upright.

"Where is it?" Milton asked Myra.

"Upstairs," she responded in a wavering voice. Although she had imagined this day for years, being there was surreal. Milton grabbed the back of Quincy's shirt and stuck the gun into the folds of fat that made up his back.

"Walk slowly up the fucking stairs straight to the money or else you die tonight, you nasty ass nigga. You really need a fucking bath!" Milton exclaimed, disgusted that he had to manhandle Quincy's filthy flesh.

Quincy began his slow climb up the weak stairs. Milton was right behind him with the gun firmly pressed into Quincy's skin. Myra followed close behind. When they finally made it to the top of the stairs, Milton could hear the dogs barking. Milton tugged on Quincy's shirt as if it were reins, bringing him to a complete stop.

"Where you got those dogs at?" Milton asked, thrusting the gun even further into his skin.

"Yo man they locked up," Quincy lied.

"Aiight, keep on walking then," Milton instructed. Quincy pushed open the door to the apartment; the smell was even worse than Myra had remembered. She started to gag, trying hard not to throw up. Milton wanted to cover his nose, but that would mean letting go of Quincy, so he endured the smell of ass and rotten food that permeated the apartment.

As soon as they stepped foot into the living room, one of the huge Rotweillers charged right at Milton. The dog had obviously been taught to protect his master. Milton gripped Quincy by the shoulders and spun him around 180 degrees. Milton used Quincy's body as a human shield, which gave him enough time to shoot the dog in mid-air as it leaped to attack. The dog whimpered as he crumpled to the floor, wounded and dying, licking wildly at his blood-soaked side until the life finally left his body.

"Noooo!" Quincy cried out, visibly upset by his dog's death.

The gunshot had shocked Myra, her heart raced and her hands shook. She bent down and began throwing up. Milton could not be distracted by any of this; he was a man on a mission.

"Muthafucka, I thought you said the dog was locked up...you wanna lie, huh? Huh?" Milton said through clinched teeth, hitting Quincy in his head with the back of the gun again, this time drawing blood.

"Get in that chair, bitch," Milton instructed him. Quincy willingly obliged. Milton pulled the extension cord out of the wall, unplugging the old 19-inch television that Quincy hadn't turned off in over ten years. They were in total darkness, except for a small bit of light that shined through the window from the lamppost outside. Milton roughly placed the cord around Quincy's neck, cutting off his oxygen as he tied in tightly around the back of the chair. Quincy couldn't move, lest risk choking himself to death.

Myra held onto her stomach, experiencing waves of nausea that seemed to come and go in quick spurts. She couldn't believe what was happening. She couldn't believe that Milton had it in him to be so diabolical; she was scared of the person she saw before her. She thought that they would just go in, take the money and leave.

"Now, I'ma ask you one more time. Where the fuck is the money or else you gonna die," Milton threatened, placing the cold steel to Quincy's lips.

"The money is in the back room. I know where it is . . . this shit is taking way too long. Let's just get it and go," Myra answered for him, in a panic stricken tone.

"Go get the shit then. We ain't come here to leave with nothing," Milton stressed.

"You gotta get it. I can't go in that back room. I just can't . . ." Myra said, her bottom lip trembling even faster now, as if she were standing on a block of ice. The other dog was in a frenzy by now, scratching fiercely at the door to the right of them. The sound of the dog clawing at the door combined with the painful memories that the back room held rendered Myra immobile. The flashbacks were clouding her vision.

Myra lay perfectly still as Quincy's huge black Rotweiller sniffed at her naked body. She was too afraid to cry out, scream, or move. Her throat began to close so that she couldn't breathe, but her better judgment prevented her from even gasping for air. Quincy stood in the corner of the room, with the other dog at his feet. He was incredibly turned on by Myra's fear.

"Whatchu mean you can't?! Don't fucking back out on me now," Milton warned, still holding the gun to Quincy. Myra remained silent, staring into space.

"Fuck it then, I'll go. Where in the back room?" Milton said, realizing that Myra meant what she said.

"At the foot of the bed, in the black trunk. The key is in his left shoe," Myra said robotically, pointing to Quincy's feet.

"Use ya other foot and take off the shoe with the key in it," Milton directed Quincy. Quincy ignored the request.

"I'ma say it one more time . . . take off the shoe with the key in it!" Milton demanded. Quincy refused to move. Milton boiled over with anger; the power he felt over Quincy made his dick hard. Milton lowered the gun toward the floor. Bang! Bang! Milton fired off two shots, one into each of Quincy's feet. Myra jumped at the sound, shaking fiercely with sweat dripping down her entire body. Sharp pains invaded her stomach.

"Agggghhhhhhhhh!" Quincy shrieked in pain. Milton envisioned his cousin Scriggy tied to the chair. He stood up and cracked Quincy across the head as hard as he could with the gun handle, causing the skin on Quincy's face to split open down to the white meat. Milton removed Quincy's shoes and retrieved the key; he didn't care about the odor or the blood.

"Here . . . hold this on his ass and make sure he doesn't try to move until I come back," Milton commanded, handing Myra the gun. She could barely stand up, she was so afraid. But she obeyed, taking the gun into her shaky hand. She placed her finger through the trigger hole and held the gun out in front of her it, even though it shook in her unsteady hand.

Milton moved mechanically, like a programmed robot, toward the back room. When he was gone, Quincy began to plead with Myra.

"C'mon baby . . . we had a good thang goin' on. You loved every minute, didn't you? I thought I treated you good. You liked when I fucked you and when the dogs did too," he snorted.

"Shut the fuck up Quincy!" Myra warned through her tears, with her entire body feeling numb.

"You is a ungrateful bitch. All the shit I done did fa you and that dope fiend bitch of a mother of yours. And now you come here with your punk ass boyfriend hiding behind a gun," Quincy retorted, spitting in Myra's direction.

"I SAID SHUT THE FUCK UP!" Myra yelled.

"Ya mother was a no good ho, and she raised you to be a no good ho too," Quincy said with so much vigor that he became short of breath.

"DON'T TALK ABOUT MY MOTHER LIKE THAT!" Myra screamed, feeling like she was having an out of body experience, like a force beyond her powers was moving her. She aimed the gun at Quincy's head and pulled the trigger. The power of the shots sent her stumbling backwards and the bullets sent blood and brain matter splattering all over the walls, the chair, and her face and clothes. Just as the shots were fired, Milton emerged with two large old fashioned mail bags filled with cash, and two saran-wrapped bricks of dope. He walked toward Myra, who was bent over in front of the door, crying hysterically. He grabbed her by the hand and pulled her up, "C'mon, it's over now . . . let's go," Milton said calmly.

Milton removed Myra's bloodied coat and shirt, leaving it behind. He wrapped her in his coat and together they rushed out of the old brownstone toward his vehicle and sped off. Myra rocked back and forth on the way home; she was traumatized by what she had just done. Of all the things she had done in her life, taking someone's life had to be the worst.

"Whew! baby, we got paid," Milton said breaking the silence, seemingly unfazed by the fact that they had just committed a crime. Myra remained silent; she couldn't bring herself to look at him. She was afraid of him, but even more afraid of herself. Thoughts of an escape flooded her brain. This was crazy—he was crazy. Myra never knew she had it in her to murder someone, but Milton seemed genuinely proud of what they had just done.

The old, ruthless Milton Roberts was back. Milton sat up all night counting and recounting his ill-gotten gains. He had big plans for the money. He felt as if he finally had enough to finance his NFL dreams. He didn't think about sharing a dime with Myra. First, he would pay Damien off and square shit away so he could get back to focusing on his career.

Myra was unable to fall asleep for several hours. Each time that she closed her eyes she relived Quincy's murder over and over again. Her body was exhausted; it had been through a tremendous amount of stress, not to mention the fact that it was already working overtime maintaining the pregnancy. Before she knew it, the sun had come up and it was time for her to get up and get dressed for the first day of her new job.

Myra did her best fixing herself up, trying desperately to mask the huge bags under her eyes. Glancing at her reflection through the passenger side window of a car parked outside of the 77th precinct on Utica Avenue in Brooklyn, she smoothed back her hair with her fingers, puckered her lips, dug in the corners of her eyes, pulled her skirt down, and walked through the precinct doors. She tried to put everything that had happened last night out of her mind.

In the dimly-lit lobby of the precinct, MOST WANTED posters and recruitment bulletins hung sloppily on the drab beige walls. A very old desk and several worn chairs was not what Myra had expected to see when she entered the building. *Damn can't NYPD afford up to date shit?* she thought to herself. Myra watched as police officers hustled prisoners in and out, making her feel slightly uneasy. *Stay calm, Myra. He got what he deserved . . . karma caught up to him.* Myra continued to reassure herself.

A young female officer approached Myra. "Can I help you?" she asked.

"Yes, I'm here for the student job—the college administrative aide job. Here is my paperwork," Myra said, extending the papers toward the officer, feeling relieved and confident that she hadn't let on that she was nervous.

"Oh ok, let me direct you to the desk sergeant. His name is Sergeant O'Shaughnessy," the officer kindly offered.

"Thank you," Myra replied.

"Hi. My name is Myra Danford . . . I'm here for the student job," she said in a polite tone to the pale, carrot top white man behind the huge desk that sat atop what appeared to be a platform.

"Who sent you over here?" he asked with an impatient undertone to his voice.

"An officer . . . I didn't get her name," Myra responded, at a loss for words.

"Go over there to your left. That's the 124 room, go in there and ask for the Principal Administrative Aide . . . that's who you need to see, not me," he snapped. Myra hadn't even been there for five minutes and she already hated her job.

"Ok, thank you," Myra said, glad to be redirected to someone else. Finally, Myra was properly given a tour and an assignment. She was responsible for answering the telephone switchboard (TS) which was located to the left of the desk sergeant. Myra was nervous about sitting next to the red-headed, blue-eyed devil of a sergeant, but she convinced herself that she could handle it.

Sitting at the switchboard, Myra was privy to all of the information that came in and out of the precinct. She heard about murders, robberies, and all sorts of criminal activities going on. She listened to all of the calls that came over the radio that day, but there was nothing about a murder on Willoughby in Bed-Stuy. She thought about calling in an anonymous tip that Quincy's body was in the house, knowing that it could be weeks before anyone found him. After fully contemplating the idea, she decided against it. She was just going to have to let things ride out. Besides, Milton promised that this would be it. All they had to do now was wait for the draft to occur. After that, it would be smooth sailing for Myra and Milton both.

Quanda walked into the Lawrence H. Woodward Funeral home on Troy Avenue and it was jam packed with people. Whenever a young guy's life was cut short by street violence, a large crowd of mourners was sure to turn up. Quanda adjusted her black shades as she moved through the crowd and made her way up to the casket. Rayon looked as if he were in a light sleep. *Damn, the undertaker did a good job with the make up,* she thought to herself. He was sharply dressed and bejeweled, even in death. *Revenge is bittersweet,* Quanda thought sadly to herself and she turned to walk away from Rayon's body.

Quanda stood at the back, watching to see who came in and out, what they wore, but mostly how they reacted. She was interested to see how many girlfriends and baby mothers who didn't know about each other would turn up. As she stood there taking in the sights, Knowledge walked in. He was flanked by ten huge dudes. *Bodyguards . . . this nigga need bodyguards. I thought he was the baddest muthafucka walking?* Quanda thought as she continued to watch his every move from behind her dark shades. She was so busy watching him that she didn't even realize that Cisco had come up and stood right beside her. When he started to put his arm around her shoulders, she jumped.

"What the fuck you doing?!" Quanda said, startled by the contact. She calmed down a bit when she realized who it was.

"Baby it's me, your man," Cisco said, reminding Quanda that she had told him she was his girlfriend.

"Yo, now is not the time Cisco . . . for real," Quanda chided. Cisco put his head down like a puppy that had just gotten whacked with a rolled up newspaper. Quanda needed to get as far away from him as she could. She was here to get Knowledge's attention, and she couldn't let anything get in her way, especially not a retard that Knowledge hated. Cisco finally got the message and left her alone for the time being.

Quanda stood in the back, waiting until the last of the mourners filed out. She had been dying to speak to Knowledge; in a way, she had sort of missed having him around. Finally, Knowledge got up from the first row of seats. He took one last look at his partner, lowering his head in sincere sorrow. As he began his amble toward the exit, the bodyguards emerged from the ends of each row of seats, one by one following him out. Quanda quickly moved toward the door so that he couldn't miss her.

"Hey," she said in a soft voice, placing her hand up against his chest, blocking his exit. Just as she touched him one of the huge dudes grabbed her wrist and began twisting it back.

"OUCH, YOU ASSHOLE!!!" she yelled, grabbing the attention of the people who still milled around the funeral home.

"It's aiight yo" Knowledge said, calling off his protectors.

"Oh, you got bodyguards now . . . even for me?" Quanda asked, her feelings genuinely hurt.

"Yo, shit is crazy right now, ma . . . you know the deal," Knowledge explained.

"I miss you . . . you haven't called or nothing," she complained.

"I know. I'm just chillin' right now. I don't know who to trust," he replied, eyes downcast.

"Trust? Well you should know you can trust me—I thought what we had was special," Quanda said, letting anxiety slip into her tone as she grabbed his wrist. She was afraid to lose her grasp on Knowledge; her plans had not been completely carried out just yet.

"Ma, just give me some time . . . I still gotchu right here," Knowledge said, placing his right hand over his heart, kissing the back of her right hand.

"Well, can I at least call you?" Quanda asked.

"I changed all of my numbers. Don't worry . . . when shit dies down, I'll holla," he assured her, leaving her standing there alone.

Quanda never noticed Cisco standing outside up against the wall watching her interaction with Knowledge. This wasn't the first time Cisco had seen Quanda with another man. He had spotted her getting out of Vell's car one night. He banged his head up against the brick wall, ignoring the pain that it caused him. He was angry and jealous. He wasn't too slow to figure out that Quanda had used him.

Knowledge had one of his bodyguards drive him to his new *Yukon Denali* that was parked in Bay Ridge, near the Verrazano Bridge. He had purchased the Denali because he felt it was low-key compared to his other cars—nobody would recognize it as being his. He drove straight to his secret estate in New Jersey. Not even Rayon had known about this spot. Knowledge rode in silence, thinking about Quanda.

He wanted so badly to bring her home with him. He was lonely and in mourning. But mostly, he was afraid for his life.

Over the years, Knowledge had convinced himself that he was untouchable. He believed that the only way to survive in the game was to have no fear. *Scared Money Don't Make Money*—was his motto. He pulled up to the black gates of his forty acre estate, and the security guard immediately opened the huge white wrought iron gates for him. He drove up to the circular drive way, leaving the car at the front door; he knew that someone would be coming to park it. Knowledge walked into the grand lobby with its expensive art hanging on the wall and Italian marble floors. Before he went any further, he rubbed his prized golden statue of *Ganesh*, the remover of obstacles. He walked straight to the spiral staircase with its gold-plated banister, and climbed the carpeted stairs, longing for his bed. He was tired, but he knew that he wouldn't get much sleep; he hadn't since the murders.

Knowledge changed into his fluffy burgundy terry cloth robe and turned on his plasma television to ESPN.

"In college sports news today, word of the upcoming NFL draft is looming. Looks like Red Storm star quarterback Milton Roberts has fallen in the picks ratings. St. John's football coach said that due to their recent string of losses, he was not confident that Roberts would be drafted. From the sports desk, I'm Rob Snow. Back to you Courtney."

"Damn, that was my team. I was betting on that nigga from BK to go all the way," Knowledge mumbled to himself, as he flicked through the channels. He couldn't stop thinking about Quanda. He just wanted to make sure that he could trust her first. He thought long and hard about things. Knowledge had decided after the back-to-back funerals that he would take Quanda on a vacation—somewhere nice, quiet, and romantic. They would make love all day, eat good food, and escape from their realities.

Cisco paced back and forth in front of the building waiting for Quanda to come home. When she arrived, he watched her long, chocolate legs descend from the cab. She was talking on her cell phone. "Shit!" Quanda exclaimed when she spotted Cisco. She continued to talk though, walking straight past him and into the lobby of her building.

"You . . . you . . . you just gonna walk by me like that?" Cisco asked, stuttering as he grabbed hold of Quanda's arm, tears collecting at the corners of his already red-rimmed eyes.

"Yo Cisco, now is not the time. I'm not in the mood," Quanda retorted, trying to go easy on him. What she really wanted to say was, "Get ya fucking retard hands off of me, simple ass! Did you really think you could ever be any man of mine?" But she kept those comments to herself.

"Quanda, I love you. I . . . I . . . I . . . th . . . th . . . thought we was close you know. We used to talk about everything," he whined, referring to all of the information he had shared with her.

"You don't love me! Stop touching me!" Quanda screamed, pushing him away from her violently.

"You gonna get yours . . . watch, Quanda. You fucked around with the wrong nigga! Cisco threatened through his tears without stuttering. His boisterous outburst caused all of people hanging around outside to run into the building. In the projects, every now and then a good one on one fight was the absolute highlight of the day.

"Don't fucking threaten me or I will beat ya ass," Quanda yelled back, stepping into the elevator, leaving Cisco alone to argue with himself.

Cisco stormed out of the building and stomped over to Myra's old building—220.

"Yo Dave!" Cisco yelled, calling out to a guy standing out front.

"What retard nigga? I don't need shit from the store right now," Dave said, giggling.

"Where Knowledge at man?" Cisco asked, with his usual slow drawl.

"What the fuck you want with Knowledge?" Dave asked, suspiciously. Everyone knew that Cisco hated Knowledge, and vice versa.

"I gotta tell him something im . . . im . . . important," Cisco stammered, anxious to purge himself of the information that was burdening his brain.

"About what?" Dave asked, not relenting.

"About Rayon and Budda get..get..getting killed," Cisco said.

"Tell me what you know," Dave said, his interest piqued.

"I can't," Cisco insisted.

"Then I can't tell you where Knowledge is muthafucka! You don't know shit no way. Getcha retard ass outta here!" Dave retorted, angry that he couldn't get the scoop.

"Forget it!" Cisco said dejectedly, walking away with his head down. He would have to think of another way.

Milton looked in the mirror one last time before he left the house. *Damn, nigga. You look good,* he thought to himself, smiling like the Cheshire cat in *Alice in Wonderland.* He had to take care of his business before Myra got home from work, but not before he got his high on.

Milton dumped his goods onto a small pocket mirror, bent down, and inhaled as he held one nostril closed; he did the same with the opposite nostril. "Ahhhhh," he exhaled, allowing the drugs to dull his senses and take him away from reality.

Milton placed the two large bundles of money into his gym bag, grabbed his brush, and headed out the door. He was feeling at ease with the knowledge that he would give Damien a big enough payment to last at least until the draft press conference was over. Once in his vehicle, Milton dialed Damien's cell phone number and listened as it rang.

"Yo, it's Milton," Milton identified himself when he heard the line pick up.

"Whatchu want nigga? This better be about my paper, faggot nigga," Damien said, chuckling wickedly at his insult.

"Yeah, I got something for you. I'll be there in twenty minutes," Milton replied, before slamming his phone shut.

"Fuck him . . . I'll get there when I get there!" Milton grumbled, angry at Damien's last comment. Milton made a screeching u-turn and headed in the opposite direction.

Milton pulled in front of the Limelight club. He checked out the sights and felt confident he would be able to find someone to fulfill his insatiable sexual needs. He knew that he wouldn't get past security with his new protection piece. He pulled out his nickel-plated beauty, handling it carefully, making sure to keep it out of the sight of passersby. Milton ran his hand up and down the cold steel, feeling omnipotent. He didn't care that there was a body on the weapon already. He needed it for protection; it was the only true friend he had. Milton quickly pulled up the small compartment between the two front seats, and placed the gun down into the empty space that usually held his CD collection. "It'll be ok for a few minutes," he reassured himself, reluctant to leave it behind.

Milton parked his vehicle and made his way to the club. Just enough men were there; it wasn't nearly as crowded as his usual spot. Milton hadn't been back 'out' (as he liked to call his extracurricular activity) since his *Webster Hall* escapade. As soon as he walked inside, he got his usual cat calls. He hated when they did that. He couldn't stand the sissy men, who were so outwardly feminine; on the other hand, he was annoyed by the dudes who only wanted to give and not receive—much like him. The constant struggle with his sexuality was a hard feat for Milton to conquer. The secret desires that he harbored toward other men bombarded his psyche with such intensity that he couldn't help but to satisfy them. It was hard for one person to play three different people—the loving boyfriend, football star, and secret man lover. Even with Damien's threats of exposing his secret life looming over his head, he could not contain or control his need. He needed to have sex with men, and he couldn't deny that.

Tonight would be different. Milton had promised himself that he would pick up someone just for a quickie. A simple tryst, maybe just a little head. Milton slid into the semi-crowded club. He sat alone, as usual, listening to Kanye West, Twistah and Jamie Fox sing and rap over Chaka Khan's classic, *Through the Fire*, as it blared through the clubs speakers.

Milton went over to the bar and ordered his usual Hennessy. On his way back to his table, he noticed someone staring at him. Eye contact was the first signal that something might jump off. When Milton made direct eye contact with his pursuer, he realized that this dude was definitely not his type. The guy was either white or Spanish, and he was dressed down. He wore a red, white, and blue striped *Gap* shirt which hung open to expose a white tee shirt underneath. His *Diesel* jeans were slightly fitted and he had on a fresh new pair of *Reebok S. Carters*. His hair was gelled in several directions, giving him a punk rocker look. He was definitely not Milton's type, but Milton couldn't help but continue to stare back. *Damn, I know this cat from somewhere,* Milton said to himself, unable to discern the guy's apparent familiarity.

For the next hour or so, the guy stared Milton down. Milton tried desperately to ignore it; he needed to find a temporary companion for the night—and quick. It was slim pickings for the night.

The strange man who had been staring at Milton all night long finally approached.

"Hi. I know this might sound weird, but aren't you Milton Roberts . . . the quarterback at St. John's?" the guy asked.

"Nah," Milton said with a dismissive air in his voice.

"My name is Frank Scarpetti . . . sports management agent with Mission Management Company," the guy explained as he extended his hand toward Milton, unabashed by Milton's demeanor.

"Yo, I said you got the wrong nigga!" Milton snapped, lowering his head to break off any direct eye contact. Milton finally figured out where he knew the audacious nuisance from. Mission Management was one of the sports management firms that had tried to get Milton to sign with them.

"Well, look man . . . me and a few of my friends are having drinks over there. Feel free to join us, on me. And here is my card . . . and it's not what you think. I don't come here to pick up men, I come to relax with my friends and feel normal. I know what it's like in our business . . . you know, being gay," Frank sympathized, extending his business card in Milton's direction.

Milton sprang to his feet in a rage. "Who the fuck you calling gay!" he yelled, pushing Frank violently in the chest. Frank was taken aback by Milton's unexpected outburst. Frank didn't have time to react before Milton began punching him in the face. The club's bouncers raced toward the mayhem, pushing and shoving their way through the crowd that had quickly formed around the two men.

Milton went berserk. He was like a madman, punching Frank's bloodied face over and over again; he was out of control. One of the bouncers hoisted Milton up from the heap of tangled arms and legs and held him in an arm lock. Milton continued to kick and fight until he was finally thrown out of the club's back door. Furious, he jogged to his car and jumped in. Milton's malevolent impulses told him to get the gun and go shoot Frank right in his smart ass mouth. Instead, he decided from that moment on that he would never pick up a dude again, no matter how bad the craving; besides, his career with the NFL was on the line now. He promised himself that first thing tomorrow morning, he would go see Damien and get things squared away, once and for all.

Myra couldn't stand being alone. The look on Quincy's face when she squeezed the trigger would forever be etched in her brain. Hoping to put her mind at ease, she decided to call Quanda.

"Hey girl, wassup?" Quanda answered the phone, seeing who it was on the caller ID. Myra immediately felt a wave of relief wash over her body.

"Nothing. Wassup with you?" Myra answered the question with a question.

"Girl, I went to the wake for Rayon yesterday—it was off the hook. Three baby mothers and two so-called wifey's showed up. The whole Tompkins, Marcy, Sumner and Roosevelt was there, enemies included," Quanda reported.

A wake or funeral was the last thing Myra wanted to hear about, but she listened anyway. Just the sound of Quanda's voice was comforting to her.

"So, they know who did it?" Myra asked suddenly, causing Quanda to stumble over her words.

"Huh? Oh girl, I don't know," Quanda answered in a low whisper.

"Let's change the subject," Myra said. Quanda breathed a sigh of relief. She hated lying to her friend.

"Aiight . . . so how you and the baby doin'?" Quanda inquired.

Myra hadn't given much thought to the baby lately. She still hadn't signed up for the free prenatal care either. Her stomach was really starting to get big.

"Oh, everything is fine," Myra lied.

"Same here girl," Quanda said, returning the lie. Both girls concealed murderous secrets, which neither dared to share.

"Where is Milton? I bet he is so happy," Quanda said enthusiastically.

"He is at practice . . . and yes, he is happy. He hugged me when I told him about it," Myra replied with her half-truths. She had no idea where Milton was and she'd be delusional to think he was happy about the baby.

"Quan, can you go check the mailbox at 220 to see if I have any mail there?" Myra asked.

"Sure girl, lemme call you back. Quame on my other line," Quanda explained as she abruptly ended the conversation.

"Ok," Myra said, wishing she didn't have to hang up so soon. Just as Myra put the phone back down, she heard Milton coming into the apartment. She quickly pulled the comforter up around her neck and pretended to sleep.

Myra had overslept again. Between working, the nightmares, and the pregnancy, it had become very arduous for her to get up in the mornings for school. On the days that she did make it class, she usually fell asleep midway through the lecture. Myra had become so dependent on Milton's dreams and aspirations that she was fast losing sight of her many goals, aspirations, and dreams.

When Myra saw what time it was, she jumped out of bed. She had to get ready for work.

"Milton!" Myra called out, shaking his sleeping form.

"Mmmm," he moaned, turning over. That's when Myra noticed all of the cuts and bruises on his face, neck, and hands. She was instantly diverted from her initial intent.

"What happened to you?!" she shrieked, shocked by his condition.

"I got hurt in practice," Milton lied.

Myra didn't really believe him. During the past months, she had grown to distrust Milton.

"Can you drive me to work? I'm going to be late if I take the train," she asked, anxious to get to work.

"Why don't you quit? When I get drafted, you won't need a job," Milton grumbled, too tired to get up.

"I can't quit. Can you drive me or not?!" Myra asked impatiently. She was sick to death of his empty promises.

They left the apartment as if they were strangers. Myra walked ahead of Milton, exiting the building while Milton locked the front door. She headed toward the garage, not waiting for him.

"Damn, say excuse me! Can't you see I'm pregnant?!" Myra yelled as three guys brushed passed her in a furious rush, almost knocking her down as they disappeared down the path toward her building. Myra waited at the entrance of the garage for Milton to emerge from around thc bushcs. Five minutes passed . . . twenty minutes passed; Myra looked at her watch, she clinched her jaw so hard it caused a sharp pain in her head.

"He can't ever do shit for me . . . after all I've done for his sorry ass!" she complained aloud, kicking up dirt as she headed back toward their building.

Myra reached the front of the building and there was still no sign of Milton. She stormed into the building in a huff. Waiting for the elevator was taking too long. She was ready to curse Milton out. As she climbed three flights of stairs, Myra mumbled the profanities that she planned to spit at Milton.

By the time she reached the last landing she was winded and out of breath. The huffing and puffing of her own breath prevented Myra from hearing the noises emanating from behind the apartment door. She swiped her key and snatched the door open, ready to let Milton have it. But before she could open her mouth, she was yanked through the doorway by her hair.

Myra had no time to react; her bladder felt like it had dropped out of her body; thoughts of her last attack clouded her senses. She felt dizzy with fear and confusion.

"Sit down!" a stocky white man with fire red hair commanded as he tossed Myra in the direction of one of the dinette chairs. Myra grabbed onto the back of the chair to keep herself from falling over. She sat up straight in the chair and looked around. She noticed that the red head was one of the guys who had pushed past her on the way to the garage. Myra looked around for Milton but she saw no signs of him. After a few seconds, she could hear loud thumping coming from the back of the apartment and the sound of muffled voices. Someone was either in the bathroom or the bedroom, but who? She was really confused about what was going down. She wondered if the same person who attacked her the first time around had finally come back for her.

After a few minutes, the noises stopped. The two other men who she had almost ran into outside emerged from the back of the apartment. Myra looked closely at each of them, trying to memorize their faces so that she could later describe them to the authorities. One guy held a large gun in his right hand and Myra noticed that he never blinked. *This all has to be a bad dream*, Myra thought to herself. Things couldn't get any worse than they already were in her life.

Damien stepped toward her. He let the fur from his white mink coat rub against her face; he was so close he could have French-kissed her. Damien took his long pinky fingernail on his left hand and rubbed it up and down Myra's cheek slowly, as if he were trying to seduce her. Myra looked disgustedly back at his double chinned, cherub-like face.

"You are prettier than I thought. No wonder ya man been making lots of dough trickin' you," Damien began. Myra could smell the cinnamon Altoids on his breath. He moved his hands from her face and began to run them over her hair. Myra was so revolted by his touch that she couldn't contain herself any longer.

"Stop fuckin' touching me!" she yelled, knowing that her comment could send him over the top.

"Oh, you a feisty one too. You know that shit really turns me on," Damien chuckled, looking around at his goons for approval. Ignoring his lewd statement, Myra kept her eyes on the guy with the gun.

"So I know all about whatchu was doin' up in here on Friday nights. Did ya sweet lover boy tell you about me?" Damien asked innocently. Myra shook her head from left to right as her legs shook fiercely. She wondered how Damien knew about her and the gambling parties, and if, in fact, Milton had shared that information with him.

"Oh well, ain't that just too bad. So you mean to tell me you just sell ya pussy and you don't know where ya pimp takes the proceeds?" Damien continued. Myra turned red with embarrassment, angry that Damien was referring to Milton as her pimp.

"Well, let's just put it this way—I'm the mothafucka that holds the puppet strings to ya man's career and his life. Now, I just added you and your baby's life to the puppet show," Damien said ominously.

"What do you want?" Myra asked, her voice shaking as her emotions bubbled to the surface. The fear in Myra's eyes was real, and Damien was glad to see it there. The fear that he evoked in Myra made him feel like his little visit to Milton's crib was well worth it.

"What do I want? Hmmmm . . . let me just tell you this—ya man 'star quarterback' done got his self into some deep shit. Let's just say he owes me big time. I'm a monster from his past, and I want my paper. Since you look like the type that stands by ya man, looks like you owe me some paper too," Damien said ruthlessly.

"How much?" Myra asked, tears streaming down her face.

"Well the price keeps going up. Believe me sweet thang, if you want to be an NFL wifey you better help ya man out cause his draft chances are slipping away. Only I hold the key to his future and to yours for that matter. There is nowhere you can or hide . . . I'm like God, I'm everywhere," Damien boasted, crouching down in front of Myra and gently caressing her stomach. Myra pushed his hands away, causing the guy with the gun to rapidly descend on her.

"I'm aiight," Damien said, calling off his goon.

"I asked you what you want—how much money?" Myra asked again.

"And I think I told you that ya man could tell you that. Listen, you should do better research on a brotha before you move in wit him and getcha self knocked up. Don't you know how many black men got AIDS these days? Maybe you should think about following yours one day . . . you know . . . check out who he keeping company wit—who he fucking wit. Ya mama didn't teach you shit girl . . . oh yeah . . . she was a crack head right? Or was that a dope fiend?" Damien said maliciously.

"Fuck you!" Myra snapped again.

"Naw, baby girl. You and ya man gonna get fucked. See, I'm content with beating his ass every now and then because what I really wanna do is fuck up his draft chances. I wanna be paid every week up until the draft. So if you can count, which I'm sure you can Ms. College Girl, ya'll got exactly two months to pay me every week on time. Oh yeah, and the payment done gone up. If I don't get my shit . . . let's just say all hell is gonna break loose," Damien replied, grabbing Myra's face and kissing her on the lips as if she were his girl. Myra struggled to break free of his grip. She scrubbed her lips viciously with the back of her hand as Damien and his crew left the apartment.

Myra did not move from the chair until she felt certain that they were gone. When she felt comfortable that they were gone, she jumped up and ran to the back of the apartment. She ran into the bedroom, but there was no sign of Milton. Myra ran into the bathroom and found Milton lying in the bathtub. He looked like he had been beaten within a half of an inch of his life.

"Oh my GOD! MILTON! Myra screamed. Milton slowly opened his bruised eyes. He was conscious but he couldn't find his voice to tell her not to call the ambulance. Milton knew that if he was taken to the hospital there would definitely be police involvement, considering his current condition.

"Shhhhh," Milton croaked, struggling to sit upright.

"Oh baby, what did they do to you?" Myra said, through her tears, on the verge of hysteria.

"Don't worry about me," Milton said in a low whisper, still finding it difficult to speak.

"C'mon, let me help you to the bed," Myra urged.

"I'm aiight. I can get up . . . aggghhhhh," Milton howled as he dragged himself out of the bathtub.

Myra had so many questions but she wanted to make sure that he was alright before she bombarded him with her concerns. She helped him get into the bed so that she could properly dress his wounds. Myra stayed by his side until the Tylenol P.M. fully took effect. With Milton knocked out, she slipped out of the bedroom down the hallway into the living room. She needed to think and plan her next move.

Myra was convinced that Milton wasn't lying to her when he told her he was in trouble; but a recurring thought kept creeping into her head—*what the hell did Milton do with the money from robbing Quincy? Why didn't he pay Damien with it?* She decided to search for the money on her own. She went through every closet, looked under the bed and couch, searched the kitchen cabinets and under the bathroom sinks . . . nothing.

Tired of searching, she sat down to catch her breath. With each minute that passed, Myra grew angrier and angrier. She clenched her fists so tightly that her fingernails dug moon-shaped craters into her palms. She didn't know what to think anymore. *Fuck this! I'm outta here . . . I had enough of this shit,* Myra decided. She jumped up and began to frantically pack her bags. She threw all of her belongings into duffle bags, plastic bags—whatever she could find.

As Myra started stacking her belongings by the door, a sharp pain invaded her lower abdomen. It was so excruciating that it took her breath away. "Aggghhhh," she screamed, clutching at her stomach. Myra fell to her knees and the pains kept coming. She kept very still, hoping and praying that they would stop. As she sat crouched on the floor, she felt the baby inside of her womb move for the first time. The movements were sharp and extremely painful. Myra grabbed a handful of the carpet and began pulling at it. She couldn't get up from the floor. The baby's movement caused reality to set in—where was she going to go? If she went back to the projects, she would definitely die; and if she left without settling the score with Damien, she would die too. *Who was she kidding? She had no place else to go. She would be better off taking her chances and staying with Milton.* Even though Myra was tempted to call Quanda, she decided against it. She didn't want Quanda to get caught up in all of this. She would just have to find a way to manage for the next two months . . . no matter how bad it got.

Knowledge dropped his rose onto Rayon's casket and walked away. He and his bodyguards headed for his private limousine. He didn't trust riding in the funeral parlor issued limo with Rayon's family, even though Rayon's mother had asked him to. As he walked away, Knowledge could see from his peripheral vision that someone was running toward him. His bodyguards reacted immediately, snatching the person up in a sleeper hold neck lock. Knowledge halted his steps in fear until he noticed that it was Cisco that they had apprehended.

"Yo, he's a harmless retard . . . ease up, son," Knowledge commanded, calling off his guard. The bodyguard immediately released Cisco, letting him fall to the ground. Cisco coughed and gasped for air.

"Yo, son why you running up on a nigga like that? Wassup with you?" Knowledge asked, puzzled by Cisco's behavior.

"I . . . I . . . I," Cisco stuttered, unable to catch his breath.

"Help him up," Knowledge ordered. Two of his bodyguards helped Cisco to his feet.

"I . . . I . . . g-g-g-g-gotta t-t-t-tell you something," Cisco said, finally getting enough air into his lungs to push the words out of his mouth.

"Whatchu gotta tell me something 'bout?" Knowledge asked, bewildered.

"It's about Rayon and Buddha . . . and Quanda from 212," Cisco said, finally getting Knowledge's full attention.

"Aiight son, get in," Knowledge instructed, his curiosity piqued. He opened his private limo door to allow Cisco access. They pulled out of Cypress Hills Cemetery, onto Jamaica Avenue. Cisco began filling Knowledge in on everything he knew, and everything he had witnessed by following Quanda around.

Knowledge played it cool the whole time Cisco was educating him. Knowledge let Cisco out of the limo on the corner of Myrtle Avenue and Broadway. He gave Cisco a hundred dollars for all of his help. Although Knowledge knew that Cisco had to die, he decided to wait until the time was right, just in case Cisco had any more important information to offer. Knowledge was furious, but more hurt than anything. He didn't want to believe what Cisco had told him about Quanda. He would have to confirm the information for himself.

Knowledge planned to continue to lay low at his estate in Jersey, so he knew that coming up with the information that he needed on Quanda would be hard. She was obviously a lot smarter than her ghetto persona let on. It kind of turned him on, the fact that a chick could be smart enough to infiltrate his set. Knowledge leaned his head back, and closed his eyes during the long ride home.

Remembering to turn his two-way pager back on, it immediately began vibrating with a new message. Knowledge scrolled down to retrieve the message—not too many people had his new number so he knew that it was probably business-related. The message read: PLEASE CALL THE SERVICE AND MANAGEMENT OFFICE OF PARK SLOPE EASY PARKING IMMEDIATELY. *What the hell?* Knowledge asked himself. He couldn't understand why he was receiving a message from the parking lot in Brooklyn, where he sometimes parked his cars. He knew that he had definitely paid his bill for the year. Knowledge dialed the number from his cell phone. The office manager answered on the second ring.

"Hello . . . somebody paged me from here?" Knowledge asked.

"Ah yes, Mr. Rose." the man began. Knowledge recognized his alias. He had taken on the identity of Drew Rose, a dead man, in order to purchase homes, cars, and other property and investments.

"This is Mr. Gurth from Park Slope," the man on the other end of the phone continued, but Knowledge cut him off.

"Yeah aiight, why did you call me?" Knowledge asked, irritated.

"Well Mr. Rose, something bad has happened," Mr. Gurth continued to beat around the bush.

"What nigga? Get to the point!" Knowledge barked.

"Mr. Rose, your cars were stolen last night during a break in at the lot," Mr. Gurth blurted out.

"WHAT?! All of them?" Knowledge yelled.

"Yes, I am sorry sir. The guard said he didn't hear a thing. In fact, only people with access cards entered and exited the lot last night," Mr. Gurth reported.

"How could that be? Only my cars were stolen?" Knowledge asked, dumbfounded.

"When we checked the records, we saw that your access card was used approximately fifteen times. All of your cars were stolen, and the security cameras were vandalized so we have no tape of the robbery," Mr. Gurth said regretfully.

Knowledge hung up the phone. He was so angry he couldn't keep his composure. He began to bang on the windows and doors. He kicked over the bottle of champagne that sat in the corner of the limo. He threw his cell phone. "Yo, hurry the fuck up and drive . . . I gotta get the fuck home!" Knowledge yelled at driver. The bodyguard that sat in the front with the limo driver asked, "Yo son, you aiight?" Knowledge remained silent.

He knew exactly who was responsible for having his cars stolen. He had only trusted one person with the location of his collection, Quanda, and she had betrayed him. He was in grave danger. He had let Quanda know a lot about him, including where he kept his stash and where he held meetings with his workers. The longer he thought about it, the more things started to come together for him. Every time he was with Quanda, shortly after, something would go wrong, including the murders. He had been set up.

When Knowledge reached his estate he called an emergency meeting with his security team. When the meeting was over, he asked the head security guy to stay behind.

"Yo man, I got a special assignment for you, worth $250,000 if all goes well," Knowledge dangled the bait out there.

"What is it boss? You know I'm game," replied the skinny bald-headed black dude with deep red-toned skin. He resembled a modern day Ghandi.

"I need to have someone followed—I'm talking day and night. I don't care if it is out of the muthfuckin' country. You need to be on her like white on rice," Knowledge explained.

"Sounds serious," the man replied curiously.

"It is very serious. I will pay you the first half of the money now and when I decide where I'ma go with it, I will pay you the rest," Knowledge clarified.

"Ok, boss," the man agreed, too afraid of his boss to question what he meant by that.

"This is a picture of her. She lives in 212 on Throop Avenue," Knowledge said, handing him the only photo that he had of Quanda. It was a small picture that they had taken together in one of those automatic photo booths while waiting in the lobby of a movie theater.

"You basically want to know all of her comings and goings, right?" the man asked.

"Yeah, and I want pictures of anybody she speaks to, meets with, or interacts with. You should have something to report to me at least twice a day." Knowledge instructed, dreading what he would find out.

Chapter 13

ALL THAT GLITTERS AIN'T GOLD

"STAND FOR THE COUNT, LADIES!" the corrections officer yelled. Myra stood upright and walked to the end of her bed. It was time for the daily headcount. Life in Dorm 9 of the Rose M. Singer jail was beginning to take its toll on Myra. She had witnessed more lesbian sex behind these steel gray walls than she had ever expected to see in her lifetime. Not only had she witnessed these unnatural couplings, but she had also been an unwary spectator of marriage ceremonies between several female inmates. Marriages between inmates were a big deal and preparations could sometimes take hours. During a formal in-house ceremony, card table chairs were lined up for guests/fellow inmates. Brides donned wedding gowns, complete with headpieces, made from the best jail-issued sheets and pillow cases one could find. To consecrate the ceremony, a small reception would be held afterward, which basically involved the sharing of commissary snacks among the attendees. Some of the more artistic inmates would present gifts to the honorees, including tee shirts made with Kool-Aid tie-dye designs. Once Myra learned that the powdered form of Kool-aid could be used to dye clothes, she vowed never to drink that stuff again.

"DANFORD . . . YOU GOT MAIL AND A COMMISSARY RECEIPT!" the mail officer shouted as he came around to pass out letters to the inmates, mostly from their loved ones or legal representatives. When Myra heard her name she thought for sure there had to be some sort of mistake. Myra never expected to receive anything in the mail; all of her "loved ones" were long gone. She grabbed the letter and the receipt and examined them both carefully. The receipt read $300. *This must be some sort of act of God,* Myra reasoned. Mr. Shepowitz couldn't have given her the money because that would have constituted a conflict of interest. *Maybe Milton had resurfaced.* Myra quickly squelched that idea. Milton would have never done something this nice for her; besides, he was technically still missing in action.

Fearing that the money would somehow disappear, she quickly went to the inmate store and purchased things she had been lacking—especially candy. When she returned to her bunk to stow away her newfound treasures, she remembered the letter. Myra looked at the name and return address, *BRADLEY HOLSON?* she questioned. Myra immediately became excited. She blissfully recalled the sexy guy that always reminded her how beautiful she was. Myra tore open the envelope, and began reading, letting herself get lost in the words. Before she could finish, she heard her name being called again.

"DANFORD! COUNSEL VISIT!" one of the C.O.s yelled.

It had been weeks since she'd last seen Mr. Shepowitz. During his previous visit, he had come bearing the bad news that the grand jury had indicted her on all charges, on the premise that there was irrefutable evidence against her. He had left her feeling hopeless and depressed, but, as always, Mr. Shepowitz promised Myra that he would come up with a plan.

"So, Ms. Danford, what you are telling me is that you were a victim of domestic violence, and that you may have been suffering from domestic violence syndrome during the time that the crime took place?" Mr. Shepowitz asked encouragingly.

"I guess so," Myra responded, uncertainty in her voice.

"No, No! Ms. Danford, this is your defense. When I ask you this in court, you have to be sure of yourself and of your answer. You cannot answer me with any hesitation in your voice. Don't you understand that a jury might think of you as stupid for not leaving Milton sooner? You have to prove that you were suffering from this syndrome, and that you felt like you had no options," Mr. Shepowitz scolded.

"Well, how do you want me to say it? You want me to start crying and slobbering or something? I didn't' have any options, I was on the run for my life for Gods sake!" Myra asked irritably.

"If you can cry, then yes! Tears never hurt anybody," Mr. Shepowitz continued, exasperated.

"Ok," Myra complied.

"Good. Now let's go over it one more time," Mr. Shepowitz began, but Myra cut him off before he could start.

"I think you need to know everything first. There are a few details that I think could help my case. I've been reading in the law library here and I read something about deals being cut for cooperation," Myra said with enthusiasm in her voice.

"Ok, Ms. Danford. Let's have it all," Mr. Shepowitz said, leaning forward on his elbows and pinching the bridge of his nose, reluctant to hear the horrors that were sure to follow.

"I have to warn you . . . it's a lot worse than before. But you know what they say, the world is three hundred and sixty degrees around . . . you can't outrun karma . . . it comes back to you every time,'" Myra preempted her story.

"Forewarned . . . please proceed," Mr. Shepowitz said with a stiff smile, waiting for her to get to the point.

A few weeks after the Damien incident, Myra decided to call Quanda. The phone rang about eight times and just as Myra was about to hang up, Quanda answered.

"Hello?" Quanda asked groggily.

"Hey Quan . . . were you sleeping?" Myra asked.

"Nah girl, wassup?" Quanda asked, clearing her throat.

"Where you been? I haven't seen you in a minute!?" Myra inquired.

"Girl, running around all over the place," Quanda replied vaguely, hoping that Myra didn't ask for more details. Quanda had been busy continuing her assault on Knowledge's business and personal life. She had arranged for all of his cars to be stolen from his secret parking garage; his Park Slope home had been raided by the narcotics cops thanks to an "anonymous" tip; his drug spot in Utica had been shut down; and the one in Newark, New Jersey had burned to the ground. Quanda was definitely a force to be reckoned with.

"Girl, I was planning on coming out there today. I got some mail for you," Quanda said, remembering her plans for the day.

"Oh? Umm . . . why don't you come by my job tomorrow?" Myra asked nervously, not wanting Quanda to come by the apartment and see the condition Milton was in, or more importantly, what condition her face was in. Myra had hoped that her face would look better after a day or two, but it didn't. She'd made the mistake of asking Milton where all the money from Quincy's robbery mysteriously disappeared to, and ended up with a black eye in response.

"Aiight, tomorrow sounds good. What time?" Quanda asked.

"One o'clock—that's when I take lunch," Myra replied.

"Ok, see you then baby girl. Oh, I forgot to ask. How's the bun in the oven?" Quanda continued.

"Oh fine, just fine," Myra lied; she had no idea how the baby was doing. She still had not gone for prenatal care. The one thing that Myra did know was that she was under a tremendous amount of stress. She had been working like a dog, bringing her entire paycheck to Milton every week so that he could pay off Damien. Since she hadn't seen or heard anything from Damien, she assumed Milton was doing the right thing with her money.

Myra sat behind her desk in the precinct. It was already two o'clock and Quanda was still a no-show. Bored, Myra turned on her personal radio and started to flip through the stations. She wasn't in the mood for listening to her usual station, WKIS. She didn't feel like hearing any talk of love, lust and lies from the male radio host on that station. She needed something entertaining to keep her awake, so she decided to tune into WBLS for all the latest gossip.

"HEY PEOPLE IT'S THE EXPERIENCE. WE ARE NOW TAKING CALLERS, HELLO?" the boisterous female radio personality chimed, allowing the first caller of the day through.

"HI HUN, FIRST LET ME SAY THAT I'M YOUR BIGGEST FAN AND I'M CALLING TO TELL IT ALL ABOUT AN UP-AND-COMING ATHLETE," said the effeminate-voiced male caller.

"OK, GO AHEAD AND DISH IT," the radio host replied.

Myra laughed at the background studio sound effects, "OOHH HOW YOU DOIN'? HOW YOU DOIN'?" resounded out of the speakers as the caller spoke.

"LET ME TELL YOU ABOUT A CERTAIN ATHLETE BY THE NAME OF . . ." but before the caller could finish, the cautious host cut him off.

"DON'T SAY THE NAME! YOU CAN TELL ME THE NAME OFF THE AIR BUT YOU CAN'T SAY THE NAME ON AIR, OK?" she rebuked the caller before she let him speak again.

"OK, WELL I WON'T SAY THE NAME BUT HE ATTENDS A COLLEGE IN JAMAICA ESTATES. HE PLAYS FOOTBALL. HE IS ABOUT TO GO PRO AND HE IS ON THE DOWN L-O-W, OK GIRL? HE SLEEPS WITH US "CHILDREN" AND PLAYS IT OFF LIKE HE IS A MANLY MAN. A FEW WEEKS AGO HE PICKED ME UP IN THE CLUB AND WHEN WE GOT BACK TO MY PLACE HE RAPED ME, OK? SO I'M ABOUT TO GET PAID . . . OK ?" the caller rambled on with the "HOW YOU DOIN'? . . . HOW YOU

DOIN'?" sound effects playing over and over in the background.

"GET OUT?! WELL, YOU KNOW YOU SHOULD REALLY REPORT THIS TO THE POLICE. WE"LL TALK OFF AIR . . . I'M PRETTY SURE I KNOW WHO THIS IS . . ." the gossipy radio personality said eagerly, just before she cut to a commercial break.

Hearing the words "football," "college," and "Jamaica Estates" together made Myra nervous. She knew that St. John's University was the only college that was located directly in the Jamaica Estates neighborhood. *What if this guy was talking about Milton?* Myra wondered to herself. Something that Damien had said to her kept resurfacing in her mind . . . *Don't you know how many black men got AIDS these days? Maybe you should think about following yours one day . . . you know . . . check out who he keeping company wit—who he fucking wit.* The words reverberated loud and clear in her ears. Myra couldn't concentrate; she was so drawn into her thoughts that she didn't even hear the precinct telephone switchboard ringing off the hook.

"Hey Danford! Don't you hear that damn phone?!" the sergeant yelled.

"Huh?" Myra responded, snapping out of her trance.

Quanda rushed down Utica Avenue. She knew that she was late for her meeting with Myra. Glancing down at her *Cartier* watch, one of the many riches she had acquired from her reign of terror, she realized she needed to pick up her pace.

When Vell had called Quanda today and asked her to meet up with him right away, she sure didn't expect him to have all of the profits from the sale of Knowledge's cars already. During her meeting with Vell, Quanda was pressed for more information on Knowledge. As usual, Vell even tried to use his relationship with her father to try to persuade her to dig up more leads, but Quanda had already told him just about everything she knew.

After her meeting with Vell, Quanda went to stash her money away before going to meet up with Myra. She knew better than to travel the streets of Brooklyn with that kind of cash on her.

Knowledge had not availed himself to Quanda as of late. As far as Quanda was concerned, he was still in mourning over Rayon and Budda. Her street connections had dried up anyway; lately, everyone was too afraid to even utter the word Knowledge.

Quanda realized that before long she would have to take her stash and disappear. She contemplated moving with Myra and Milton whenever they purchased their mansion, hopefully in a state far from New York.

Quanda made it to the precinct without ever noticing the guy snapping pictures of her—capturing her every move—including her meeting with Vell under the Williamsburg Bridge and her entrance into the police precinct.

Myra was listening so intently to the "*Experience*" that she didn't notice when Quanda walked in.

"Ahem . . . Ahem . . ." Quanda cleared her throat, as she moved to stand in front of Myra's desk. Myra looked up from under her dark shades.

"Hey sis!" Myra squealed out of surprise, happy to see Quanda's face.

Myra stood up from her desk to give her friend a hug. As soon as Quanda saw Myra's belly, she yelled out.

"Daaaaaaaaayum, girl! You got big as a house . . . look at this belly!" Quanda said reaching out and patting Myra's bulging stomach.

"I know girl, right," Myra responded, moving her friend's hand away from her stomach so that she could properly give her a hug.

The girls tightly embraced each other. It had been weeks since they'd last seen one another.

"Why the hell you got shades on inside in the damn dead of winter?" Quanda asked, finally addressing the obvious. She was the same sagacious Quanda Myra remembered. She didn't miss a beat.

"Girl, I was doing laundry, bent down to put clothes in the washer and as I came up the door hit me in the face," Myra lied.

"Lemme see," Quanda said, snatching the glasses off of Myra's face before Myra could respond.

"OH, HELL NO!" Quanda shouted in outrage. "I know that nigga Milton ain't beatin' on you?!" Quanda continued, yelling at the top of her lungs.

"Shhhhh," Myra said trying to quiet her friend down, pushing her friend toward the door.

The two left the precinct engrossed in conversation, as Quanda inquired about the black eye, they were oblivious to the fact that they were being followed.

"Where you wanna go eat?" Myra asked, changing the subject.

"I'm not hungry. I wanna know what the fuck happened to ya face," Quanda demanded.

"Quan, I swear, that's what happened," Myra continued with the lie, feeling emptiness in her heart. Myra had never told her friend such a bold-faced lie. It was a testament really to what direction her life was taking—lies and deceit dictated everything that Myra did nowadays.

"Word to who?" Quanda asked, still not convinced.

"To my unborn child," Myra responded, crossing her fingers in her pocket.

"Aiight, MyMy. If you say so," Quanda relented, taking her best friend's word as bond.

Myra felt guilty about lying to her friend, but she knew that if she told Quanda the truth all hell would break loose. The pair walked up Utica Avenue until they reached St. John's Place. There, they found a small West Indian restaurant to have lunch in.

"So, wassup otherwise?" Myra asked, breaking the uneasy silence that had formed between her and Quanda.

"Same shit . . . the hood is the hood. They found that dirty ass Quincy dead! Girl, somebody shot his ass in the head and the body was mad decomposed n' shit. They said he was in the house for like weeks or months before anyone found him," Quanda reported.

Myra's blood ran cold through her veins. She didn't respond to the news, but her mind raced and her heart pounded. She forced herself to calm down. If Quanda even picked up that something was wrong, Myra would have some serious explaining to do.

"I'm about to move up outta Tompkins. It's just the same shit day in and day out. Girl, you are so lucky that you got school and a good man on ya side . . . that is if he ain't hittin' on you or nothing," Quanda added sarcastically, still not entirely convinced.

"He's not hitting on me, Quan," Myra reiterated, slightly annoyed that Quanda had brought it up again.

"Ok girl, I'm just messin with ya. Speaking of school . . . I gotcha mail," Quanda said, reaching into her new pink Christian Dior girlie saddlebag and handing Myra a stack of unopened letters. Myra was too preoccupied with keeping her lies together to comment on Quanda's obviously expensive accessories.

"Oh thanks. I'll read them later," Myra said, stuffing the letters into her bag.

After being reminded about Quincy, Myra didn't really have much of an appetite anymore. Picking over her food, she couldn't wait for her hour lunch break to be over. As they sat in the restaurant, Quanda continued to ramble on. Myra barely listened to a word she was saying. This was the first time she could remember when seeing Quanda hadn't eased mind or her troubles.

"It's time for me to go back to work," Myra said in a somber tone as she glanced down at her watch.

"Oh aiight, I'm skating home then," Quanda replied. The girls hugged one last time before they parted ways, heading in opposite directions.

Back at her desk, Myra went through her stack of mail, one letter at a time. As soon as she spotted a letter from St. John's University in the stack, her hands began to shake. She tore at the sealed envelope, anxious to reveal its content.

Dear Ms. Danford,

It is with regret that I write to inform you that your eligibility for the St. Vincent's Academic Scholarship has been revoked. This decision was based on your poor academic achievement and attendance history. The St. Vincent's Academic Scholarship requires that you maintain a 3.5 overall GPA; your GPA has fallen significantly lower than this standard requirement. If you wish to continue your academic study at St. John's University, you must wait for the next semester to qualify for financial aid by filling out a FAFSA, or you may apply for our student loan program. If you have any questions or concerns, please can contact your student advisor.

Sincerely,
Robert Harriman, President

Myra felt her heart sinking. *How much can one person take?* Myra put her head in her hands and began to sob loudly. No one in the crowded precinct seemed to notice, or if they did they simply didn't care to comment on it; this was the story of her life. Myra had traded in her dreams of college and a successful future for inconsequentiality.

Quanda stopped at a newsstand and picked up a copy of the *Amsterdam News.* She planned on taking the money she had made from robbing Knowledge to get an apartment for herself, maybe in Harlem. Quanda heard that there were luxurious, newly rehabilitated brownstones in Harlem and several owners were looking to rent out their apartments.

Knowledge handed his provisional private investigator a rubber-banded stack of money in exchange for the photographs of Quanda. Knowledge went through each picture carefully, carefully analyzing each shot. There were pictures of Quanda leaving her building, meeting with Vell, and accepting money from him. However, none of the pictures infuriated Knowledge more than the ones of Quanda entering the precinct and exiting with Myra. He grew hot inside with anger. He had just come to terms with the fact that Quanda had set him up, but to learn that she was still in contact with Myra after all of this time pushed him over the edge.

Knowledge seethed with anger over the fact that Quanda had always vehemently denied knowing Myra's whereabouts. He couldn't believe that he had allowed himself to become so vulnerable to the machinations of a mere woman. He had never really cared for or loved a woman as much as he had Quanda, not even his own mother.

"I got something for this bitch!" Knowledge declared, throwing the pictures all over the room.

It never occurred to Knowledge that what Quanda had unleashed on him was karma.

Myra arrived home from work mentally and physically exhausted. All she wanted to do was lie down and never get up. Milton was leaving just as Myra entered the apartment.

"Oh," Myra said, shocked to see him up and about.

"I'm going out. You got the check?" Milton asked, not wasting his time on small talk.

Myra dug into her purse and handed him her earnings. She wanted him to take the money and simply disappear from her life. As she watched the door close behind him, she prayed that he would never return.

With Milton gone, Myra found herself thinking about Damien's words and what she had heard on the radio. Even though she tried to put her outrageous thoughts out of her mind, she found that she could not.

Driven by pure instinct, Myra rushed to the phone and dialed the Jewel car service. She knew that one day it would come in handy—plus, it was free. The driver informed her that he would be there in two minutes. Myra wobbled down the stairs as fast as her pregnant body allowed. She knew that Milton had to walk to the parking lot, which would give her time. She planned to follow his ass, and perform a little P.I. work.

The cab was in front of the gates by the time she stepped outside. Myra jumped into the black *Cadillac Sedan Deville* and noticed that Milton's truck was still stopped at the traffic light on the corner of the block.

"Follow that silver Navigator . . . but try not to get noticed," Myra ordered the driver.

The cab weaved in and out of traffic trying to keep up with Milton without being obvious that they were tailing him. Myra made certain to keep her eyes dead and center on his vehicle.

The Navigator made its way onto the Grand Central Parkway. Milton paid his toll at the Triboro Bridge toll plaza and continued up past Randall's Island onto the lead way ramp into Harlem.

"Where the fuck is he going?" Myra questioned out loud. The cab driver was having a difficult time keeping up with Milton.

"Hurry up!" Myra yelled at the driver, starting to panic. The cabbie obeyed; he didn't really care how far Myra wanted to go because he was getting paid by the mile.

Milton finally came to a stop on a decrepit block in Harlem. He parked his car and entered into a seedy-looking bar/club.

"You got a pen?" Myra asked the driver. He handed her a pen and she scribbled down the name of the club—Ebony Lounge, on a piece of napkin.

As Myra sat waiting for Milton to leave the building, the cab driver started to complain, reminding Myra that what she was doing would probably be considered illegal. She had to quiet him with the 100 dollars that she had set aside from her paycheck today for her secret stash. She couldn't allow her 007 mission to be compromised.

After approximately forty-five minutes, Milton emerged from the club with a guy in tow. When the two rushed toward Milton's SUV, Myra shook the cabbie awake. "Yo Mohammad, get ready to drive," she instructed. The driver obliged, staying a car length behind.

"I need more money," the driver grumbled, dutifully following the Navigator.

"Ok, when I get back . . . and remember you're going to get paid off of the voucher too," Myra reminded him, making sure he didn't try to fleece her.

Milton was too preoccupied with fulfilling his insatiable sexual appetite to even notice that the same car had been following him since he'd left *Dara Gardens*.

Milton drove back onto the highway and headed into an area in Queens that was very close to Brooklyn—Cross Bay. Myra grew more and more anxious. *Maybe Milton was just trying to meet up with Damien to drop off his payment?*

Milton turned into the Cross Bay Motel parking lot. Myra had the cab driver stop at the corner of the block; she didn't want to chance being noticed. She watched patiently, taking in an eyeful of Milton and his companion. The man Milton was with sashayed worse than a woman. Milton looked around nervously before he entered the motel. What she had heard that day on the radio was true—Milton Roberts, the man she had been dying to marry, was on the down-low!

Myra had heard stories about men who slept with both women and men, and claimed to be straight, but she never thought that Milton would be one of them. Her tears had long dried up; all that remained was pure rage. Myra's blood pumped so fast that she began to hyperventilate. Out of frustration, she pounded her fist on the seat of the cab. She contemplated whether or not she should rush into the motel and bust in on Milton's nasty ass.

"Back to Dara Gardens!" Myra commanded, before she gave in to her impulses. Myra was fuming with anger during her entire cab ride home. *I'm out . . . I'm fuckin' out! Whatever happens will happen. How dare this bastard use and abuse me and all along his ass is gay. No wonder Damien is blackmailing him; he probably knows all about this. I guess everything that glitter ain't gold!* Myra had finally hit rock bottom; she was ready to leave.

Myra exited the cab in a hurry. She sped as fast as she could down the path to the building. Nothing mattered anymore—where she would go, whether she lived or died. She just had to get away from Milton and fast.

Myra finally reached the door to the apartment. She ran inside and, in a frenzied rush, tried to pack everything that she would need. She had to get out of there before Milton returned. As she made her way through each room, trying to gather just the essentials, Myra felt a gush of hot fluid run down her legs. At first she thought that she'd just pissed on herself, but this felt different. A sharp pain in her stomach brought her packing to an abrupt halt. Myra was terrified by what was happening to her body. She was going into labor, and from what she had calculated, the baby was at least six weeks early.

Myra thought fast and decided to call Quanda. She knew that she could depend on Quanda, no matter what.

After about six rings, Quanda answered.

"Hello?" Quanda answered.

"Hello?! Quanda?!" Myra asked, the panic evident in her high-pitched voice, followed by a resounding scream.

"MyMy, what's wrong?!" Quanda asked, scared to death for her friend's safety. When Myra did not respond, Quanda dropped the phone and ran out of the house half-crazed and half-dressed. She flew down the stairs of her building and ran to the corner of Throop and Myrtle Avenues to hail a cab. A dark blue car with black tinted windows pulled up beside her. With the window slightly cracked . . .

"Where you headed?" the driver asked.

"To Queens . . . Dara Gardens!" Quanda yelled, jumping into the car and thinking she was on her way to save her best friend.

Chapter 14

A RUDE AWAKENING

The automatic door locks activated as Quanda closed the cab door. She didn't pay it any mind; it was common practice where she came from for taxi drivers to lock their passengers in the vehicle until they received payment for the ride. Before Quanda could give the driver her exact destination she was startled by a deep Lou Rawls sounding voice resonating from the far left corner of the car.

"So you hang out in Queens now?" the voice boomed.

"Shit Knowledge . . . don't scare me like that!" Quanda squealed, her voice quivering with panic. Her stomach immediately felt squeamish and her heart pounded ferociously against her sternum.

"Why you so nervous? I thought you missed me?" Knowledge asked, emitting a shrill maniacal laugh.

"Yes baby, of course I did," Quanda replied mendaciously. She immediately fell into character, unaware of the fact that Knowledge knew all about her coup to overthrow him. Knowledge decided to play along to see just how far Quanda would take her charade.

"So who you goin ta see in Queens, ma?" he quizzed.

"Oh my sister . . . you know my pops had mad kids everywhere. I just found out about this sister in Queens, so I'm headed there. But now that you back, I'm goin' wherever you goin'," Quanda said flirtatiously, the lies rolling off of her tongue even though her nerves were on edge.

"Aiight, you visiting family. I'll take you there and then I can meet your peeps," Knowledge said, rubbing his newly grown goatee as he watched Quanda fidget in her seat.

"Nah baby, I missed you so much. Forget about it . . . let's just go to your crib," Quanda suggested. Her audacity and continued duplicity incensed Knowledge; he was sure she had been the one to tip off the police, resulting in his Park Slope brownstone being raided and seized as evidence.

"How about this . . . me and you just get on a plane right now and go someplace nice and warm," he said being equally deceitful. The nerve above Quanda's right eye began to twitch. Sweat dripped from every pore on her body.

"I can't go no where looking like this," Quanda said, gesturing at her house clothes. "At least let me go back to Tompkins to change my clothes and do my hair," Quanda recommended, bidding for time. She was so consumed by her dilemma that Myra had totally slipped from her mind.

Knowledge looked through the front windshield and realized that they had arrived at the instructed destination. He was glad, because he'd grown weary of playing lie swap with Quanda. When the cab came to an abrupt halt, it didn't take Quanda long to figure out what was going on; she had enough street savvy to know that the gig was up. Instinctively, she dashed for the door handles, but they were missing. As she began to bang frantically on the door and windows, Knowledge reached over to grab her.

"HELLLPPP!!!" Quanda screamed as Knowledge grabbed a handful of her hair and yanked it back viciously. Her screams were bloodcurdling; she screamed until her chocolate face turned red.

"BITCH WHERE THE FUCK YOU GOIN'?!" Knowledge spat, snapping her head back.

"YOU WANNA SET NIGGAS UP?! YOU THOUGHT YOU COULD PLAY THE GAME?! NOW BITCH, YOU IN FOR A RUDE

AWAKENING FOR REAL!" Knowledge's voice roared like a lion ready to devour his prey.

"Wait a minute! Whatchu' talkin' about?! Baby, I love you!" Quanda declared, her pleas falling on deaf ears. Quanda and Knowledge struggled in the back seat. Quanda ripped off his platinum and diamond chain and clawed chunks of his skin from his face and neck, but her efforts was no match for Knowledge's strength and fury.

Knowledge balled up his huge gorilla hand and punched Quanda's delicate face until her cheek bones shattered, continuing to unleash his wrath on her body. Even with her face bleeding and the pain beginning to saturate her senses, Quanda refused to surrender to Knowledge's brutal assault. She kicked, clawed, and bit any piece of Knowledge's skin that she came in contact with.

"Yo, son! Come around and open the fucking door!" Knowledge yelled to his driver. "I'ma torture this bitch before I kill her! She thought she could take me down slow, so I'ma give this bitch one slow painful death!" Knowledge avowed.

"Why you doin' this shit?! I never did nothing but love you . . . you gonna believe some shit you heard around the way over my word?!" Quanda whined in a last-ditch effort to save herself.

Knowledge's driver assisted him with pulling Quanda from the car. The driver opened the door and grabbed at Quanda, but she kicked him in the chin before he could reach her.

"AWWW SHIT! YOU LITTLE BITCH!" the driver cried out in pain.

"STOP BEING FUCKIN' WEAK AND GRAB THIS BITCH OUT BEFORE I SHOOT YOU!" Knowledge yelled.

Quanda continued to fight as they tugged and wrenched at her; she had an unwavering will to live. Knowledge sustained his tight grip on Quanda's hair as he pulled her out of the vehicle. The driver held onto her flailing legs as Knowledge exited behind her.

"Drag her to the spot . . . I got something to show her," Knowledge instructed the driver. He was unnervingly calm and that frightened both Quanda and the driver immensely. Both wondered why Knowledge didn't just shoot her and get it over with.

Quanda kept her eyes open as the two men carted her body off. She could see the two famous red and white smoke stacks in the distance. Quanda knew she was still in Brooklyn.

They entered a building that resembled a factory and several men came rushing toward them. Knowledge immediately dropped his portion of Quanda's body, causing her head and shoulders to collide with the concrete floors.

"Take her to the room," Knowledge instructed the goons. Suddenly, Quanda was surrounded by several pairs of feet. A sharp pain invaded her rib cage as one of the men kicked her in the side. She didn't bother to scream. One of the goons covered her eyes with a blindfold and hauled Quanda over his shoulders. She managed to peek from under her blindfold and what she saw left her breathless—the building wasn't a regular factory, it was a drug factory! Quanda could see assembly lines with actual workers chopping, bagging, and capping drugs. There were three separate lines, one for cocaine, one for heroin and one for weed.

Knowledge was not the person she thought he was; his enterprise was much bigger than he had let on. Quanda had been under the impression that the hit on Rayon and Budda had put Knowledge out of commission for a while, but now she realized that the drop off at the apartment in Tompkins was a front; just like the apartment in Park slope, the cars, and the operation out in Utica. Knowledge didn't need any of those assets to survive; they were merely front businesses. He didn't need to employ all of those corner hustlers; he did it for entertainment. Knowledge was a millionaire many times over.

As they carried Quanda to her execution, it dawned on her that she would take Knowledge's secret with her to the grave. She just couldn't figure out why a big time drug Kingpin would have wasted so much time with her and why he had assaulted Myra and killed Vidal. Unless she was really the one who had been set-up.

"We had to provide general anesthesia to the mother. The mother was pre-eclamptic and the umbilical cord was wrapped around the baby's neck, which caused a drastic decrease in his heart rate," a petite Asian female resident reported to the head obstetrician.

"The patient was given a cesarean section with a mid-line bikini cut. The abdomen remains guarded and the patient will experience residual contractions for approximately two days as the uterus rebounds," a male Indian resident continued.

The group of doctors and residents conferred at the foot of Myra's hospital bed. Myra could hear their voices but was unable to see their faces. Her abdomen was tightly wrapped in gauze which rendered her incapable of sitting up. As the anesthesia started to wear off, she could feel the pain permeating her lower abdomen.

"Hi, Ms. Danford," the Asian doctor chimed when she noticed that Myra was fully conscious.

"Ahem . . . hello," Myra responded, clearing her throat.

"How are you feeling?" the doctor asked as the others began to huddle around the woman in the bed next to Myra.

"I'm in a lot of pain," Myra groaned in reply.

"Yes, that's quite normal after a C-section. You will have pain for a few more days, but you have to get up and walk or else your cut will get stiff and you'll be stuck here longer than you need to be," the doctor explained.

"What happened? Why'd I get a C-section?" Myra asked, trying to remember.

"When your husband called the ambulance your baby was in danger. Your blood pressure was elevated to a dangerous level and your baby was tangled in his umbilical cord. We had to sedate you and perform an immediate C-section in order to save your baby," the doctor informed Myra.

"How is the baby?" Myra asked, afraid to learn the truth.

"He is touch and go. He appeared to be premature at about 32 weeks of gestational age. He weighs two and a half pounds, but he is a fighter. He is already trying very hard to breathe on his own, but for now we have to keep him on a breathing tube. He'll be here for a while, at least until he reaches five pounds and is breathing without assistance. You, on the other hand, will be discharged in a few days," the doctor said.

"Can I see him?" Myra asked, anxious to see her son. All Myra could think of right now was seeing her baby—touching him, hugging him, loving him.

"The nurse will help you down to the neonatal ICU. Your husband has been there since the baby's birth," the doctor said with a smile.

The man the doctor kept referring to as her "husband" must be Milton. He must have been the one to call the ambulance. None of this made sense to Myra. The last person Myra had spoken to was Quanda, so why wasn't Quanda here instead? All Myra could think of at that moment was her son.

Myra lay back down in pain, waiting for the nurse to come so that she could get out of this bed and visit her baby. In the meantime, Myra closed her eyes and said a prayer:

Dear God, I haven't forgotten about the things I learned about Milton. But God, I need to do what is best for my baby. If I let Milton know that I know his secret, he will go crazy—he might even kill me. Lord, I'm lost. I want to take my baby and run, but I have nowhere to go. I know Quanda will help me, but I'm not sure if we can live with her . . . her house is already so crowded. Besides, I can't go back to Tompkins. Please give me the strength to get through this, Lord. Please rescue me from myself. If it's time for me to be out on my own Lord, please make a way for me and my son. Please Lord; remove Milton from my life for good. In Jesus name I pray, Amen.

"What up?" Milton's words startled Myra out of her reverie. She opened her eyes and looked at Milton square in the face. It was like looking into the eyes of the devil himself.

"Hey," Myra responded, hesitant to even talk to him.

"Yo, thank you, man. He looks just like me . . . even as small as he is," Milton beamed, surprisingly out of character.

"And thanks for giving me a reason to continue living," Myra snapped, with a slight attitude. She was disgusted by the mere sight of Milton because every time she saw him she was reminded of his duplicitous lifestyle.

"So when they say you gettin' out?" Milton questioned, ignoring her hostility.

"They didn't say," Myra said, evasively.

"Aiight, well the draft is in like three weeks. I figure we can give—" Milton started, but Myra cut him off.

"Are you fuckin' kidding me?! We've just experienced the birth of our son, who is barely holding onto his life, and you got the fucking nerve to come up in here talking about how we gonna make money to pay off a debt that has nothing to do with me! Get the fuck out! I don't even want to see your face right now!" Myra screamed at the top of her lungs. She couldn't control the emotion that had come over her. All of the anger that she had suppressed during these last few months had bubbled to the surface. Myra felt as if everything she had done for him—giving up on her dreams, lying to her friend, stripping, stealing, murdering—was for nothing. Milton's words meant zilch to her now. He was just a low-down, dirty bastard, so low he could suck an earthworm's dick.

"What the fuck is wrong with you?" Milton asked, taken aback by Myra's sudden outburst.

"You . . . you are what's wrong with me and with the world. You're a lying sack of shit and me and my son don't need your ass anymore!" Myra continued on with her verbal assault.

"Listen, this must be your hormones talkin' or something. You ain't goin' no where with my son. We gonna be a happy family in the next couple of weeks. Tom hooked me up with a sure way to get some big chips," Milton said grabbing Myra's face, attempting to kiss her.

"Milton, don't you dare put your faggot hands on me!" Myra screamed, turning her face away. She could not believe his nerve.

"What the fuck did you say?!" Milton barked, moving closer to Myra's bed.

"I want to be alone," Myra said flatly, realizing what she had just said.

"I asked you a fucking question!" Milton continued, getting up in Myra's face.

"Milton, please. I'm in pain . . . please leave me alone," Myra cried out of desperation.

"If you ever talk breezy again, you will fuckin' die! I already told you that I don't love no hos," Milton warned, lifting the bottom of his shirt to expose the handle of a gun he had stuffed in the front of his jeans.

"I'll be back to pick you up. We got some unfinished business. You can either come easy or we can both go out with a bang!" Milton threatened before he stomped out of the hospital room.

Myra remained hospitalized for the rest of the week. She visited her baby boy every day and was astonished at how fast he was making progress. In just one week, his body had begun to regulate its own temperature, which was a great accomplishment for a preemie, according to the doctors.

Myra sat close to the small incubator that served as an artificial womb for her son. She put her sterilized hands through the two small holes in the glass so that her baby could feel human contact, her loving contact, which the doctors had explained was better for him than any medicine. As she sat there rubbing the new love of her life, a short lady with African braids and a thick Nigerian accent approached her.

"Hi, Ms. Danford. I'm Ms. Obeke, a pediatric social worker," the woman said introducing herself.

"Hello," Myra replied guardedly; she was leery of social workers of any kind.

"I need to ask you a few questions before you leave today. Can we talk?" Ms. Obeke asked.

"Sure," Myra responded.

"Are you married?" asked Ms. Obeke

"No," Myra replied.

"Ok, is the baby's father involved?" Ms. Obeke asked.

"Yes," Myra replied, afraid that if she said no it would count against her in some way.

"Do you live together?" the social worker asked.

"Yes," Myra responded. *But not for long,* Myra thought to herself.

"I need you to fill out these papers. They are emergency contact papers for the baby. In case you are not available, we need alternate contacts. The baby will be here for a little while. He seems to be doing better, but before he comes home we will need to make a home visit to see that you have a stable home, supplies for the child, and sufficient resources to raise this child. He will probably also require nurse visits every once in a while—most preemies do," Ms. Obeke explained.

Myra had zoned as the social worker rambled. Myra had not planned on staying with Milton, but she knew that if she didn't have a stable place to stay they would never let her baby come home. She also knew that going to Quanda's crowded house with a preemie would be out of the question in the eyes of the Social Service system.

“Ms. Danford . . . do you understand what I’m saying to you?” Ms. Obeke asked after noticing that Myra was gazing blankly into the distance.

“Huh? Oh yeah . . . I do. What paperwork do you need me to fill out?” Myra asked, snapping out of her trance to focus on what the social worker was saying.

Myra quickly filled out the paperwork, putting Quanda and Ms. Brenda down as the alternate emergency contacts for the baby. When the social worker left, Myra went back to touching her baby’s soft skin. Tears streamed down her face. Quanda hadn’t showed up at the hospital even once, and Myra found that to be very strange. She had tried calling Quanda and Ms. Brenda several times during her stay in the hospital but she never got through. Myra promised to try again as soon as she got home, sure that there must have been some sort of an emergency in Quanda’s family. *Maybe Quanda’s sister Quil had a chronic asthma attack again,* Myra speculated. Myra needed to talk to Ms. Brenda to weigh her options about where to go with her baby and how they could both get away from Milton.

Milton sat in his vehicle in front of the hospital waiting for Myra to emerge. He knew that Myra had no idea that he was aware of her discharge date. He hadn’t been back to see her at the hospital since their last tiff. Milton figured that all of the urgent messages on his answering machine from Ms. Brenda meant that Ms. Brenda and Quanda were planning to help Myra leave him. With his cocaine habit and the constant threats he received from Damien, he was becoming paranoid—borderline crazy.

Myra left the hospital carrying a bag filled with things she had been given in the hospital. She planned to get on the train and go straight to Quanda’s house; she had given up on the idea of retrieving her belongings from the apartment that she shared with Milton. She was leaving Milton for good; Myra had already contacted her job and let them know that she would be returning to work. She needed an income so that she could get a place before it was time for her baby boy—Kyle David Danford—to be released.

"Going somewhere?" Milton whispered, pushing the cold steel against her spine, causing her to drop her bags in surrender. Myra was too stunned to respond. She hadn't seen him lurking.

"I don't want to hurt you . . . just get in the truck so we can talk," Milton instructed, pushing her forward with the barrel of the gun. Myra never uttered a word; she did as she was told.

"Here is the plan . . . Milton began as they both settled into the front seat of the car. Myra didn't hear his words; she was too busy reading the headlines of the newspaper that lay on the dashboard, "SPORTS MANAGEMENT FIRM CEO FILES CRIMINAL ASSAULT CHARGES AGAINST NFL PROSPECT MILTON ROBERTS." The article went on to say:

A week before the draft, Roberts stands accused of assaulting an unnamed complainant last month in a well-known gay bar. Another man has also come forward with allegations that Roberts picked him up in a different gay bar and raped him. Police are currently seeking Roberts for questioning.

Myra had a rude awakening, as she sat held at gunpoint by a wanted man.

Chapter 15

THE BEGINNING OF THE END

"So did you enjoy the dick? Wasn't it you that said it was so good?" Knowledge asked sarcastically as he pulled himself up off the floor where Quanda lay swimming in a fetid mixture of her own bodily fluids.

Quanda could not respond. Her naked, bruised, and beaten body shook uncontrollably and she had stopped trying to scream. The handkerchief was tied so tightly between her top and bottom lips, each time she screamed the material cut further into the corners of her mouth.

"ANSWER ME BITCH!!!! YOU SO FUCKING BIG AND BAD . . . YOU WANTED TO GET IN THE GAME, NOW PLAY!!!" Knowledge screamed as he stomped Quanda's thigh leaving his *Nike* sneaker print embedded in her skin.

Quanda had begun to go into shock, therefore she was numb. Knowledge had been holding her captive for a week. He had seen the MISSING posters hanging up all over Tompkins, but he had other plans for Quanda. Knowledge had never felt as much love for anyone as he had felt for Quanda, but that love had instantly turned to hate. He remembered something that an older woman once told him IT AIN'T NO DEEPER ROOTED HATE THAN LOVE TURNED TO HATE, and he was definitely feeling that right now.

"Get the fuck up . . . I'm not finished with you yet" Knowledge growled as he yanked Quanda's battered body up off the floor. She was unable to stand and she fell forward on her face.

"You not so big and bad now right . . . I got a surprise for you," Knowledge spat as he dragged Quanda's mortally injured body. He was amazed that Quanda had retained her consciousness this long.

"OPEN YA FUCKING EYES AND LOOK AT WHAT DADDY GOT FOR YOU, SINCE YOU L-O-V-E ME SO MUCH!!!" he barked, holding Quanda's face forcefully and simultaneously removing the blindfold and mouth gag from her face. Quanda struggled to lift her battered eyelids; she wanted to obey his every command hoping that he would have mercy on her.

"I SAID OPEN YA EYES!!!" Knowledge continued. As Quanda finally opened her eyes she let out a deafening scream at what she saw hanging above her.

"QUAMEEE!!!!!!!!!!! NOOO!!!!!!! AGGGGHHHHHH!!!" Quanda screamed, her heart ached and she forgot about the pain that pervaded her body as she stared at her brother's eviscerated remains. "YOU FUCKING ANIMAL!!!!! I HATE YOU!!!!" she screamed at Knowledge.

"HAHAHAHAHAHAHHA!!!!" Knowledge cackled taking pleasure in her pain. "Now it's your turn . . . but first tell me that you love me one more time" he said, suddenly becoming serious.

"Do it . . . just do it" Quanda sobbed, begging for death. She closed her eyes tightly and before the words could fully leave her mouth . . . BANG, BANG, BANG, BANG, BANG, BANG the shots rang out.

Myra looked up at the sky as the sun peeked through the dark clouds. Her eyes burned with exhaustion and the bikini cut in her abdomen throbbed with sharp pains. She had been in the car with Milton for eighteen hours as he devised his "plan." Several times during their practice run through, Myra contemplated jumping out of the vehicle and making a run for it, but the opportunity never presented itself. Milton must have also anticipated Myra's surreptitious plan, therefore he forced her to drive while he held her at gunpoint.

The area they cased was desolate at that hour of morning, and the only pulse of life visible were the huge sewer rats scrambling for their daily meal. Myra had heard enough "turn here" and "reverse this way" for an entire lifetime. Milton made her go over his plan at least twenty five times. She knew Kent Avenue, in the Greenpoint section of Brooklyn like the back of her hand by now. They drove past the *Brinks* armored car facility at least twenty times. Milton pointed out truck number 2137.

"That's the truck we need to follow. It will pull out at five o'clock" Milton reported.

"Look, Milton, there has to be a better way. I'll go back to the apartment with you and I'll do more parties, but please don't do this," Myra pleaded.

"Shut up!!! You never have faith in me and you are weak. Tom gave me the ins and outs of this shit. Do you realize that the draft is today? If I can get a big payment to Damien I can still be drafted. We can also take some of the money and just live," Milton rambled, sounding like a deranged madman and looking like one also.

"Milton, it's over. You got people suing you and your draft chances are gone so please turn yourself in to the police and let me go be a mother to our son" Myra implored.

"SEE, I KNEW YOU WAS A QUITTER . . . YOU MAKE ME FUCKING SICK! THAT IS WHY I KEPT A LITTLE INSURANCE ON YOUR ASS" he barked, pulling a small plastic bag from under the front seat of the vehicle. "CHECK THIS SHIT OUT" Milton commanded.

Myra slowly opened the bag, the barrel of the gun visible in her peripheral vision. She lost her breath as she viewed the contents.

She had been sure that Milton had left her bloody shirt and jacket at Quincy's house the night of the murder. Myra stared at cold hard evidence that she was a murderer. Her blood ran cold, and the hairs on her skin stood up.

"YOU LIKE THAT SHIT . . . I'M SURE THE POLICE WOULD LOVE TO HAVE THEIR HANDS ON THIS SHIT . . . NOW JUST SHUT THE FUCK UP AND DRIVE!!!" Milton screamed, shoving the cold steel of the Heckler and Koch 45mm up against Myra's temple.

Myra continued to drive. When the clock on the dashboard read 5:00, Milton began to fidget in his seat as he dug into a black duffel bag and pulled out a ski-mask.

I cannot believe that he is serious . . . he is actually going to rob an armored truck at 5 o'clock in the morning in Brooklyn, Myra thought to herself.

Myra watched closely as truck number 2137 pulled out of the heavily gated Brinks facility on Kent Avenue.

"Drive!!!" Milton yelled. He was racked with panic and the gun shook between his fingers. Myra obeyed his command, and as the truck made is way down Kent Avenue, toward the Brooklyn-Queens Expressway she followed.

"Ok, it's gonna stop right at that twenty-four hour check cashing place on Flushing Avenue," Milton reported. And just like he said the truck stopped. Myra realized that Milton had been given inside information. There was no other way he would know the precise times and stops of the truck. Her body began to tremble and she was no longer tired. She was awake and wired like she had downed a Red Bull mixed with Pepsi and coffee.

"Milton, please think about this . . . I don't feel right" Myra begged.

"Ok, now the first driver will get out of the front. The second driver has a 9mm glock in the back . . . this truck is only carrying a million dollars so there are no NYPD escorts necessary." Milton reported in a mechanical drone, ignoring Myra's pleas.

Myra began to sweat and her palms slipped around the steering wheel. She looked over at the demon sitting next to her and envisioned horns protruding from his head. The clock now read 5:21.

"In one minute the driver will exit . . . he will get the bag from the inside man, he will then take out his gun and carry the bag into the check cashing place, except he won't make it because I will be there . . . and you know the rest of plan, right?" Milton continued, but Myra couldn't hear him. She was too nervous to focus and she stared straight ahead.

Myra was jolted out of her trance by a sudden outburst. "NOW!!!" Milton screamed, as he jumped from the vehicle. Myra stepped on the gas and rammed the back of the *Brinks* truck as she had been instructed. The airbag in the Navigator did not deploy as she had hoped. Myra figured that if the airbag had come out it would have hit her hard in the chest, either knocking her unconscious or killing her, which at this point seemed like the better alternatives.

"GIVE ME THE FUCKING BAG!!!" Milton screamed, as he pointed the gun at the guard. The guard immediately dropped the bag and proceeded to raise his gun in Milton's direction but Milton shot him four times . . . *POW, POW, POW, POW* hitting the guard in the face. The remaining guard opened fired on the vehicle in Myra's direction. She ducked as shards of shattered glass rained down on her body. Milton turned from his first victim and proceeded to fire on the second guard. As the life left the second guard's body he fell from the back of the armored truck and landed on the hood of the *Navigator*. Myra covered her ears and screamed as the botched robbery took place in what seemed like slow motion. Milton wasn't satisfied with one bag of money.

"REVERSE THE TRUCK NOW!!!" he yelled, pointing his weapon in her direction. Myra sat up like the exorcist and threw the truck in reverse, and as the vehicle moved the guard's body fell to the ground.

Milton jumped into the *Brinks* truck and retrieved three more bags of money. Myra was trembling and her entire body felt numb. She watched as Milton prepared to exit the back of the battered truck, and just as he made it to the back, an NYPD vehicle drove by slowly. Myra noticed the police car but she was in too much shock to motion for Milton to hurry up. She watched in horror as the NYPD car reversed and pulled up beside the *Brinks* truck. Just as Milton jumped to the ground two police officers, one in a white uniform shirt and one in a navy blue uniform shirt, drew their weapons and screamed for Milton to FREEZE!!!!

Myra quickly realized that one of the officer's was a Captain. Milton bent down and grabbed the dead guard's gun. The officers immediately opened fire, hitting the side of the *Brinks* truck, but missing their intended target. With guns in both hands Milton returned fire, shooting wildly.

POP! POP! POP! Six rounds from the nickel plated 45mm Heckler and Koch handgun sounded off into the still morning air. Myra watched as bright blood gushed out of the hole in the Captain's neck. With pure terror etched on every line of his face, his body folded like an accordion to the ground. The officer who had been the Captain's assigned driver lay wounded by his side unable to reach his radio to call for back up. Milton jumped into the passenger seat and Myra floored the accelerator.

"WHEW WEEE DID YOU SEE HOW I DROPPED THOSE NIGGAS, BABY!!" Milton exclaimed breathlessly, excited by his murderous deed.

"YOU KILLED A POLICE CAPTAIN! FOR GODS SAKE, MILTON, WHAT IS WRONG WITH YOU?!!" Myra screamed, disregarding her own safety as she rode with the psychopath.

"YEAH, AND NOBODY KNOWS WHO DID IT, AND NOBODY WILL KNOW" Milton growled lowering his voice to a threatening whisper as he reached over and placed the gun to Myra's lips. Tears streamed down her face and she realized that this was the beginning of the end for her. Milton and Myra had both forgotten to check the check cashing place for surveillance cameras.

"We got one more place to go, baby girl" Milton chimed, seemingly unfazed by his recent activity.

"WHAT?!" Myra screamed she couldn't believe her ears.

"Yeah we got unfinished business with a certain person remember the nigga that caused all of this?" Milton replied. "So pull over and I'll drive," he continued.

Myra was more than happy to relinquish the wheel of the battered crime vehicle. She put the SUV in park and went for the door.

"Oh hell no . . . I'll get out and you climb over to the passenger seat I'm a little smarter than you think, baby. See I know you might try to make a run for it," Milton said, still waving the gun in Myra's direction.

The drive from Brooklyn into Queens seemed to take forever. People along the highway stared and pointed to the vehicle with its smashed windshield and blood stained and dented grill. One man glared at the vehicle in horror and, sensing something was wrong, he began dialing 911 on his cell phone. Milton noticed the driver, and extended the gun in the man's direction. The concerned driver immediately dropped his phone and the call.

Milton sped the entire distance to the next destination of his crime spree. Myra was still shell shocked. The clock read 6:12. Myra realized that she had aided and abetted Milton in committing three, possibly four, murders and one of the victims was a NYPD captain. She was sure that this story would be all over the media in no time. All she could do was close her eyes and try to picture her baby boy's face.

"Aiight this fat nigga should be leaving his crib in like five minutes . . . he goes to the gym. Huh, the gym, as fat as his ass is," Milton stated, laughing hysterically at the irony. Milton pulled the Navigator along side a cherry red drop top Jaguar XK8. Myra peered out of the window and looked at a house on the opposite side of the street. She watched as the timed lawn sprinklers came on and spun around and around covering the well-manicured lawn with a fine mist. Myra saw her dreams of having a house with grass disintegrate each time the sprinkler rotated.

"Look, just like clockwork," Milton hissed as he retrieved and cocked his weapon of choice. Damien was alone. He usually went to the gym by himself. In fact, the goons Milton was accustomed to seeing Damien with were all for hire, they weren't real bodyguards.

"Yo Damien!!" Milton shouted. Myra jumped. She noticed Damien stop dead in his tracks.

"Ay, Milton . . . wassup?" Damien responded, with an unsuspecting nervous giggle.

"I gotcha payment . . . today is the draft too," Milton replied calmly.

"Aiight" Damien said.

"Wrong fucking answer, nigga . . ." Milton screamed as he pumped Damien's portly body full of lead. "HOLD THAT YOU FAT BITCH!!!!" Milton yelled, as he jumped out of the vehicle. He grabbed Damien's car keys from his lifeless hands and ran back to the Navigator. Milton yanked Myra out of the passenger seat, retrieved the three bags of money and opened the doors of the Jaguar. Milton grabbed Myra's neck and forced her into Damien's car.

"Nice new ride for us, baby girl" Milton beamed as he peeled out, leaving his truck, void of the license plates, in front of Damien's house, which was now the scene of another crime.

"So what now?" Myra asked as they pulled up at the *Dara Gardens* apartment.

"Whatchu mean, what now?" Milton asked in return.

"Yeah, what happens now? Oh wait let me see. You're going to kill the commissioner of the NFL and we will live happily ever after, right?" Myra retorted sarcastically.

"NO . . . we gonna lay low for a few days and then we outta here. Now help me put this money in these gym bags and let's go upstairs and make hot passionate love," Milton replied, laughing uncontrollably.

Myra was more than afraid of him as she helped him stuff the money into the bags. When they were done they drove up to the gate.

"Hello Mr. Roberts . . . nice new car" the security guard complimented.

"Thanks, Musan . . . man it cost me a fortune, make sure you watch me get drafted tonight," Milton replied, smiling brightly as the security let him in as usual. He'd definitely lost his mind.

A combination of shock and sleep deprivation had Myra hallucinating. Every car she passed in the parking garage resembled an NYPD vehicle. She shook her head several times to try to shake the images.

When they got into the apartment Milton instructed Myra to come into the small hallway between the bathroom and the bedroom. He opened the linen closet and removed a stack of towels from the shelf. He hit the back of the wall several times and the sheet rock came loose revealing a hidden compartment.

"See baby, this wasn't all for nothing . . . this is OUR stash" Milton assured her.

Myra gaped at the amount of money in the wall. She had never thought to look there, and she realized that almost every dollar she'd made for Milton was stashed there. Myra immediately felt entitled to a cut of the money. Even though most of it was blood money, she was desperate at this point. She needed to get her hands on some of the cash so she could escape, get an apartment, and await the release of her baby boy.

Myra planned to stay awake until Milton fell asleep, take some of the money and make a run for it. But Milton would not let her out of his sight. If she went to the bathroom he followed. He would not allow her to turn on the television. He told her that she didn't need to hear news about the crimes and he did not particularly want to watch the draft.

Myra watched as Milton snorted line after line of cocaine. She was appalled, but now she had the answers to most of her questions she had regarding his recent erratic behavior. *I need to get to the phone to call Quanda, she'll know what to do,* Myra thought. She still hadn't heard anything from Quanda and the recent turn of events hadn't allowed her to focus on it either.

Milton paced up and down the apartment, drinking glass after glass of ice water and sniffing cocaine. Myra sat stiffly on the sofa, fighting a losing battle against the melatonin saturating her brain. Finally, her brain and eyelids relented.

Bliiiiiingggggg, Bllllinnnnggggggg, Blinnngggggggg, the sound of the telephone startled Myra out of her sleep. She jumped up, looking around frantically trying to get her bearings. When she realized where she was, she got up from the couch. Myra didn't see any sign of Milton. She tiptoed down the hallway into the bedroom, being careful not to wake him if it happened that he had gone to sleep.

Milton was not in the bedroom. The room appeared untouched and the television was on, but muted. Myra walked to the bathroom door and placed her ear up against it. She didn't hear any noises. She gently pushed it open but he was not there. Myra decided that she would finally make a run for it but not before she took some of the money. She rushed into the hallway and yanked open the door to the linen closet. The secret compartment was exposed and the makeshift wall was gone. Myra stuck her head in the closet and realized that every dime of the money was gone. Her heart began to race. She ran to into the bedroom and opened Milton's walk-in closet. It was empty. She noticed that all of his framed NFL posters were also gone. So was his expensive shoe collection. Myra pulled open dresser drawers and . . . nothing. Milton was gone. Sweat drenched her body and her body temperature rose. As she ran around the bedroom in a panic, the television screen caught her attention. Myra touched the remote and raised the volume . . . she listened to the breaking news on NY 1.

"In breaking news today police report that they have a witness in what has become known as the crime of the century case. Police say an unamed homeless man came forward yesterday stating that he witnessed the daring early morning armored car robbery that left two armed brinks guards and a police captain dead. Police report that the unidentified witness saw the two suspects. Police will not release any further information at this time."

Myra's knees became weak and she collapsed.

Bllllinnnngggg, Bliiinnggggg, Myra almost jumped out of her skin when the phone rang. She looked up at the window; darkness had engulfed the sky. Myra didn't realize how long she had been out. The phone continued to ring . . . Blliinnnnnnngggggg, Bllllllinggggg, Myra peered at the nightstand contemplating whether or not to answer it. *Maybe it's Milton telling me to meet him somewhere* she thought. She crawled over to the side of the bed and reached up for the phone.

"Hello" she whispered dryly into the phone. "Quil? Why are you screaming at me? What are you talking about? I missed . . . who?? NO!!!!! NO!!!!! NO!!!!! NO!!!!!!!!! NOT THE ONLY PERSON I HAVE LEFT IN THE WORLD!!!!"

Myra screamed as her blood pressure rose. She dropped the phone. She was dizzy, she couldn't process anymore information. She began to tremble all over and black spots clouded her vision.

"ARRGGGGHHHH!!!!!" Myra screamed as she began throwing things around the bedroom. With one swipe everything on the dresser went crashing to the floor. Myra pulled the telephone from the wall and threw it into the mirror. As she walked toward the bathroom in a zombie-like daze, she stepped on a thin piece of paper. She picked it up and read the words: FLIGHT 1102 CABO SAN LUCAS, MEXICO. She placed the paper in the back pocket of her jeans. Tears ran down her face like a waterfall. The news she had received on the phone made her heart ache and she was losing touch with reality. She realized that Milton had left her holding the bag and it would be just a matter of time before the police closed in on her.

Myra moved like a robot toward the bathroom, simultaneously removing her clothing. She turned on the water in the bathtub, chose her weapon and sat down. As she did the deed, she heard the helicopters hovering outside the window.

"POLICE! WARRANT FOR MYRA DANFORD AND MILTON ROBERTS!" Myra heard the words echoing loudly through her apartment door, followed quickly by the brutal force of the battering ram as the door gave away at the hinges. The sound of hard black combat boots thundered unrepentantly down the hallway, and reminded her of the rhythmic pounding of a fraternity step show . . . *STOMP, STOMP, STOMP.* As the hammering of footsteps grew louder and louder, Myra closed her eyes and whispered in prayer, "Please God, take me now. I've had enough of this life. I surrender to you."

The warm water enveloped her body, easing her like the comfort only a baby in its mother's womb could feel. Pink tinged water cascaded over the sides of the porcelain tub, forming a makeshift waterfall onto the linoleum floor, which ran into a stream under the door. Myra had orchestrated her own watery grave.

"I THINK SOMEONE'S IN HERE!" an officer yelled as he sloshed through the flooded hallway, motioning rapidly for the other officers to bring the battering ram for the door. Voices faded in and out. Myra's heart beat loudly and rhythmically in her ear, like the sweetest African drum music.

Slowly, Myra succumbed to the hypnotic beats, setting her soul free from the confines of her body. She was escaping this hell of a world. Her spirit emerged from her body, hovering over the pitiful sight. "You did it now . . . you fucked yourself outta the game," it taunted.

As the door to her self-made sanctuary came crashing down, the reality of her situation became alarmingly clear.

"HEY IT'S THE GIRL AND SHE'S IN A TUB FULL OF BLOOD .

.. GET A BUS UP HERE RIGHT NOW!" the sergeant barked orders to the other officers. Navy blue uniforms began to pillage the apartment for evidence of the crime.

"EMERGENCY SERVICE UNIT TO CENTRAL K . . . WE NEED A BUS AT THE LOCATION . . . ONE FEMALE PERP, 18-25 YEARS OLD, WITH APPARENT SELF-INFLICTED INJURIES, LENGTH OF TIME IN CONDITION UNKNOWN, APPEARS TO BE SEMI-CONCIOUS, STILL HAS A PULSE," the officer shouted into his two-way radio.

The ambulance arrived in less than three minutes. Paramedics rushed Myra out of the building, navigating their way through the gathering crowd of onlookers. A murmur of hushed whispers and speculation passed between the wealthy residents of Dara Gardens as they took in the nightmarish scene. ESU, S.W.A.T., and WARRANT SQUAD were just a few of the titles that the neighbors read out loud as blue and white NYPD vehicles swarmed the area.

The EMTs carefully loaded the stretcher carrying Myra's body onto the back of the vehicle. Doors closed, the ambulance squealed to life as it pulled away from the curb, leaving behind the wide-eyed and open-mouthed residents of the Jamaica Estates neighborhood.

"She's lost a lot of blood . . . I don't know if she is going to make it. Her blood pressure is steadily plummeting," one of the EMTs reported to the accompanying officer.

"She is important to us right now, so you better find a way to save her," the officer responded coldly.

"The next thing I remember is waking up strapped to the hospital bed in a strait jacket." Myra said, finally getting to the end of the story.

"I know everything after that." Mr. Shepowitz replied in response to Myra's conclusion. "But something you said caught my attention" he continued. "The piece of paper that you put in your pocket, the airline ticket receipt . . . where is it"? he asked.

"I guess it's with my clothes that the police seized as evidence . . . why?" Myra replied.

"I've gotta go . . . Ms. Danford, things might work out after all," Mr. Shepowitz chimed with newfound hope in his attitude. "One more question . . . how did you find out all about your best friend and what happened to her?" Mr. Shepowitz inquired, as he stood to leave.

"After I was transferred to Rikers Island, before I spoke with you the first time, I received a package with Quanda's journal in it. Both of us always kept a journal of our daily activity. The things I didn't find out from her journal, I found out through a secret source, who has been very good to me since I've been locked up . . . he is an angel." Myra reported dreamily.

"Ok, Ms. Danford, I've have to run. I think things will work out just fine," Mr. Shepowitz assured before turning on his heels to exit, leaving Myra with a small glimmer of hope.

Chapter 16

BUSTED!!

Milton stood on the balcony of his beach-front villa and let the warm sea breeze wisp around his nude body. He'd decided that today would be his last day in Cabo San Lucas. He hadn't initially intended on staying there as long as he did. Six months was long enough. Besides when he ended up in Mexico, it was just because he had needed a quick flight out of New York. His ultimate plan was to take up residence in a country that did not have extradition laws. Milton never wondered how things had turned out with Myra or the baby. In fact, he didn't care. He was rich and reasoned that he could buy himself a family if he wanted one.

Milton walked back through the sliding glass patio doors, stepping into the luxurious master bedroom. He had one last desire he had to fulfill before he left Mexico. He picked up the gold-plated old-fashioned rotary phone and dialed a familiar number.

"Hola, Manuel," Milton said, with a horrible Spanglish accent.

"Hola, Senor Juan," the man at the other end replied, calling Milton the alias he had taken on since being in Mexico.

"What time will you be here for the massage?" Milton asked, using code the word.

"Soon," the man replied, hanging up the phone.

Milton was immensely excited. In Mexico male prostitution was a big business and it was cheap. Milton was elated that he didn't have to sneak around anymore, and with the money he had, any service he wanted would be provided. He never even had to leave his villa. Milton took a long hot shower in anticipation of the salacious escapade he was about to experience. As the water cascaded over his well-toned body, Milton stroked his penis while simultaneously squeezing his testicles. The pain gave him great pleasure. He continued until his balls were numb; this way he'd perform longer with his 'date.'

As Milton exited the glass-encased shower, he heard the knock at his villa door. A pang of nervousness flitted through is stomach, as usual. Milton padded over to the door and yanked it open. Manuel looked just as good as usual if not better. The five-foot-nine inch Mexican had the most beautiful tanned olive colored skin. His well-oiled hair lay slicked against his perfectly round head. Milton licked his lips in anticipation; he stepped aside, allowing Manuel into the villa. Manuel knew the drill; he immediately disrobed, exposing his fourteen inch dick, which seemed out of place on his short, stacked body. Milton really liked Manuel. He was obedient, never said more than two words, and allowed Milton to do almost anything to him.

Milton snapped his fingers, as if he were commanding a dog, and Manuel immediately dropped to his knees. The obedient sex-slave crawled over to Milton and bounced up and down like a dog waiting for a bone. Milton removed the towel from his waist, rolled it up tight and slapped Manuel across the face with it. Manuel did not move or flinch. Milton then grabbed Manuel by the hair and dragged him over to the side of the bed. He sat down on the bed and forced Manuel's head between his legs. Manuel immediately took Milton's swollen dick into his mouth. Milton laid back and rolled his eyes in ecstasy.

As the Mexican slurped on Milton's erect tool, Milton heard a noise outside of his villa door. It sounded like more than one pair of feet of feet, which was distracting. He was sure that he had put the DO NOT DISTURB sign on the door to keep Marta the housekeeper out while Manuel was there. To regain his focus, Milton grabbed Manuel's hair tightly and continued to enjoy the deviant act.

Milton felt himself ready to explode. He wanted to stand up and shoot his load in Manuel's face. Milton knew that would degrade the man, but he didn't care. His cousin Scriggy had degraded him the same way many times during his young life. As Milton hurried to get to his feet before his hot juices escaped, he heard a noise outside of the door again. This time he did not have time to think before . . . *BANG!!! CRASH!!!* The villa door came crashing in. "POLICE!!! DON'T MOVE!!!!" several officers shouted in unison.

Milton stood in shock, throwing his hands up; he surrendered. Manuel immediately retreated toward the throngs of police that bombarded the villa, leaving Milton standing butt naked, with a hard dick, and BUSTED!

Myra sat in front of Mr. Shepowitz in shock. She couldn't believe the words he had just uttered. She replayed them in her mind "*The prosecutor has agreed to the cooperation deal and will grant you full immunity if you agree to testify in court. The information you provided, especially the airline ticket receipt, led to the capture of Milton Roberts, the most wanted man in New York City. They took our word for it, Ms. Danford. Based on the domestic violence reports your co-workers at the precinct provided stating that you were a victim of domestic violence and the surveillance video from the check cashing place that shows you were held at gunpoint, which exhibits that you participated under duress, and not of your own free will, you will be granted full immunity from the crime so long as you testify.*

"Ms. Danford . . . are you listening to me?" Mr. Shepowitz asked, breaking Myra's trance.

"My friends call me Myra!" she said exuberantly, jumping to her feet hugging him tightly around the neck.

"You better sit down," Mr. Shepowitz said, blushing at her uncharacteristic show of affection. In reaction to Myra's sudden movement, the C.O.s moved in closer to the table in the council visit area.

"Being in here, I've heard horror stories about public defenders . . . but you were the best. You didn't have to . . . but you did," Myra professed, on the verge of tears.

"Yeah . . . think nothing of it. Your story made me realize why I became a lawyer. Besides this case put me to work and made a real lawyer out of me. Oh, one more thing, I have something to show you," Mr. Shepowitz chimed, pulling a folder from his briefcase. "Just remain calm, as if I'm showing you court documents," he warned as he furtively pushed the folder in Myra's direction.

Myra did as she was told, opening the folder slowly. Tears immediately welled up in her eyes. She looked up from the folder into Mr. Shepowitz's face.

"You are an angel. God sent you," she whispered, as she examined the picture of her baby boy. She looked into his eyes, familiar eyes. Myra examined his face, wanting so badly to kiss his fat cheeks. Mr. Shepowitz had given her the will to live. He had shown her that life is not always as bad as it seems. Her time in jail had served its purpose in her life. Myra had learned that no amount of money could buy her love. After all of this time and heartache, she'd finally found her true love and he was staring right at her from a small 5X7 photograph.

"Court is in two weeks . . . so as usual, my advice is stay out of trouble, kiddo, and keep that beautiful head of yours up," Mr. Shepowitz encouraged, as he stood up to leave.

Myra was so happy when she returned to general population that her surroundings didn't bother her nearly as much as they usually did. She headed toward the dayroom area of the dorm, and just as she settled into on of the plastic chairs, the afternoon news flashed onto the television screen. Myra was too busy daydreaming about

Kyle to really pay attention to the television, but when she heard a familiar name, her mind immediately snapped back. Myra listened intently to what the reporter was saying.

"Travis Danford, the president and owner of the Stringer Danford Sports Management Firm was arrested today in his mid-town manhattan office. He was busted on charges of money-laundering, blackmail, extortion and racketeering. Sources say that Danford, a former on again off again NBA player, bilked millions of dollars from numerous professional athletes to build and maintain his business. Police say the investigation began after one of his employees, Damien Fuller, was found dead in his posh Flushing, Queens neighborhood. Since then numerous athletes and witnesses have come forward with allegations that they were blackmailed, beaten, extorted, and threatened by Danford and employees of his firm. Danford's lawyer says the charges are preposterous and that his client will be proven innocent."

Myra took did a double-take as she watched her father being led out of Manhattan Criminal Court in handcuffs flanked by detectives and reporters. She couldn't believe her eyes or her ears. Myra was astonished at the fact that Damien had worked for her father all of that time. More importantly, she couldn't believe that her father was filthy rich, and living the high life, all the while she and her mother suffered. Myra refused to feel sorry for herself. Her crying days were over. Instead, she smiled to herself and whispered, "See Daddy? You left us and you thought life would be better, but what you forgot was . . . karma is a bitch when it catches up to you."

Chapter 17

KARMA

"Please raise your right hand. Do you swear to tell the whole truth and nothing but the truth so help you God?" the court officer asked.

"I do," Myra replied.

Myra placed her body in the tight leather swivel chair behind the witness stand. Her hands shook, and sweat drenched her back as she offered up two hours of testimony. Myra endured a harrowing cross examination from Milton's defense attorney. The prosecutor

re-crossed and the defense did the same. Myra remained calm. Each time she answered the questions, she looked over at Milton; a sense of redemption swept over her. Myra had promised herself that she would look him in the eyes every time she spoke, so that he could feel the pain that she had endured.

Throughout her pointed testimony, Myra watched Milton lean in several times to speak to his attorney, no doubt refuting her words. Myra knew that those were points where she'd embellished the story a bit—Mr. Shepowitz had prepared her well. She and her public defender rehearsed her testimony several times over before the trial. Myra had it so down packed that she saw doubt clouding the eyes of the defense team.

The prosecution presented witness after witness. Myra shook her head as she saw Craig, Milton's friend who had given him the gun, being brought in to testify—in handcuffs. She later found out that the only way Craig could get off for providing Milton with the murder weapon was to testify against him.

After six weeks of testimony and one day of jury deliberations, the courtroom was packed. Police officers from all over the city turned out. They wanted to witness Milton get what he deserved. They didn't take too kindly to cop killers. Milton sat stone-faced as the jury filed into the jury box. Throughout the trail he hadn't shown any signs of remorse.

A deadly hush fell over the court room as Judge Rowley slammed his gavel, bringing everyone to order. Myra sat on the front pew next to Mr. Shepowitz and the prosecutor.

"Has the jury reached a verdict?" Judge Rowley called out.

"Yes, your honor, we have," the female jury foreperson affirmed, handing the paper that held Milton's fate to the court officer. The judge read the jury's decision and handed the paper back to the court officer.

"Ladies and gentlemen of the jury, what say you?" Judge Rowley asked.

Mr. Shepowitz grabbed Myra's hand. Myra squeezed his hand in return, and her nerves twitched as the jury foreperson stood to read the verdict.

"We, the jury, find the defendant Milton Roberts guilty of first degree murder," she read. The courtroom erupted in cheers and screams. The family of the police captain and all of his fellow comrades jumped to their feet in victory.

"ORDER! ORDER!!" Judge Rowley yelled, banging his gavel.

Tears streamed down Myra's face, as Mr. Shepowitz hugged her tightly. These tears were not of sorrow but of joy. Milton's guilty verdict had just made her a free woman.

Myra opened her eyes and focused on the back of the courtroom.

She immediately became antsy. Myra shook as she sat back down on the bench and waited for the jury to read the remainder of their verdict. She couldn't wait to get to the back of the courtroom.

Once court was dismissed, Myra looked over at the defense table. Milton's ankles were being shackled. As the court officers led him out of the courtroom, Milton lifted his head and Myra's eyes locked with his. They stared at each for a long five seconds; just enough time for Myra to mouth the words *"karma comes full circle."* Milton hung his head as one lone tear escaped his left eye.

"You are free to go, Ms. Danford" the District Attorney informed Myra.

"Yup, you are finally free," Mr. Shepowitz said, extending his arm toward the end of the pew. Myra took his cue and inched her way to the end of the wooden pew. As soon as she made it to the aisle, she bolted to the back of the courtroom.

Ms. Brenda saw Myra running toward her. Ms. Brenda picked up baby Kyle and extended him toward his mother. Myra grabbed her baby boy. Holding him close to her body, she showered his fat cheeks with kisses. Myra held him close to her heart; promising never to leave him again.

"So you don't see nobody else?" an all too familiar voice questioned from a distance.

"QUANNNDAAA!!!! Myra screamed out, quickly running over to her best friend.

Ms. Brenda moved close to them, grabbing Kyle from Myra so the girls could properly embrace. Myra bent down and grabbed her best friend tightly around the neck.

"I'm so sorry this had to happen to you. Quan, I love you" Myra sobbed.

"Girl, it's just a wheel chair . . . that ain't stoppin' a bitch like me from getting my swerve on," Quanda joked, immediately putting her best friend at ease.

"I will never lie to you again. I swear, and we will never be apart again either," Myra whispered.

"Fo' sho," Quanda replied in agreement.

Myra held her baby boy closely as they all exited the criminal court building in downtown Brooklyn. Throngs of reporters screamed questions and shoved microphones in her face. Cameras flashed one after the other. Mr. Shepowitz shooed them away, making a clear path for Myra, Kyle, Quanda, and Ms. Brenda to escape. Before he completely dismissed the hungry crowd, he turned around to make a statement:

"My client has asked me to read this statement on her behalf:" *The world is a 360 degree circle; therefore what goes around comes around. It's called karma and it always comes full circle."*

Myra smiled as she heard her attorney uttering the words that saved her life. Just as they made it past the reporters, a long black stretch Hummer H2 pulled up to them.

"Who the hell is that?" Quanda asked, knowing the answer.

"I think I have an idea," Myra chimed, smiling brightly.

They all watched as two long legs emerged from the back of the Hummer. Quanda sized up the beautiful man before her as he straightened his tie and swiped the wrinkles from his pants.

"Are you ready to start a new life . . . with a real man?" he asked, looking directly into Myra's eyes.

"Yes, Bradley Holson, I am," Myra replied, running toward her 'angel'. Brad hugged her tight, and lifted her off of her feet. He looked down into her eyes and said, "I thought this day would never come, I've read your letters over and over again. The wait was well worth it," Myra kissed him deeply, allowing her heart to feel real love.

"Ya'll got a crippled bitch cryin' over here," Quanda joked through her own tears.

"Come on, we got a few stops to make before we head home—to OUR HOME," Brad said, gesturing for everyone to load into the Hummer.

As they all got comfortable on the butter leather seats, everyone seemed overjoyed.

"I'm so glad you stayed in touch with Myra all of this time," Ms. Brenda said to Brad.

"Ms. Brenda, I've been in love with her from the moment I met her. After we began writing each other and keeping in touch, I made sure her lawyer did the right thing . . . and with a few phone calls to the right people, I knew she would be fine," Brad replied.

"Don't forget that you kept my commissary piling," Myra said, smiling.

"Oh yeah, in the words of Foxxy Brown, her 'commissary stayed piling,'" Brad chuckled.

Myra gazed out of the window as the Hummer made its way down Myrtle Avenue. Her heat began to pound as the vehicle came to the corner of Throop Avenue. She peered out of the window and noticed a colorful graffiti mural painted on the wall beside the corner bodega. It read: R.I.P KNOWLEDGE, SCARED MONEY DON'T MAKE MONEY . . . LIVE BY THE GUN DIE BY IT.

A somber overcame Myra as she surveyed the neighborhood that she grew up in. Crack heads continued to crawl the streets in search of their next hit. The corner and building hustlers remained, only they were younger than she'd remembered. Myra eyed all of the luxury cars lined up for the "floss show." One car stood out. It was a black Mercedes Benz Maybach. She peered out the window at the driver, it was Rell.

"Yeah, girl . . . after he killed Knowledge and saved my life he took over Tompkins. He is the new kingpin," Quanda whispered to Myra after noticing her friend staring at the vehicle.

"History repeats itself," Myra whispered in return.

The H2 pulled up in front of 212 Throop Avenue. Ms. Brenda inhaled deeply and exhaled slowly as she opened the door to exit.

"Hurry up and get whatever you want to take. Tell the rest of your children to hurry up also," Brad instructed.

"I will," Ms. Brenda said somberly.

"What's going on?" Myra asked, confused by the conversation.

"Girl, your man is the truth; he is moving us all out of this hell hole." Quanda chimed in, addressing her friends concern.

"Moving everyone?" Myra questioned, astonished.

"Hell, yeah . . . don't you know he is the star forward for the New Jersey Nets? Soon to be Brooklyn Nets? Quanda replied, dumbfounded by Myra's ignorance.

"That's right, baby. You won't be a NFL wife, but how does the wife of an NBA player sound to you?" Brad chimed.

"YES . . . YES . . . it sounds absolutely wonderful!!" Myra screamed, as she handed Kyle to Quanda and jumped into Brad's arms.

Myra had just finished reading Kyle a bed time story when Zaida, the hired help entered

Kyle's bedroom.

"Senora Holson, you have mail," Zaida said, handing Myra an envelope.

"Thank you, Zaida. Keep an eye on my baby until he falls asleep. I'll be in my bedroom," Myra replied.

Myra walked along the grand hallway to her and Brad's quadrant of their 30,000 square foot mansion. Sitting on her specially made circular bed, Myra tore open the envelope and began to read,

Dear Mrs. Holson,

We regret to inform you that Mr. Travis Danford com-

mitted suicide while being contained at the Manhattan House of Detention.

At this time you are his only next of kin. We ask that you come to identify the body, at which time you will be allowed to claim his remains for a proper committal.

Please contact our office at 718-546-9600, upon receipt of this letter. The Department of Corrections offers you and your family our deepest condolences.

Respectfully,
Warden William Ugghi

Myra closed her eyes and pictured her mother's face the day that Vidal realized that Travis was not coming back home. She remembered how her mother had cried and cried. Myra looked down at the letter in her lap. She picked up the paper and ripped it to shreds.

"Closure . . . finally," Myra mumbled to herself. She walked over to the massive audio surround system built into the wall of the bedroom. She changed the 100-disc CD changer until she found disc three. It was her Alicia Keys CD. Myra skipped songs until she found the one she was looking for and pressed play.

"What goes around comes around
What goes up must come down . . .
It's called KARMA b-a-b-y . . . what goes around" . . .

Myra relaxed on her plush chaise lounge, soothed by the lyrics. Just as she closed her eyes her husband came into their bedroom.

"Is everything alright?" Brad asked.

"Yup . . . just fine," Myra replied and meant it. She picked up the phone and dialed Quanda's number. She wanted to find out how Quanda's physical therapy was coming along. Myra knew that with money anything was possible, she truly believed that one day her best friend would walk again.

Dear Bertha,

I heard you was sick and that your precious nephew Scriggy won't even wipe your shitty ass. Good for you. You are a hateful bitch, always was and always will be. I hope you die a long, slow, and painful death.

I just wanted you to know that you ruined my life. I was an innocent little boy. All I ever wanted was people to love me and accept me. All I ever wanted was love. Because of you I will never find love.

I hate you and everything you stand for. If I could get out of this jail I would come kill you myself. Do you know that I just got sentenced to three consecutive life sentences, which means that I'll never see the light of day.

All because of you, bitch! All because you refused to love me and protect me from your perverted, sick, bastard nephew. Oh yeah, I heard Scriggy got AIDS . . . good for that nasty nigga. I hope his dick falls off!!

Well I hope this letter finds you half dead, suffering in a lot of pain.

With Much Hate,
Milton.

Bertha gasped her last breath as she finished reading Milton's letter. Her body went limp, as her soul left it. Slumped over in her bed, Bertha died, all alone.

MELODRAMA PUBLISHING ORDER FORM

WWW.MELODRAMAPUBLISHING.COM

Title	ISBN	QTY	PRICE	TOTAL
Myra	1-934157-20-1		$15.00	$
Menace	1-934157-16-3		$15.00	$
Cartier Cartel	1-934157-18-X		$15.00	$
10 Crack Commandments	1-934157-21-X		$15.00	$
Jealousy: The Complete Saga	1-934157-13-9		$15.00	$
Wifey	0-971702-18-7		$15.00	$
I'm Still Wifey	0-971702-15-2		$15.00	$
Life After Wifey	1-934157-04-X		$15.00	$
Still Wifey Material	1-934157-10-4		$15.00	$
Eva: First Lady of Sin	1-934157-01-5		$15.00	$
Eva 2: First Lady of Sin	1-934157-11-2		$15.00	$
Den of Sin	1-934157-08-2		$15.00	$
Shot Glass Diva	1-934157-14-7		$15.00	$
Dirty Little Angel	1-934157-19-8		$15.00	$
Histress	1-934157-03-1		$15.00	$
In My Hood	0-971702-19-5		$15.00	$
In My Hood 2	1-934157-06-6		$15.00	$
A Deal With Death	1-934157-12-0		$15.00	$
Tale of a Train Wreck Lifestyle	1-934157-15-5		$15.00	$
A Sticky Situation	1-934157-09-0		$15.00	$
Jealousy	1-934157-07-4		$15.00	$
Life, Love & Loneliness	0-971702-10-1		$15.00	$
The Criss Cross	0-971702-12-8		$15.00	$

(GO TO THE NEXT PAGE)

MELODRAMA PUBLISHING ORDER FORM
(CONTINUED)

Title/Author	ISBN	QTY	PRICE	TOTAL
Stripped	1-934157-00-7		$15.00	$
The Candy Shop	1-934157-02-3		$15.00	$
Sex, Sin & Brooklyn	0-971702-16-0		$15.00	$
Up, Close & Personal	0-971702-11-X		$9.95	$
				$
			Subtotal	
			Shipping**	
			Tax*	
	Total			

Instructions:

*NY residents please add $1.79 Tax per book.

**Shipping costs: $3.00 first book, any additional books please add $1.00 per book.

Incarcerated readers receive a 25% discount. Please pay $11.25 per book and apply the same shipping terms as stated above.

Mail to:

MELODRAMA PUBLISHING

P.O. BOX 522

BELLPORT, NY 11713

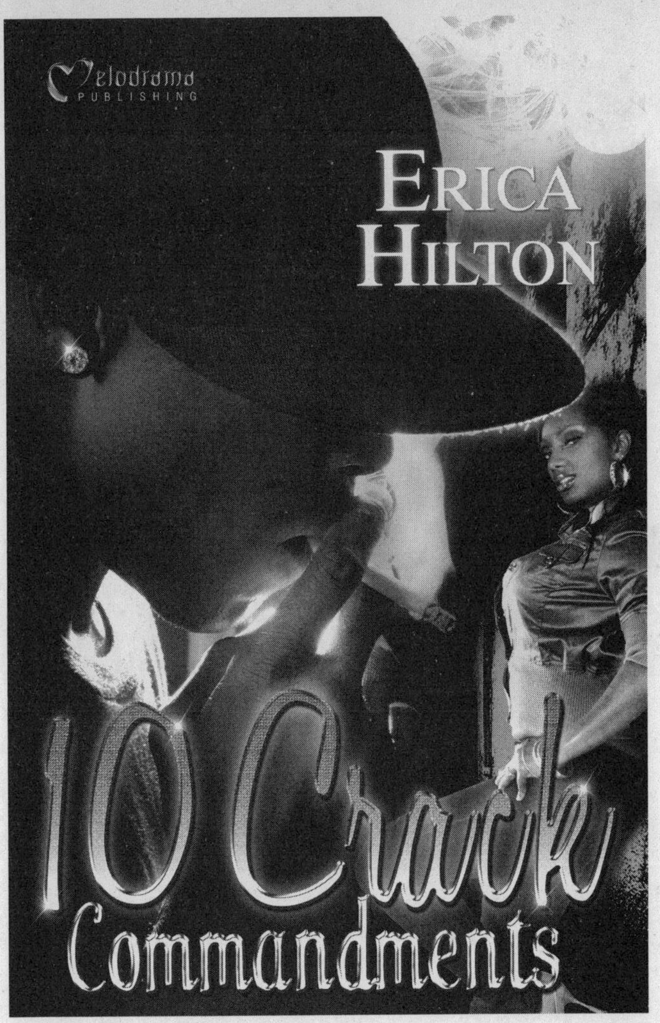

One...two...three...Follow Lil Nut as he maneuvers through his hood in a quest to attain ghetto riches. In order to dodge all the usual pitfalls that come when hugging the block, Lil Nut assumes that he'll be all right as long as he follows the hustlers rule book. The streets say that once you get into the game, the only way out is death or incarceration. Vying to stay one step ahead, Lil Nut is determined to follow the ten crack commandments.

Release Date: April 2009

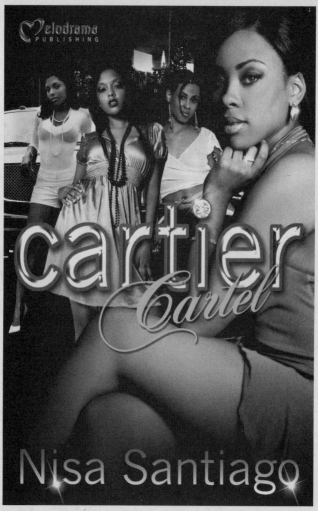

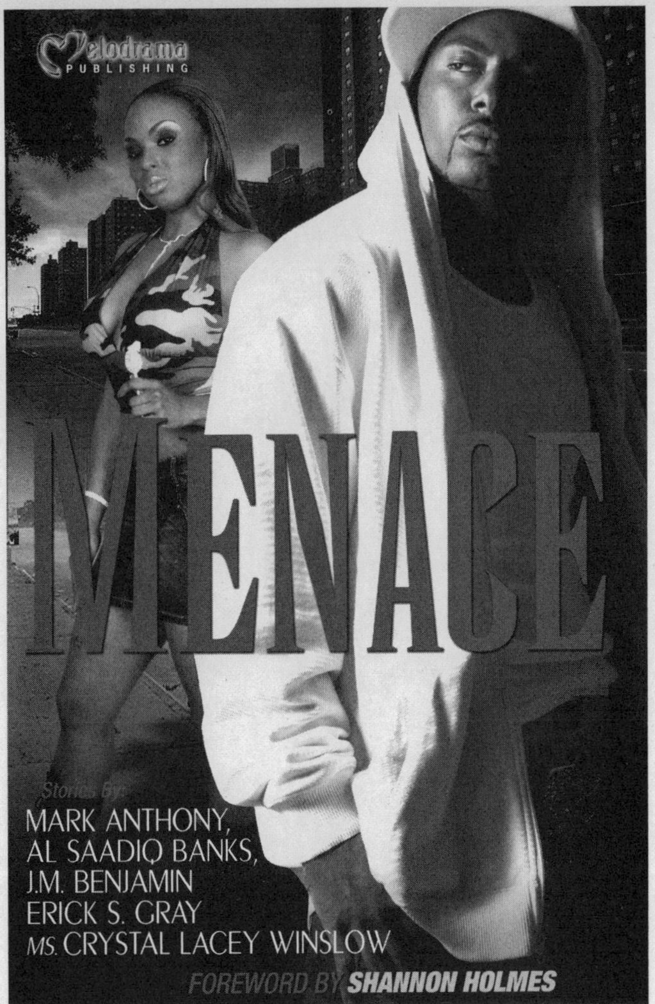

With the Foreword written by Shannon Holmes, this is a gritty work of fiction that captures the allure of sex, money, murder and power. "Snake Eyes" by Mark Anthony explores the old adage about keeping your friends close and your enemies closer. "Cagney & Lacey" by Crystal Lacey Winslow is just like a modern day Bonnie and Clyde, with two criminals embarking on a killing spree. "Walk with Me" by Al-Saadiq Banks walks you through the seemingly dark life of Miracle, capturing the ironic circumstance of being in the wrong place at the wrong time. "Keepin' it Gangsta" by JM Benjamin is about the notorious "Dicer". Feared by many because of his murderous and infamous reputation—he still finds a soft spot in his black heart to hold down the only woman that ever truly loved him.

Release Date: March 2009

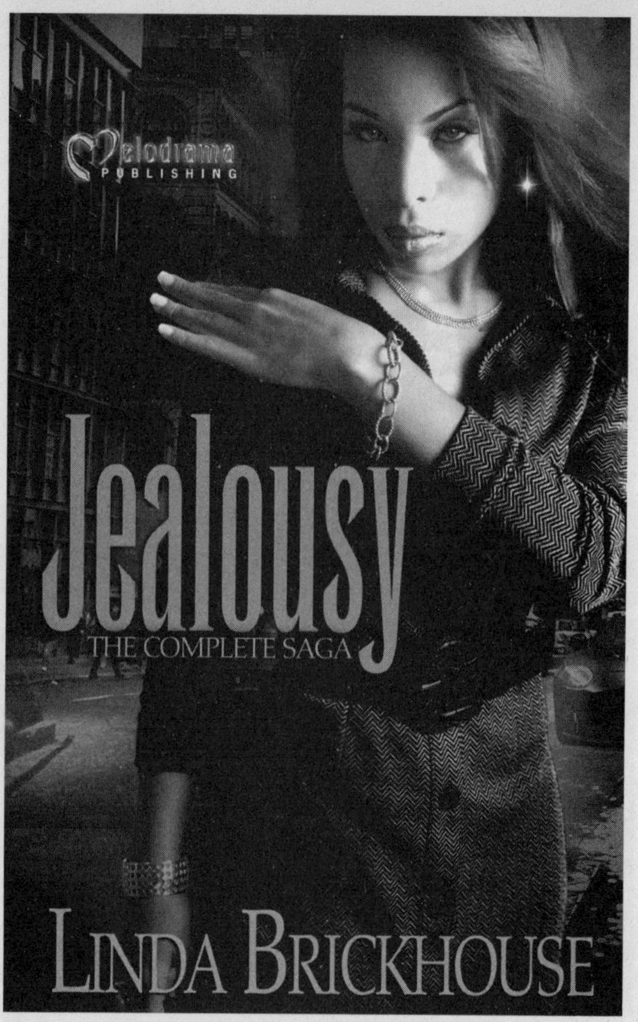

Eve, the sexy vixen narrowly escapes death because of Jealousy. You would think she'd learn her lesson and stay out of grown men business. When being a rich man's mistress wasn't quenching her thirst, she set her evil eyes on his enemy, Earl Clement and they embark on a tumultuous affair. When Chaka's dead body is found all roads lead to Earl and Eve.

Chaka's crew, the Baker Boys, are dead-set on avenging their leaders death; with bounties on each man's head it's Guerilla Warfare on the streets of New York. Money, power and respect are at stake—and jealousy runs rampant inside the once tight crew. Nevertheless, Eve has an agenda all her own. She doesn't need power and respect as long as she walks away with the money!

Release Date: May 2009